SHEPHERD'S WAKE

A DETECTIVE HARPER NOVEL

SHEPHERD'S WAKE

J.K. WOLFE

SHEPHERD'S WAKE

Published by Deep Watch Press

Cover Design by Ambient Pixel Design

https://JKWolfeBooks.com

ISBN: 979-8-9990159-7-6

DEDICATION

For my father,

who taught me the value of hard work,

of integrity,

and of loving your family.

Author's Foreword

This is a work of fiction. But again, the truth runs just beneath the surface.

Shepherd's Wake is about more than a case, more than evidence and manhunts and courtroom justice. At its heart, it's about the things that anchor us when the world tries to drag us under. Family. Faith. Integrity.

For me, those themes are not abstract. They've been tested in the real world, in the moments when the job pressed hardest against the people I loved, and when I saw faith used as both a light, and a weapon. Some of what you'll read here is drawn from those tensions. From the cult-like grip of manipulative leaders, to the quiet courage of officers who carried their families in one hand and their badge in the other.

Detective Jake Harper isn't perfect. He stumbles, he doubts, and he carries scars. But like many of us, he keeps showing up. He learns that family is both his strength and his responsibility, that faith can wound and heal, and that integrity isn't measured when it's easy.

The truth behind the fiction is simple: doing the right thing always comes at a price. And yet, that is where meaning is found.

— J.K. Wolfe

"The ocean is more ancient than the mountains, and freighted with the memories and the dreams of Time."
- H.P. Lovecraft

PROLOGUE

The yacht floated alone in the shifting mist, its white hull soft against the bruised blue of the Sound. Dawn was breaking slowly across the water, pale sunlight bleeding through the low cloud cover. Off in the distance, barely visible through the layered fog, the Space Needle pierced the skyline like a ghost.

Seattle Harbor Patrol Officer Mike Crenshaw eased off the throttles as he circled the vessel in a wide horseshoe. Textbook approach. Old Coast Guard habits died hard. The call had come in twenty minutes ago from a commuter ferry. An unmanned yacht, drifting just outside the traffic lanes of Elliott Bay. No lights. No response to repeated radio hails.

Crenshaw pushed his sunglasses up onto his forehead and scanned the vessel. The name was stenciled cleanly across the transom in black block lettering: *The Halcyon Way.*

"Nice boat," said Officer Jules Ferris, standing beside him on the patrol boat's console. "Looks clean. Doesn't look stolen."

Crenshaw shook his head. "No nav lights. No motion. Anchor's not down," he paused. "Something's off."

The officers completed their slow sweep around the fifty-six-foot Sea Ray. No movement. No visible damage. No one waving from the bridge or deck. The yacht tender—the small dinghy often secured on the bow—was either missing or didn't come with this model.

Crenshaw keyed the mic. "Halcyon Way, Halcyon Way, this is Seattle Harbor Patrol, Harbor-One, hailing you on channel one-six. Do you copy? Over."

No answer.

Crenshaw keyed the mic again. "Halcyon Way, Halcyon Way, Harbor-One hailing you on one-six. Do you read?"

Silence.

Crenshaw brought the patrol boat alongside the stern. Ferris caught the rail and tied them off as the engines idled down. The air was still, the water slapping gently against fiberglass.

"Seattle Police! Harbor Patrol! Is anyone aboard?" Ferris called out.

Still, no answer.

They stepped over the gunwale and onto the back deck of *The Halcyon Way.*

"Harbor Police!" Crenshaw shouted. "If you're on board, make yourself known!"

Yet more silence.

The deck was pristine. They climbed up to the flybridge. Nothing out of place. No wet towels, no sandals, no coffee mugs, no fishing gear. No signs of a lazy morning or rushed departure. Just sun-bleached teak and silence. It looked...sterile.

Inside was worse.

As they entered the galley, it was empty. Spotless. Cupboards bare. Below deck, the berths had been stripped of all bedding. No clothing, no bags, no signs of habitation. The heads were empty, no toothbrushes, towels, no toiletries.

There wasn't even a fingerprint on the mirror. A faint, acrid tang of bleach lingered in the air.

Crenshaw crouched at the helm and picked up a tablet. When he powered it on, the screen flashed and loaded to the setup screen. Factory reset.

Ferris's voice echoed from below. "There's nothing anywhere. No bags. No ID. No signs anyone's even been on this thing."

He reappeared on the stairs as Crenshaw pulled a small packet of documents from the helm cubby. Vessel registration.

"2003 Sea Ray 560, *The Halcyon Way*," Crenshaw read aloud. "Registered to a Daniel and Malia Rainier."

Ferris took the papers, scanning. "Late twenties. Bellevue address."

Crenshaw pulled out his phone. "I know that name."

He tapped through a few apps. "Here. Social media."

He turned the screen toward Ferris. Photo after photo. The same yacht, the same couple. Smiling. Holding hands. Toasting on the deck. The woman's hands covering a small bump on her belly. "Looks like the San Juan Islands. All posted in the last few weeks."

Ferris leaned in. "Babymoon?"

"Looks like it," Crenshaw said. He swiped again. One image showed the man in uniform. Crenshaw stopped. "That's it."

"Coast Guard?" Ferris asked.

"Yeah. Daniel Rainier. Lieutenant. JAG Corps." Crenshaw's jaw tightened. "We need to call this in."

Ferris nodded. "And notify the Coast Guard."

Crenshaw stood slowly, staring out into the Sound. The fog was lifting now, light bleeding through.

"CGIS is going to want in on this."

Part One: Signs and Wonders

"The purposes of a person's heart are deep waters, but one who has insight draws them out."
— Proverbs 20:5

CHAPTER
ONE

September 10.

The cell phone buzzed on the dresser, vibrating against wood. After a few rings, it silenced. Then it started again. And again. A fourth time broke through the steam just as Jake Harper stepped out of the shower.

He grabbed a towel, wrapped it low around his waist, and picked up the phone. 6:07am.

"Harper," he said, dripping onto the carpet.

"Good, you're up," came the voice of Supervisory Special Agent Easton. "Need you out at Pier 36 ASAP."

"What happened?" asked Harper, wiping steam from the mirror.

"Missing couple. Coastie and his wife. Their yacht was found adrift out in Elliott Bay."

"Who found it?"

"Seattle PD Harbor Patrol. Officer Crenshaw and his partner. Crenshaw's a reservist out of Station Seattle. Said it didn't feel right, asked for us specifically."

Harper paused, running a hand through his wet hair. "What makes Crenshaw think CGIS needs in on it?"

"For starters, the yacht was wiped clean. No personal effects. Nothing. Just a tablet reset to factory default. Oh, and the smell of bleach. Crenshaw recognized the missing Coastie, LT Daniel Rainier."

Harper's eyebrows raised in recognition. "Rainier...I knew him. He was involved in—"

"I know," Easton interrupted. "That's why I want you on this."

Harper exhaled slowly.

"Listen, I know you and Alyssa are due to head back home next week," Easton added, voice softening. "I'm not asking for the whole case. Just eyes on the scene. See if Crenshaw's instincts check out. If it looks like something we need to stay on, I'll reassign it, pull a couple full-time agents and put 'em on it."

"Roger that," Harper said. "I'll keep you posted."

He dressed quickly, pulling on khakis, a polo, and his worn black Chucks. His badge clipped to his belt, sliding his holstered Glock 19 onto his left hip.

The house was quiet. Harper moved carefully down the hall, stepping around the creaky floorboards outside his daughter's room. Adelyn—Addie—was four and a half years old, wild, and whip-smart, with a mop of curly blond hair and ice-blue eyes that lit up like her mother's.

In so many ways, she was Alyssa in miniature. The same spark in her smile. The same serious goofiness that turned into full-belly laughter when it broke loose. She wrinkled her nose the same way when she was thinking. Asked the same quiet questions before bed. Sometimes, Harper caught her watching the world the way Alyssa did, like she already understood more than she let on.

But when she was grumpy... that was him. The scowl, the stubborn set of her jaw, that was pure Harper.

He loved it. All of it. The way they lived in her, woven together in curls and attitude and too-big pajamas. The only real difference was her hair: sunlit blond, where Alyssa's had always been fire.

From the kitchen, the scent of fresh coffee drifted in, strong and dark. Alyssa was already up.

Harper stepped into the kitchen and slid his arms around her from behind, just above the swell of her belly, and kissed her neck. At eight months pregnant, he could no longer fit his arms all the way around her, but that only made him hold her closer. She was petite, barely five-foot-one, but pregnancy had filled out her figure in ways that stopped him in his tracks more than once. Her auburn hair fell loose around her shoulders, and her bright blue eyes met his with that quiet mix of knowing and calm that had always steadied him.

She turned in his arms and kissed him on the lips, slow and warm, savoring the stillness of the hour before the world woke up.

"Where you off to so early?" she asked, her voice low.

"Easton called. There's a missing couple, a Coastie and his wife. Their yacht was found adrift in Elliott Bay. Locals flagged it. He wants me to go check it out, see if it's actually a CGIS case."

Alyssa raised an eyebrow, skeptical.

Harper grinned and raised his hands in mock surrender. "Easton said if it looks like anything serious, he'll hand it off to the full-timers. He's *well aware* we're both itching to get back home."

She laughed, brushing her hair behind one ear. "I'm just giving you shit, mister. I don't want to be giving birth in base housing."

He smiled and kissed her forehead. "Wouldn't be the worst delivery room I've seen."

"You say that now," she muttered, heading toward the coffeemaker. "Just come back in one piece."

•••••

Harper was lost in thought during the ten-minute drive from the Coast Guard-provided rental house to USCG Base Seattle. The streets were quiet this early, just the occasional ferry horn echoing across Elliott Bay. Low clouds clung to the skyline, mist curling off the water in long, silver tendrils.

Seven months ago, he was a Detective at Stonehaven PD. He'd just started digging into a pretty heavy sexual abuse case when the call came in. Official, clipped, and unmistakably federal. The Coast Guard needed him to mobilize, not as a Maritime Enforcement Specialist, which he had been serving as in the CG Reserve for several years, but as an Investigator First Class—a Reserve Special Agent with the Coast Guard Investigative Service. The case involved someone Harper knew better than most: BMC Logan Cross.

The two had served together years earlier in the Coast Guard's elite MSRT East—the Maritime Security Response Team— running anti-terrorism and anti-piracy ops. Afterwards, their paths diverged, but they kept in touch. Harper went on to work at Stonehaven PD, working his way from patrol to detective while continuing to drill as a reservist. Cross transferred to a small boat station, trading the tactical world for SAR cases and routine law enforcement while he and his wife focused on starting a family.

Then came the call. CGIS told him little at first, only that Cross had stumbled into something bigger than anyone expected. Irregularities. Dead bodies. Whispers of a shadow network calling itself *Blackwake*. The network reached higher than it should have, and there were attempts on the lives of Cross and those around him. CGIS needed another investigator, someone Cross trusted. He had asked for Harper by name.

It had been a hell of a thing. Harper came in at the tail end, but he saw enough. Enough to know the threat was real. Enough to know it wasn't over the moment the gun smoke cleared. And now, even back in Seattle, he was bracing for the years of testimony and trials still to come.

Alyssa had made it possible for Harper to go. She took leave from work, packed their lives, and flew east with Harper and Addie. He wouldn't have gone otherwise, not with a pregnant wife and a young daughter. They made it work: quiet dinners in a rental house near base, morning cartoons before Harper geared up for long briefings and even longer operations.

When the East Coast case finally wrapped, CGIS reassigned him to Seattle to finish his mobilization. Just a month, they said, to finish up a few lingering paperwork issues. They furnished a rental house close to Base Seattle for a soft landing before the family would head back home to Stonehaven, Oregon.

That had been the plan.

Now, as he pulled into the lot at Pier 36, Harper had the feeling he wasn't done yet. Not with this case. Not with what was waiting on board *The Halcyon Way*. Not with potential ghosts following him to the West Coast.

He flashed his creds to the armed guard at the gate, then drove through and parked his government-issued Ford sedan in the nearest spot to the Coast Guard pier. As he stepped out, the sharp scent of saltwater met him on the breeze, carried inland off the Sound.

I do love late summer up here, he thought absently.

The yacht was moored alongside the dock, sleek, quiet, and perfectly still. Next to it, a Seattle Harbor Patrol boat bobbed gently, tied off to the pier. Two SPD officers stood nearby, flanking the pier. Yellow crime scene tape stretched across the gunwale of the yacht, fluttering in the breeze. An active-duty Coast Guardsman stood in front of it, armed and in blues, posture squared beside the city cops.

Harper approached the group, holding up his credentials. "Special Agent Harper, CGIS."

"Officer Crenshaw, and my partner Officer Ferris," said one of the officers, stepping forward with a firm handshake. Harper shook both their hands, then turned to the Coastie.

"BM2 Irons," the petty officer said. "I was instructed to stand by with the officers until jurisdiction was established."

"Appreciate it," Harper said to Irons with a nod, then turned back to Crenshaw. "Walk me through what you found."

Crenshaw adjusted his duty belt slightly and stepped forward, squaring his shoulders with habitual precision.

"Harbor Patrol was dispatched at 0442 hours," he began. "Initial call came from a commuter ferry captain. Reported an uncrewed vessel drifting just outside the lanes in Elliott Bay. No running lights, no movement, no response to hails."

He gestured to *The Halcyon Way*. "We arrived on scene at 0503. Circled the vessel. Fifty-six-foot Sea Ray, name on the transom matched registry logs. No visible damage, no one on deck. Yacht tender was missing. No anchor in the water."

Harper nodded. "You hailed them?"

"Twice," Crenshaw confirmed. "VHF channel one-six. No response. The vessel was unsecured and unmanned. Per protocol, we boarded."

Ferris spoke up, tone more casual. "Was weird from the get-go. Looked too clean. Not 'left in a hurry' clean. Like showroom clean. You could eat off the damn flybridge."

"We conducted a standard sweep," Crenshaw continued, ignoring the comment. "No personal effects aboard. Galley and berthing areas were stripped. Heads were clean. Cupboards empty. No luggage, no ID, no food, no toiletries. No trace of habitation."

"No toothbrush, no coffee mug, nothing," Ferris added. "Hell, there wasn't even a pair of shoes on board. Just that tablet by the helm, and it was wiped."

"Factory reset," Crenshaw clarified. "We powered it on, confirmed the status. Also noted a faint odor of cleaning agents. Bleach, possibly diluted."

Harper's brow furrowed. "No blood?"

"Negative," Crenshaw said. "No physical signs of violence. But the absence of evidence was... noticeable."

"It didn't feel right," Ferris said, rubbing the back of his neck. "I mean, I've seen folks abandon boats before. This wasn't that."

"I located the ship's registration in a cubby near the helm," Crenshaw went on. "Daniel and Malia Rainier, registered owners. West Seattle address. Names rang a bell, so I ran a quick check. That's when I found out about Lieutenant Rainier."

"You know him?" Harper asked.

Crenshaw shook his head. "Not personally. But I recognized him from a case briefing a few months back. He's JAG, helped prosecute some major players in that mess back east. Murders, corruption, people higher up than they should've been."

Harper nodded once. "Yeah, I was pulled into that too."

Ferris frowned. "Didn't know the Coast Guard had cases like that."

"They shouldn't have," Harper said. "But it happened."

Ferris blew out a breath. "Damn. No wonder the names rang a bell. After that, Crenshaw pulled up their socials."

Crenshaw nodded. "Public profiles. Recent posts. Photos aboard *The Halcyon Way*. Scenic shots from the San Juans. Dates indicate they were out just a few weeks ago. Appeared to be a vacation or extended leave."

"Yeah, after that mess back east, he transferred out here," Harper said.

"Looked like a babymoon," Ferris said, softer now. "Malia was visibly pregnant in the photos. Holding her belly. Posed together on deck, sunset shots... smiling."

Harper didn't respond. Something twisted low in his gut, quiet and sharp. His hand drifted to his belt, thumb brushing against the smooth edge of his badge. For a moment, he wasn't standing on the pier. He was back in the kitchen, arms wrapped around Alyssa's swollen belly, her laughter still warm in his chest.

Crenshaw's expression hardened. "Given the condition of the vessel versus the recency of those images, we suspected foul play. That's when I called CGIS."

Harper exhaled, slow and steady. The wind kicked up slightly, lifting a corner of the yellow tape on the yacht's rail. He cleared his throat. "How recent were the photos?"

Crenshaw, ever precise, answered. "Last post was dated sixteen days ago. Metadata confirms it was geotagged near Orcas Island."

"Anyone try calling them?"

"Yeah, found their numbers in Lexus-Nexus, gave them a call. No answer. Had dispatch try and ping them. Last location was somewhere north of where the boat was found."

Harper gave a slow nod. "You did good work, both of you. Let's take a closer look."

As they stepped aboard *The Halcyon Way*, Harper saw the same thing Crenshaw and Ferris had: absence.

Not just the lack of people, but the lack of life.

No personal items. No clothing left draped over railings. No dishes in the sink or towels clipped to the stern rails. Just polished fiberglass and an unnatural stillness, like the boat had been staged for sale or sanitized for a showing.

He moved into the interior cabin. The faint odor of bleach hit him immediately, even through the salt-heavy breeze drifting through the open deck hatches. It wasn't strong, but it was there, lingering like something that didn't want to be forgotten.

Harper pulled on a pair of blue nitrile gloves and began moving through the space methodically. He lifted seat cushions.

Checked cabinets. Opened drawers. Every compartment told the same story: nothing.

No travel bags. No receipts. No hairbrush. No crumbs tucked into corners. Not even a stray coin in a cupholder.

He paused near the galley sink, eyes flicking over the glossy countertop.

If Alyssa had packed for a trip like this, there'd be snacks stashed somewhere, a blanket she liked to curl up in, books she never quite got around to reading. Addie's stuffed dolphin would be lying in the middle of the floor. A pair of little shoes kicked under the bench. Chaos, the soft, familiar kind.

Here, there was nothing but precision and silence.

Harper exhaled through his nose and kept moving.

Crenshaw suddenly stopped moving and tilted his head to the side. Ferris did the same. Harper recognized the posture immediately, that familiar, distant stare as a patrol officer listened through one ear to a voice no one else could hear.

He paused mid-step, waiting, watching Crenshaw's expression shift from neutral to curious to something sharper. The sergeant's voice, no doubt. Crenshaw flipped open his notebook and jotted something down.

Crenshaw straightened and looked over at Harper. "You're not gonna believe this."

Harper said nothing. Just gave him the look that said *try me*.

"Someone just reported *The Halcyon Way* stolen."

Harper's brow furrowed. "The Rainiers?"

"Nope." Crenshaw shared a glance with Ferris. "Some local guy. Says he's the new owner. Claims he bought it earlier this week."

Harper's eyes narrowed. "Name?"

Crenshaw flipped open his notebook. "Asher Kincaid."

Ferris added, "Apparently, he's kind of a big deal around here. Family pastor at one of those mega-churches on the east side. Community outreach, podcasts, charity galas, the whole polished package."

Harper glanced at the helm, then at the lifeless decks. The yacht looked like a postcard, but something about it felt posed. Like a crime scene dressed for Sunday service. *This just got interesting.*

"Pastor Kincaid, huh," he said. "Interesting choice of vessel for a man of God."

Crenshaw handed over a slip of paper. "My sergeant asked me to have you call him. Says there's more you'll want to hear."

Harper took it, already reaching for his phone. "Thanks."

Whatever this was, it had just turned a corner.

He gave *The Halcyon Way* one last look, all clean lines and curated silence, and felt it again: that quiet pressure in his chest that came when something didn't add up.

Whatever this was, it wasn't just a stolen boat.

CHAPTER
TWO

arper stepped away from *The Halcyon Way*, the hum of the harbor fading as he put the phone to his ear. The number Crenshaw had given him rang twice before a gravel-lined voice picked up.

"Sergeant Nolan."

"Sergeant, this is Special Agent Jake Harper, CGIS. You asked for me to call."

"Appreciate it," Nolan said. "Crenshaw filled you in on the stolen boat report?"

"He did." Harper glanced back at the yacht, sleek and silent at the pier.

"Well, our higher ups are wanting us to help you guys out any way we can. Anything you need, Special Agent?"

"We're a little short staffed. Any chance you could send out a crime scene unit? Full sweep. If there's any forensic evidence on that boat, I want it found."

There was a pause. Harper could almost hear the man weighing what to say next.

"Well, you're in luck," Nolan said. "Detective Maguire already beat you to it. He has a CSI team en route, and drew up a warrant just in case. They've got another scene to hit, but should get to your boat later this morning. Should cover you for a deeper look."

Harper pursed his lips. "Detective Maguire?"

"Well, given the nature of things, a missing Coast Guard Officer, the lack of a body, the mess with this bill of sale and stolen boat, my lieutenant wants us to keep a foot in the door. So we're assigning one of ours. Detective Tate Maguire."

Harper chewed his cheek, trying to keep the frustration out of his voice. "You're assigning a Detective? I thought this was a CGIS case."

"It may be. But until we have a clear homicide, and *where* it may have happened, or other proof of federal jurisdiction, this still potentially falls within SPD's lane. My higher-ups want to treat it as a joint-investigation."

Harper stared out across the pier, jaw grinding slowly. He didn't like sharing cases, especially not ones that already felt personal.

"And this Maguire?" he asked. "He any good?"

There was a dry chuckle on the other end. "Maguire's been around longer than most of my unit's been out of diapers. Homicide since '04. He's unconventional, but solid. You'll like him. Or hate him. Probably both."

Harper didn't respond right away. He didn't need a partner. He needed clarity. Answers. Not hand-holding from the local brass.

Still, he'd been in the game long enough to know when to push, and when to play ball.

"Alright," he said finally. "Let me know where to meet him."

•••••

They met just after 9:00 a.m. at *The Shanty,* an old coffee shack tucked near the marina. It was the kind of place built for dockhands and daybreak fishermen, not tourists. Salt clung to the window glass. The air smelled like tidewater and burnt espresso.

Harper arrived to find a man already seated at a sun-bleached table just outside, a newspaper folded neatly next to a half-empty mug. He looked up as Harper approached.

He was tall. Harper could tell that even while seated. A gray beard framed a face lined with sun and time. His full head of hair, still thick and spiked up, gave him an edge that hadn't dulled. He had on stylish tortoiseshell glasses and a smartwatch on his left wrist. He exuded a calm that didn't ask for attention.

"You Harper?" the man asked, voice like sandpaper wrapped in silk.

Harper nodded. "Yeah."

"Tate Maguire." He extended a hand, with a firm grip. *No bullshit.* "Grab a coffee if you need one. I'm not in a rush."

Harper didn't sit yet. "I was told you've been assigned to this case."

Maguire tilted his head. "'Assigned' is a generous term. I was *voluntold.* Politics. You know how it goes."

"I do," Harper said flatly.

Maguire gestured to the open chair with two fingers. "Sit. Relax. I don't bite. Not unless provoked."

Harper sat, back straight, eyes steady. "So why you?"

Maguire leaned back, one arm resting on the chair beside him. His sleeve rode up, revealing ink. Interlocking spirals. A stag. A sunburst in knotwork. Irish paganism woven in skin.

"Two people vanish from a spotless boat," he said. "No blood. No struggle. No goodbye. Then some holy man shows up waving a bill of sale and a halo. You don't need to be a mystic to smell bullshit."

21

Harper allowed the corner of his mouth to lift. Just slightly.

Maguire watched him with the ease of a man who missed nothing. "You're not like the other Feds," he said.

"Wasn't always one. Not really one now, to be honest."

Maguire raised an eyebrow. "Oh?" he said, bringing his coffee cup up for another drink.

"I'm a reservist, on active-duty orders. Just finished up a case back East, was supposed to head back to work next week."

"What do you do when you're not playing Coastie?" Maguire asked.

"Detective, Stonehaven PD," Harper said.

"Ah, yes. I thought your name sounded familiar. I read about that human trafficking case in the news. Redhouse or something?"

Harper leaned back, stretching his back. "Redhaven."

"Ah, that's right."

"Yeah. It was a hell of a thing."

"Sounds like it."

Harper didn't offer more. The headlines had called him a hero, but they hadn't printed the long nights, the mistakes, the girls they hadn't reached in time. None of them had printed the cost. Not the missed chances. Not the girls they couldn't save. Not the weight of losing Detective Sergeant Foster. Of watching his murder, unable to stop it. That wound was still raw, and hadn't closed.

"What about you? What's your story?" Harper asked.

Maguire tapped the side of his mug. "Homicide division since 'oh four. Navy, before that."

Harper laughed. "I thought I smelled a squid."

Maguire choked on his coffee. "Been a minute since a puddle pirate called me that."

"What'd you do in the Navy?"

22

"Got out a lieutenant commander in 'ninety-eight. Got tired of hiding who I was."

Harper tilted his head and raised an eyebrow of his own, but stayed silent.

"Don't ask, don't tell. My now-husband, Thomas, proposed, and I didn't want to hide anymore. Got out after twelve years, joined Seattle PD, and got married in ninety-nine. Been married since."

Harper nodded, the image of Alyssa flickering across his mind, barefoot in the kitchen that morning, mug in hand, belly full with their son. He felt it settle in his chest like warmth, the quiet gratitude of being seen and loved without condition.

"Seems fair to me. No one should have to hide who they are."

For a moment, there was nothing but the wind brushing through halyards and the distant cry of gulls.

Then Maguire said, "So. Want to find out where the bodies are buried?"

Harper met his eyes. "Only if we're the ones digging."

Maguire smiled, and for the first time, it wasn't sharp. It was knowing.

"Good," he said. "Then let's get to work. I'd like to get eyes on the boat, be there for the forensics."

"Let's get to it, then," Harper said.

•••••

The late morning sun cut hard angles across the pier as Harper and Maguire stepped back aboard *The Halcyon Way*. The forensic unit had arrived ten minutes prior—two techs in charcoal jumpsuits and nitrile gloves, their equipment cases already open on the dock.

Maguire stepped over the gunwale and onto the aft deck, eyes sweeping the immaculate surface. "Damn," he muttered. "Looks more like a showroom than a crime scene."

Harper said nothing, but he felt it again. The tightness in his chest. The sterile wrongness that clung to the boat like static.

One of the CSI techs, a young woman with short black hair tucked under a cap, stepped out of the galley. "We've started prints in the main cabin," she said. "Prelim sweep's coming back clean so far. Not smudged. Not partials. Just...nothing."

Maguire raised an eyebrow. "You saying nobody's touched a surface on this entire boat?"

"Well, it's either that," she said, "or someone went through with gloves and bleach. Which coincidentally, it smells like. The chem test will tell us for sure."

They moved inside. Harper could feel it growing. The absence. There was no dust, no clutter, and no grime in the crevices. The place didn't feel used.

The second tech emerged from below deck with a notepad. "Bedrooms are empty. Cabinets are wiped. Drawers have a few utensils, but no personal effects. No clothes. No toothbrush. Nothing in the medicine cabinet, and nothing in the head. You sure this wasn't just a demo yacht?"

Harper walked slowly toward the helm, his eyes tracing the panels. "No. There were signs it was lived in. Photos on social. A trip logged."

The first tech held up a fingerprint card. "We'll still process the helm, exterior railings, and cabin handles. But so far? This boat's a ghost."

Harper nodded. "Then we treat it like one. Document every absence. Every silence. A lived-in boat should look lived in."

Maguire looked out toward the shimmering horizon.

"Where the hell are they?"

"Time to find out."

CHAPTER 3

CHAPTER
THREE

September 10. Noon.

Before chasing any other leads or theories, they had agreed on the next most logical starting point: the Rainers' residence.

They drove separately. Harper, in his nondescript federal sedan, trailed Maguire in his city-issued unmarked Caprice through the midday Seattle traffic. Harper kept the radio on low, static blending with soft-spoken weather updates and the occasional pop-country ballad. A gray marine layer hung over the Sound, and a light mist dusted the windshield, more suggestion than rain.

On the drive, Harper tapped his speed dial.

"Jake! How are ya buddy?" Chief Boatswain's Mate Logan Cross answered, his voice familiar and steady.

"I'm alright. Listen—I'm working a missing persons case. It may brush up against all that shit we just dealt with."

"I'm listening,"

"Daniel and Malia Rainier," Harper said.

There was a brief silence. Then: "Fuck." Cross' tone sharpened. "Tell me everything."

Harper ran through what they had so far.

"This doesn't sound like them," Cross said finally. "But I'll make a few calls. So far, it's been quiet back here."

"Appreciate it, buddy." Harper ended the call.

The West Seattle neighborhood where Daniel and Malia Rainier lived was quiet, tucked into a residential pocket just far enough from the bustle to feel insulated. Shinkle Place SW curved gently through a row of modern two-story townhomes, each painted in muted earth tones, like sage green, terracotta red, and slate gray. Clean sidewalks and tidy landscaping on rain-glossed pavement.

Harper parked behind Maguire at the end of the row. The Rainiers' unit sat at the corner, an end-unit with no backyard neighbors, just a stand of fir trees and a sloping greenbelt beyond the fence.

They stepped out, shutting their doors softly in the hush of the cul-de-sac. Harper pulled on a light jacket against the unexpected cool in the air. *Summer in Seattle, where the sun never made any promises.*

Maguire glanced toward the house. "How do you wanna play this?"

Harper adjusted his jacket. "Figured we'd start simple. Knock, listen, look for anything out of place. But it's your city. I'll follow your lead."

Maguire gave a short nod. "Then let's see if anyone's home."

As they walked up the steps, he could see the lights were off inside. They knocked with authority.

Only silence answered.

They waited a beat. Then another.

"I'll circle around," Harper said. "Check the garage windows."

Maguire nodded and knocked again.

Harper stepped off the stoop and followed the path along the side of the house. Ground-level windows looked into the garage. He cupped a hand to the glass and peered in. Inside, a red Honda sat neatly parked. The rest of the garage was tidy—storage shelves, labeled bins, and a single bike hanging from wall hooks.

He continued around back. The rear garage door was shut. A narrow patch of grass led to a small fenced patio. Above, the second-floor balcony was empty save for a lone lounge chair, a faded cushion drooping over one side. The sliding door was closed.

Harper circled back to the front, where Maguire stood with arms crossed, knocking rhythm replaced by stillness.

"Anything?" Harper asked.

Maguire shook his head. "Nada. No answer. No movement."

"Garage is shut. No one on the balcony. Saw a red Civic in the garage."

"Malia's car," Maguire said without hesitation. At Harper's raised eyebrow, he added, "Pulled DMV records as soon as I got the case. Malia owns a red Civic. Daniel drove a black Raptor."

"They probably took the Raptor to the marina," Harper said. "Either way, we'll need a warrant to get inside."

Maguire smiled, slipping a folded sheet of paper from his briefcase.

"You mean like this?"

Harper blinked, then arched a brow.

"Pays to be prepared, Coastie. Isn't that your motto? Semper...something?"

"Paratus," Harper answered dryly. "Do you have a key by any chance?"

Maguire smiled again, and pulled one out of the briefcase.

"How—?"

"I stopped by the HOA office earlier," he said, matter-of-fact. "They keep a copy of the keys for each unit in case of emergency. Figured it couldn't hurt to ask." He wiggled the key between his fingers, then added with a smirk, "Pays to be *pa-ra-tus*," emphasizing each syllable like a schoolteacher, his tone just shy of smug.

Harper gave a small shake of his head. "You're enjoying this."

"Little bit."

Maguire stepped forward and slid the key into the lock. The deadbolt gave with a solid *click*. As the door creaked open, Harper instinctively braced himself for the worst. He'd walked into enough death scenes to know the scent: sweet rot, sour breath, something that clung to your clothes no matter how fast you left. It was a smell no cop could ever forget.

But the smell did not come.

Instead, the air held the stillness of vacancy. He smelled stale carpet, a faint trace of citrus cleaner beneath the undisturbed air.

"Smells like they've been gone a while," Maguire said behind him.

"Yeah," Harper said. "Let's see what they left behind."

Maguire called out, "Seattle PD! Malia, Daniel, are you in here?"

His voice echoed through the house. Silence answered.

They stepped into the entryway and ascended a short flight of steps. Hardwood creaked faintly beneath their shoes as they entered a small living room. To the left, a modest couch and worn leather chair flanked a low wood coffee table. A waist-high divider separated the space from the dining area, where a long wooden table sat undisturbed, a vase of wilted flowers slumping at its center like a memory long forgotten.

30

They passed another staircase, this one leading down, as they entered the kitchen. The balcony Harper had seen from the street loomed just beyond the sliding glass door, still empty. The half-bath tucked off the kitchen was clean. Lifeless. Everything was still, too still.

They took the stairs down and entered the garage. Malia's red Honda Civic sat idle, dust settled on the hood. Parked just behind it was a black Harley Davidson.

"Daniel's," Maguire said, nodding toward the bike.

They popped the Civic's door. Nothing suspicious. Parking passes for downtown, a coffee shop punch card, and a receipt from Pike Place folded in the glove box. Mundane artifacts of daily life.

Back upstairs, they headed up the second flight of stairs to the top floor. The hallway branched left and right. Straight ahead was a small office, cozy and cluttered. A desk with an open laptop sat beside a compact vinyl cutter. Shelves overflowed with craft supplies: sticker paper, heat transfer vinyl, and ink refills.

Folded baby clothes were stacked neatly beside the desk on a small white shelf. Harper picked one up.

"*Cute-tea*," it read, with a smiling cartoon iced tea. He set it down and picked up another. "*I woke up this cute*." And a third. "*Protected by a U.S. Coast Guard Officer*." His fingers paused on the last one.

He folded them gently and placed them back, something tightening in his chest.

A cluster of photographs lined the hallway wall. Harper paused. One showed Daniel in dress whites, receiving his law diploma from a historically Black college, his proud father standing

31

just behind him in Navy blues. Beside it hung a photo of Malia as a teenager, barefoot in a patterned sundress, standing with her arms around a group of women on a cliff above the ocean. A fresh lei rested on her shoulders, her smile easy and unguarded. There was something rooted in her even then. Something joyful, grounded, and utterly at home.

Down the hallway, they passed a bathroom, standard and unremarkable, then found the master bedroom. A king-sized bed stood in the center. Two nightstands flanked it. On one lay a bible, bookmarked near the back, and a copy of *Black's Law Dictionary*. Daniel's, Harper guessed.

On the other was a water bottle, a folded blanket, and *What to Expect when You're Expecting*. Malia's.

The room felt hollow. What was noteworthy wasn't what they were seeing, it was what *wasn't* there. No suitcases in the closets. No unpacked clothes. The closet doors stood half open, with space in the hangers and empty divots in the shoe racks. Drawers with gaps where clothes had once been folded and stacked.

"They never unpacked," Maguire replied.

Harper said nothing, just nodded and moved into the hallway.

They crossed to the far end of the hall and opened the final door. A nursery. Harper stopped short.

The room was painted in soft blush tones, filled with quiet anticipation. A white crib stood along the far wall, draped in a pink sheet patterned with clouds and stars. A matching dresser sat beneath a mounted pink changing pad. Between the two was a plush pink glider chair, its seat still slightly indented.

A stuffed pink swan was mounted on the wall; its wings spread in mid-flight. Below it, a small bookshelf held empty photo frames, waiting for memories that might never come.

Harper looked again at the glider with its indented seat. He pictured Malia there, one hand on her belly, the other resting on the armrest. He imagined her taking in the room with quiet joy, eyes full of hope and love for a child not yet born. Planning a future that now hovered on the edge of vanishing.

Harper exhaled slowly, the silence around them thick and reverent.

"They were ready," he said.

Maguire gave a faint nod. "And now they're just...gone."

They finished the search through the house, finding no sign the Rainiers had returned since leaving for their trip. Nothing suggested they'd been planning to sell the yacht, either.

Back in the kitchen, Harper stared through the sliding glass door to the alley below. Maguire was on the phone in the living room. After he hung up, he joined Harper by the door.

"I've got one of our guys digging into their finances," Maguire said, "but our preliminary appears clean. No debt, no missed payments. I checked with narcotics and organized crime, and they had nothing on them either. I'm not seeing any reason the Rainiers would be in a sudden need for cash or were in any trouble. At least locally."

Harper nodded. "He wasn't on our radar either. I'll talk to his command, but from what I know, Daniel's record is solid. Highly regarded."

"What about that thing back east?" Maguire asked. "Black water or something?"

"Blackwake," Harper said. He gave a small shake of his head. "I already called back East, spoke with some of my old contacts.

They're going to double check, but so far they have nothing, no chatter, no whispers, no loose ends. Far as anyone can tell, they're done. What's left of them scattered to the wind, the rest dead or awaiting trial."

"Couldn't be retaliation?"

"Not their style," Harper said. "They killed with purpose, when someone was in their way. Once the threat was gone, they moved on. Daniel's part ended when he transferred out here. It's been quiet ever since."

"What about his current case load?"

"Nothing heavy. He was mostly supervising junior JAGs, keeping the Coast Guard out of litigation. Risk management, liability work. My guess is he was easing into a quieter life with the baby on the way."

"Makes sense," Maguire said. "Guess that means it's time we checked out this so-called yacht sale."

"Sounds like the best next step as any," Harper paused. "What do you know about this Pastor Kincaid?"

"Family pastor over at *Living Water*. Big church on the east side, real polished, real connected. A lot of brass go there, rub elbows. A lot of Seattle's political set."

"But not you."

"Nah," Maguire said with a smirk. "Grew up Catholic. Spent enough time in the military hiding who I was. Not doing that anymore."

Harper gave a slight nod. "I hear that."

"Kincaid's a climber," Maguire went on. "He's not lead pastor yet, but he's angling for it. Thinks in soundbites. Smooth. The type who knows which camera to smile for."

They walked to the front door. Harper stopped and took one last look around, eyes sweeping the empty space. The house felt hollow now, stripped of the life it once held. The future they were building. The family they were preparing for. All their hopes and dreams.

I'll find you, Harper promised silently.

He stepped outside and pulled the door shut behind him, quiet as a prayer.

CHAPTER
FOUR

They pulled into the lot just after three.

The church sat on a wide stretch of well-kept property, framed by evergreens and freshly mulched flower beds. The smell of bark dust hung thick in the warm air. There was a row of identical SUVs in the parking lot, branded with the church logo—a stylized symbol of a river flowing. *Living Water Church.* Not quite a megachurch, but close. It was big enough to house hundreds, with room to grow. The building had a modern-rustic facade, with warm stonework, wooden beams, and the kind of welcoming signage that felt curated for social media.

The parking lot stretched wide, lined with reserved spaces for *First-Time Guests* and *Expectant Mothers.* A directional sign pointed toward the gymnasium, children's ministry wing, and cafe. Another pointed inward: *Main Sanctuary - This Way to Worship.*

"Jesus has an ecosystem," Maguire said under his breath as they walked up the front steps.

Harper gave a quiet grunt. "Looks like it."

Inside, the lobby was cavernous and tastefully lit. Pendant lamps hung low over rustic tables. A coffee bar sat to the right. Beyond it, a hallway led toward classrooms and ministry offices. Everything smelled faintly of cinnamon, fresh carpet, and copy paper. Somewhere down the hall came the faint strum of a guitar and the muffled thrum of bass, like background music bleeding from a coffee shop. It lent the place a polished warmth, but to Harper it sounded more curated than spontaneous, ambiance on a timer.

A receptionist greeted them with a bright smile. "Can I help you?" The woman looked to be in her early thirties, with blonde hair that looked professionally bleached and styled. She wore a tight, knee-length skirt and plaid blouse styled to look modest but carried a boutique tag he recognized from Alyssa's magazines; two hundred bucks disguised as humility. Her shiny brow did not move an inch with her smile, showing the botox injections she likely regularly received.

"We're here to see Pastor Kincaid," Harper said, flashing his credentials. "The family pastor."

Her smile tightened slightly. "He's in his office. One moment, I'll let him know you're here."

A few minutes later, a door down the hall opened, and Asher Kincaid stepped out.

He was taller than Harper expected, lean but not frail. Early forties, with short-cropped sandy hair and a neatly trimmed beard. He wore dark jeans, polished brown leather boots, and a slate-gray button-down rolled at the sleeves. He looked like the kind of man who could just as easily sell you a house or pitch you a startup. He looked smooth, polished, the look of an approachable professional.

"Officers," he said, voice warm and rehearsed. "I'm Asher Kincaid. Appreciate you coming by. Always happy to help our public servants." Harper wasn't sure, but he thought he caught the faintest flicker of Kincaid's eyes. As if he was quickly sizing them up, like a salesman taking the measure of a buyer. Or a boxer sizing up his opponent in the ring.

"Detective," Maguire corrected, his smile polite but tight.

"Special Agent Harper, CGIS," Harper added, showing his ID.

"My apologies, gentlemen. I'm not used to dealing with law enforcement, outside of the pews, of course. We do have several of Seattle and King County's finest as a part of our congregation." He shook hands with both of them. His grip was firm and practiced, but his smile lingered a half-second too long, as if rehearsed in a mirror.

He ushered them into his office. "Right this way."

His office was modest, smaller than expected. Tastefully minimal. Bible college diplomas were neatly framed besides certificates in family counseling. The details of the office were meticulously ordered, yet one diploma frame was slightly crooked. Harper filed it away. A verse stretched across the wall behind the desk: *"Train up a child in the way he should go..."*

Harper scanned the bookshelf. Row after row of books on purity culture, courtship, and marriage theology. *Dating with an Eternity Mindset. Courtship in the Modern Era.* He recognized a few from his own youth.

Harper clocked it all with a glance. So did Maguire, though his poker face was better.

"Please, have a seat," Kincaid said, gesturing to the two chairs across from his desk. "What can I do for you?"

"We're following up on your report," Harper said, sliding out his notebook. "*The Halcyon Way.* You claimed you purchased it?"

"That's correct," Kincaid said smoothly. "I was hoping to restore it. Beautiful vessel. Terrible shame it was stolen." The corner of his mouth twitched before settling back into the smooth smile.

"Restore it?" Maguire asked.

"Why, yes. It just needed some refinishing. Nothing major, just some upkeep—woodwork, polish. A good cleaning."

Harper made a note. *Refinishing, or cleaning?* The downgrade was subtle, but shifts in someone's story always mattered.

"Where and when did the sale take place?" Maguire asked.

"Here in Seattle. Couple days ago," Kincaid replied. "I'd been in contact with through my agent for about a week. We agreed on terms. I paid in full, cash, as requested. I have the bill of sale if you need it."

Harper studied him. "Do you know Daniel or Malia Rainier personally?"

Kincaid blinked, then tilted his head slightly, as if trying to recall. "Rainier...yes, that was the name of the previous owners. At least, that was their names on the paperwork. But no, we never met face-to-face. All communication was through the broker." His blink was a fraction too long, the pause just noticeable enough to make Harper wonder if he was recalling, or inventing.

Harper and Maguire shared a look. "Name of the broker?" Harper asked.

"Yes, of course." Kincaid turned to a drawer and flipped through a small stack of papers. "Here—Trevor Oliver. He attended our church briefly, but I wouldn't say we were close." Kincaid said the last part quickly, as though putting distance between them. But his tone seemed to carry a trace of familiarity that didn't match the words.

Kincaid continued. "When I mentioned wanting to buy a vessel for the church, someone mentioned he worked in yacht brokerage. So I reached out."

He handed them a business card. Harper took it. No website, just a name and a phone number.

"And the pick up?" Harper asked. "When and where did you take possession?"

"Supposed to be right at the marina. Where they had been keeping it, the Shilshole Point Marina. No one was there, and the yacht was missing. They were supposed to leave the keys in the galley before they headed out of town. They were going to walk me through it." He paused, then added with a hint of irritation. "Still waiting on that tour."

The certainty in his tone didn't match the word supposed. Harper marked it. It was one of those slips he recognized as a man claiming ignorance but knowing more than he should.

"What do you mean?" Maguire asked.

"Well, I was supposed to meet them to go over the systems. You know, the quirks of the boat. Always easier when the prior owners walk you through it. I'd hate to sue for breach of contract," he added lightly. "When you find them, please tell them to give me a call."

Maguire snorted. "Suing someone for skipping a boat tour? That very Christlike of you?"

Kincaid didn't blink. "The justice system exists to serve everyone, Detective. Including the church."

There was a beat of silence.

Harper flipped his notebook closed. "We've located *The Halcyon Way*." He studied Kincaid's reaction.

Kincaid perked up. "That's wonderful! Where is it?" His pupils seemed to flare just briefly before his expression softened again.

"Secured at Coast Guard Base Seattle," Harper replied. "Until further notice, it's being held as part of an ongoing investigation."

Kincaid's smile wavered slightly. "You're holding it?"

"Standard procedure," Harper said evenly. "We're treating this as a possible missing persons case."

"Missing persons?" Kincaid asked.

Maguire looked at the pastor. "The Rainiers. They're currently missing."

Kincaid's brow furrowed just enough to register concern. "Oh. That's... awful. I'm sorry to hear that." He offered a small, practiced smile. "I'm sure you'll get to the bottom of it. Truth has a way of surfacing."

Harper didn't respond right away. Just let the silence stretch.

Then Maguire leaned forward slightly, his tone polite but edged. "With all due respect, Pastor... what exactly does a family minister need with a yacht like *The Halcyon Way*?"

Kincaid's smile didn't falter. "A fair question. I understand how that might look from the outside."

Harper tilted his head, watching him.

Kincaid folded his hands over his knee, settling in. "Our church believes in stewardship. And we believe God blesses faithful servants. Sometimes those blessings come in ways that allow us to bless others. That yacht, well, it's not about luxury. It's about opportunity."

"Opportunity for...?" Maguire prompted.

Kincaid's voice warmed. "We do a lot of outreach. Host donor couples, ministry partners. When you take someone out on the water—give them space to breathe, to feel God's peace—it opens doors. It softens hearts. A relaxed donor is a generous donor. And generous donors let us feed more families, support more missions, fund more counseling scholarships." His voice warmed as if he'd given the pitch before, polished from repetition.

Harper stayed quiet. Maguire didn't.

"What about the other side of that coin?" he asked. "Jesus said it's easier for a camel to pass through the eye of a needle than for a rich man to enter the kingdom of heaven."

Harper let Maguire press the point, content to watch how Kincaid handled friction.

A faint tightness flickered around Kincaid's eyes before he chuckled, like a teacher humoring a thoughtful student. He leaned forward slightly, palms open like a professor steering a seminar. "That's one interpretation. But Scripture has layers. Context. The message isn't about condemning wealth, it's about how you use it. We're not building empires. We're building bridges."

Maguire raised an eyebrow. "Expensive bridges."

Kincaid spread his hands slightly. "Look, gentlemen. We serve a diverse congregation. Wealthy families, struggling single moms, everyone in between. Some of our largest donors don't respond to Sunday morning handshakes. But an afternoon on the water? That creates connection. And connection creates mission."

Harper glanced again at the books on the shelf. The verse on the wall. The polished smile on Kincaid's face.

"I'm sure you do a lot of good," Harper said, voice neutral.

Kincaid nodded solemnly. "We try to. The harvest is plentiful."

The room sat quiet for half a beat before Maguire stood.

"Well, Pastor, thanks for your time. We'll be in touch."

Kincaid stood, offering his hand again. "Of course."

Harper shook it. So did Maguire. The second shake was cooler than the first. Harper felt it, even if Kincaid's smile hadn't dimmed.

They turned to leave, but Harper paused at the door and looked back.

"Mr. Kincaid, could I get that bill of sale?"

"Oh, yes. One moment." Kincaid opened a drawer and thumbed through a small stack of papers. "Ah, here it is." He handed over a sealed manila envelope. "I'll get that back, I'm assuming?"

"When we're done with it, yes."

"Perfect. And thank you for your service, gentlemen." His smile didn't falter for a second.

As they made their way back down the hallway, the sound of laughter and guitar drifted faintly from a nearby classroom.

Maguire muttered just loud enough for Harper to hear, "Nothing to hide, my ass."

Back at their cars, they stopped briefly while putting their notebooks back in their cars. Harper spoke first.

"That verse you quoted to Kincaid. About the camel and the needle. You remember it well."

Maguire turned and looked back at the church, but the corner of his mouth tugged into something between a smile and a grimace. "Confirmation class. I had to memorize whole passages. Did the altar boy thing. Communion, the works."

"That's right. You're Catholic."

"Was," Maguire said. "Grew up in Long Beach. Irish neighborhood. Whole family was Mass-on-Sundays, don't-dare-miss-Lent type."

"What changed?"

Maguire was quiet a beat. "I fell in love."

Harper said nothing. Just listened.

"I was twenty. In the Navy. Officer training. Met Thomas at a bar in Norfolk. Two weeks later, I knew. Two years later, we got married in Canada, because back home it wasn't legal yet." Maguire glanced at Harper. "Church didn't exactly send a wedding gift."

Harper's brow creased slightly. "They cut you off?"

"They didn't need to. I left before they could. Got tired of pretending every Sunday. Tired of confessions that felt more like blackmail than grace."

"And your family?"

Maguire took a long breath. "My mom came around. My sisters too. But my father... he was the Chief of Police back in Long Beach. Old-school. Held respect like a badge and shame like a sword. Never forgave me."

"I'm sorry."

Maguire waved it off. "That's not why I left the church. I left because it stopped feeling like God and started feeling like control. Just another system that made you lie about who you were. And I'd already seen too much of that in uniform."

"I hear that," Harper said.

Maguire glanced over, reading something in Harper's expression. "You too, huh?"

Harper didn't answer right away. Just stared at the steeple rising against the sky, then back toward the road.

"I grew up Baptist, small-town church. Summers were revivals and Bible camp, winters were potlucks in the fellowship hall. Youth group, Bible club in high school. My dad was an elder, my mom sang in the choir. Back then it felt simple. God. Family. Community. But somewhere along the line, simple...changed."

Maguire gave a small nod. No judgement, just understanding. "Guess we both know what it's like to have the ground shift beneath your feet. For me, it was incense and Latin every Sunday, kneeling till my knees went numb."

Harper's gaze lingered on the clouds beyond the church. A faint memory stirred—the smell of pine and sawdust from Bible camp, hymnals pressed into his hands. "Let's just say I've spent a lot of time figuring out which parts of my faith were mine...and which parts were somebody else's leash."

The two men stood quietly for a moment, the church behind them still glowing with soft light, the sound of distant music floating faintly through the parking lot like some curated echo of peace. But Harper could feel the dissonance beneath it, the way charm could be a mask, and righteousness a costume.

Charm was easy. Righteousness was even easier. But truth was something that could not be counterfeited.

CHAPTER
FIVE

Harper was quiet on the drive east, the skyline falling behind him as the city gave way to forest-lined highways and open hills. He and Maguire had decided to split the work, cover more ground, and keep the pressure on. Something about the bill of sale was too clean, too convenient. The whole transaction reeked of forethought.

Maguire would stay in Seattle to dig into Asher Kincaid and the so-called broker, Trevor Oliver.

Harper had drawn the harder hand.

He was headed to Snoqualmie to meet Malia Rainier's parents.

The Rainiers' cell phones had gone straight to voicemail every time they tried. No pings. No movement. Just silence and two full inboxes.

Harper reached for the coin he kept in his pocket without thinking, thumbing it once, then letting it drop back. Foster's words, the same etched on the coin, echoed quietly in his head.

Right is right. No matter the cost.

He didn't know what the Rainiers had stumbled into. Not yet. But he was starting to believe they hadn't just vanished.

As the SUV hummed along I-90, Harper's mind replayed the interview with Kincaid. The smug composure, the practiced warmth, like a politician giving a eulogy for someone he'd never met.

There was something about that kind of performance, something familiar. A mask worn too well.

The religious veneer didn't bother Harper on the surface. He'd grown up in churches. He knew the rhythms of Scripture, the weight of guilt, the scent of wood polish and bad coffee in fellowship halls. Hell, at one point he'd wanted to *be* a pastor. But he also knew the men who learned to weaponize it, men who hid ambition behind pulpits and used God as cover for control.

He'd seen it too many times before: the charm that sold obedience as love.

And once, a long time ago, he nearly bought it himself.

•••••

Then.

The air smelled like pine needles, dust, and campfire smoke. *Taps* played in the background over the camp speakers, signaling lights out, but the cabins were still buzzing with half-whispered stories and stifled laughter. Fourteen-year-old Jake Harper lay in his bunk, staring at the rafters. His chest felt tight, but not from the heat. From what had just happened. From the pure excitement of it all.

They'd kissed. His heart thundered as he remembered how soft her lips felt against his.

Melissa Whitley. A sweet girl with a soft laugh. Jake was smitten. They'd talked all week during Bible study breakouts and camp games, drifting a little farther from the group each day. Until today, the first day week two, he'd mustered up the courage to kiss her. One kiss, quick and nervous. Electric. One turned into two. Then ten minutes under the stars, wrapped in the kind of magic only first love could conjure.

They'd walked back, hand in hand, dropping them quickly when passing camp counselors. No one saw. They were sure of it. At the steps of her cabin, Melissa looked both ways, then kissed him again. With intent. Like she meant it. Then she disappeared behind the door.

Jake floated back to his own cabin. He felt like he could fly.

The next morning, at breakfast, Jake and Melissa couldn't stop stealing glances. Across the boys' table. Across the chapel crowd. She blushed every time. Jake was already daydreaming about the next two weeks at camp. His first girlfriend.

Then his counselor, Kevin, pulled him aside. Said Pastor Rick wanted a word. Rick had a tan like polished leather and a voice built for sermons and shame. He filled pulpits and silence with equal weight. Kids cried during his altar calls nightly. Some collapsed under it.

Jake sat alone in his office, heart pounding again, for a different reason. He ran through every camp rule in his head. He hadn't broken any. Had he?

The overhead light buzzed faintly. A Bible lay open on the desk beside a worn copy of *Every Young Man's Battle*.

Pastor Rick soon joined, sitting in his chair with a rusty creak. He folded his hands and gave Jake a sympathetic smile, the kind that wasn't quite kind.

"Jake," he said. "Do you know why you're here? Why I asked to speak with you?"

Jake shook his head, throat tight.

"I understand there was some...unwise behavior last night."

Jake didn't answer.

"You and Melissa. What happened?"

Jake's blood ran cold, numbness spreading through his chest. Before he could speak, Pastor Rick continued.

"Your counselor, Kevin, followed you when you wandered off. Saw you two through the trees."

He was spying on us? Jake felt his ears burn hot as he looked down at his feet.

"Now's the time to be honest, Jake. You two were being untoward. Being *sexual* with each other."

Jake's head snapped up. "All we did was kiss!"

"And did you feel anything during that kiss?"

Jake blinked. "What?"

"I mean physically. Emotionally. Did it stir up anything in you that shouldn't have been there?"

He felt his face burning. "I...I don't know."

Pastor Rick tapped the Bible. "Scripture tells us to flee youthful lusts. Not manage them. Not excuse them. *Flee.*"

Jake stared at the pastor in confusion. "Pastor, it wasn't lust...it was just kissing. I—I like her. She likes me. We're just...gonna be boyfriend and girlfriend."

Rick shook his head. "Jake, Jake. *Fleeing* means no dating without the intention of marriage. Hand-holding, kissing, those are distractions. You're called to purity, Jake. Not confusion. Are you planning on marrying Melissa?"

"I don't know. I'm just fourteen!" Jake said, tears welling.

"If you don't know," Rick said gently, "let me tell you. I've been in this business a long time. I've seen these things. Middle and high school romances don't lead to marriage. Which means—"

"But—"

"Let me finish, son. It means when you kissed Melissa, you were kissing another man's wife. And that's serious. Jesus tells us that

50

even *looking* at another man's wife is to commit adultery in your heart. And you kissed her."

Jake broke and began sobbing, his head in his hands.

"I want you to picture your future wife watching you right now. Watching while you're at camp. Would she be proud? Watching you kiss another man's bride?"

"No," Jake choked out.

Rick's voice softened. "God has a plan for you. I see it. But sin wants to derail that plan early. The Enemy knows where we're weak. Right now? That's your heart. Your body. Your discipline."

He handed Jake a worksheet: *Accountability Questions for Young Men.* Checkboxes for *impure thoughts. Sexual temptation. Guarding your heart.*

"Take this. Fill it out. I'll check in tomorrow before morning worship."

Jake took it numbly. "What about Melissa?"

"I'm afraid our code of conduct is clear. She led her brother in Christ to stumble. She'll be going home. Her parents are already on the way."

"What? Why punish her? We both—" Jake's voice cracked with outrage, the injustice boiling in his veins. "We both kissed each other!"

Rick sighed. "Her responsibility was modesty. She failed. We can't have temptation spreading. Reflect on how to spend the rest of camp in purity."

Outside, the moon still lingered in the daylight sky. The pine trees whispered above the chapel.

Jake didn't return to his cabin right away. He sat on a rock near the flagpole, knees pulled to his chest, the worksheet clutched in his hand.

His heart was broken, over Melissa, over the next two weeks alone, over the injustice of it all. She was being sent home. He got a worksheet.

He cried, knowing he did nothing wrong, but feeling filthy anyway.

•••••

Now.

The road curved east. Harper blinked, clearing the memory like fog from glass. The past wasn't something you escaped. You just learned where to set it down.

As Harper drove into Snoqualmie, he was struck by the town's idyllic architecture, nestled beneath the shadow of the Cascades. It looked like something out of a postcard, with quaint streets, carefully preserved Craftsman homes, and flower boxes bursting with late summer color.

There was a slow rhythm here. Cars moved deliberately. Storefronts bore names instead of brands. Kids rode bikes down the sidewalk without helmets, and an old man waved from a rocking chair outside a barber shop that hadn't changed its signage since 1974.

It felt untouched. Or, at least, like it wanted to be.

Harper had always found towns like this harder in cases like these. The grief hit different. More concentrated. It seeped into the corners, into swing sets that wouldn't be used, porches that wouldn't be paced, dinner tables still set for two.

He turned off the main drag and followed a tree-lined street that sloped gently up toward the residential ridge. The Kaluas lived in a cedar-sided home with soft blue trim and a wide porch draped in hanging baskets. A red Subaru sat in the driveway. A garden flag fluttered near the front step, *Aloha, Welcome Home* spelled out in cheerful script above a wreath of painted daisies.

Harper parked at the curb. He cut the engine and sat still for a moment, hand resting lightly on the key.

He hated this part.

The part where he had to knock on a door and maybe not have answers. The part where a mother's eyes searched his face for hope and a father tried not to look broken.

The part where *missing* edged closer to *already gone.*

He stepped out of the sedan, adjusted his badge, and made his way to the front porch. The porch boards creaked beneath his shoes. The hanging baskets swayed slightly in the mountain breeze.

The door was answered almost immediately after he knocked, the door opening to a woman in her late fifties. She had warm brown skin, her black hair streaked with silver and swept into a loose bun. She wore soft scrubs and a worried expression that didn't ease when she saw Harper's badge.

"Mrs. Kalua?" Harper asked, holding up his badge wallet. "My name is Jake Harper. I'm a Special Agent with the Coast Guard Investigative Service. May I come in?"

"Call me Leina. Please, come in."

Harper stepped into the house. It smelled faintly of lemon and fabric softener. Family photos lined the hallway: Malia at her wedding, Malia in college, Malia on a horse as a small child. Another showed her on a beach in Maui, hair windblown, feet in the sand, holding a cracked coconut and grinning like it was treasure. Yet another showed Malia in a college cap and gown, grinning between two proud parents. Her smile didn't change much.

"Ron's out back," Leina said, leading Harper through the kitchen. "He's tuning up a customer's bike. It's how he copes."

She guided him into a modest backyard with a view facing the mountains. Ron Kalua stood beside a bike stand, tightening cables with quiet precision. He was tall, still solidly built, his skin sun-darkened, curls tied back into a short ponytail. Years of cycling had carved lean strength into him, but the worry etched around his eyes was new.

"What's this about?" Ron asked, letting go of the bike cables. "Why is the Coast Guard here? Did something happen to Malia and Daniel?"

Harper folded his hands. "We found a yacht adrift yesterday morning—*The Halcyon Way*. It was floating in Elliott Bay, just outside Seattle. No one was on board. We believe it was their vessel. Can you confirm?"

Leina gasped, her hand flying to her mouth. "That was their boat!"

"Were they recently on a trip?" Harper asked.

"Yes," Ron said. "Two weeks cruising the San Juans. Kind of a honeymoon continuation."

"They were celebrating," Leina added, her voice catching. "She's pregnant. It's their first. They've been trying for a while."

Harper felt a sharp tug in his chest. He thought of Alyssa. Her belly. Their son.

"How far along is she?" he asked gently.

"Five months," Leina said.

Ron had his phone out, already trying. He pressed it to his ear. "No answer."

"We haven't been able to reach them either," Harper said. "Can you confirm their phone numbers for me?"

Ron handed over his phone. Harper quickly noted the numbers, Daniel's and Malia's. Both matched what they had.

"When were they supposed to return?"

"Yesterday," Ron said. "We figured they extended their trip. They do that sometimes."

"Oh God..." Leina's voice cracked. She turned toward Harper, tears beginning to spill. "Do you think something's happened to them? My baby girl..."

"That's what we're trying to find out, ma'am," Harper said softly. "We're following every lead. That's why I'm here. Can you tell me a bit more about Daniel? About their relationship?"

Ron leaned forward in his chair. "Daniel's a solid guy. Coast Guard Academy, law school, then commissioned officer. Smart. Steady. The best we could ask for in a son-in-law."

"She always said he made her feel safe," Leina added, dabbing her eyes with a tissue. "He's like a son to us."

"He's always treated her with respect," Ron added. "A man knows."

"They're so in love," Leina whispered. Then, with trembling hands, she opened a drawer on the side table and pulled out a photo. It showed Malia and Daniel grinning, holding up a black-and-white sonogram beside a letterboard sign: *Baby Rainier - Coming Soon!* Daniel's arm was wrapped protectively around her shoulders, in dress whites, his uniform cap pushed back just enough to show his eyes. Malia wore a flowery blue dress and a plumeria tucked behind one ear, her long dark hair cascading over her shoulder.

Harper stared at the image. Malia's eyes sparkled with joy. Daniel stood proud, protective, the kind of man who already saw himself as a father. There was a joy in both of them, real and unguarded. The kind of happiness people couldn't fake.

It hit like a weight to the chest.

He cleared his throat and gently accepted the photo. "Would you mind if I scanned this for our case file?"

Leina nodded, her fingers lingering on the frame before she let go.

"Can you think of anyone who'd want to hurt them?"

"No—no, everyone loves them," Leina said, voice trembling. "Why? Do you think something's happened?"

"We're just following every possible lead right now, ma'am," Harper said, keeping his tone level.

Ron jumped in. "Well, aside from that ugly business back East, there's been nothing. Nothing like that out here."

"Anywhere else they'd go?" Harper asked. "A cabin? Friends in the area?"

"That boat was their get-away," Ron said. "If they wanted quiet, that's where they'd be."

"I don't know much about their friends here," Leina added. "Daniel's parents passed a few years ago. He always said we were his second parents. Always happy to see us."

She hesitated, then added, "Malia did mention she had a close friend from college who lives nearby. They'd got back in touch after she and Daniel moved back here. They'd, go get coffee, go for walks. Sadie something. I think she lived up toward Kirkland for a while, and just moved downtown."

Harper looked at the Kaluas. "How did they keep the boat? Was it neat? Messy?"

"Oh, they were fastidious," Ron said. "Daniel kept it all top-notch. Everything was in working order and clean. Him being in the Coast Guard and all."

"What about personal effects on board?" Harper asked.

"That was clean too. They always put stuff away," Leina said, then paused. "Although... they usually had a few things left out after a trip. Malia's sandals, Daniel's travel mug, that kind of thing."

"Did they keep it show-ready?"

"No," Ron said slowly. "It was clean, but lived in. They weren't prepping it for charter guests or anything."

"Were they thinking about selling it?"

"They didn't say so directly," Leina said. "But they'd talked about needing more space. Bigger house down the line. Maybe even a second baby someday."

Ron added, "With the baby coming, I think they knew the boat might get used less. Could've been thinking ahead."

Harper nodded slowly, absorbing it all. Then he stood, pulling two cards from his wallet and handing one to each of them.

"If you hear anything, anything at all, please call me directly. I'll make sure you're updated the moment we know more."

"Please do, Agent," Ron said.

Leina stepped forward and took Harper's hand in both of hers. "Please. Find my baby."

Harper held her gaze. "I'll do my very best, ma'am."

Outside, the air had cooled. The sun was beginning to dip behind the ridgeline, casting long shadows across the quiet street.

Harper slid into the driver's seat and started the engine. He sat there for a moment, hands on the wheel, clenching his jaw.

He knew.

He was in it now.

No way he could walk away. Not with this. Not with *them*.

He was supposed to return to Stonehaven next week.

But he wasn't going anywhere.

Not until the Rainiers were found.

He just had to tell Alyssa.

CHAPTER
SIX

Harper pulled into the driveway of their rental home, nestled near the end of a quiet cul-de-sac in a tree-lined suburban neighborhood. It was the kind of place where porch swings creaked in the wind and chalk drawings faded slowly on the sidewalks. A wind chime stirred lazily on the neighbor's porch.

The house itself was modest: one story, light gray with navy trim, with a small covered porch and a patch of hydrangeas that Alyssa had coaxed into bloom. It wasn't permanent. The furniture didn't all match. But it was theirs for now. A pocket of peace, borrowed time before everything changed again.

Harper cut the engine and sat for a moment, fingers still resting on the key. Inside, he knew Alyssa would be making dinner or coaxing Addie into picking up her crayons. Maybe humming to herself. Maybe resting. He wasn't sure.

He knew what he had to say. But he wasn't sure how to say it.

As Harper opened the door and set his keys in the bowl by the entry table, he heard the unmistakable squeal of delight from down the hall.

"Daddy!" Addie came barreling toward him, arms wide, socks sliding on the hardwood.

"Baby girl!" Harper grinned, scooping her up mid-sprint and spinning her in a wide circle. Her giggles echoed through the house like music, warm and wild.

Alyssa leaned in from the kitchen, a dish towel slung over her shoulder. "Hey, you."

He met her halfway for a quick kiss, Addie still clinging to his neck. "How's the day?" she asked.

Harper hesitated just a beat too long. "Let's talk after Addie goes to bed."

Alyssa raised an eyebrow, reading more in his eyes than he said aloud. She nodded. "Okay."

Harper grilled steaks and zucchini out back while Alyssa prepped Addie's mac and cheese, her favorite, the kind shaped like little characters from her favorite movie. The sun dipped behind the trees, casting amber light across the deck.

At dinner, Addie held court with tales from her playdate.

"And then," she said, eyes huge, "Cayden jumped up on the slide and, and—" She dissolved into giggles, trying to get the words out. "He burped! *Really loud!*"

Harper laughed. Alyssa laughed harder.

It was simple. Perfect, in its own fleeting way. A moment that grounded him, anchored him, just long enough to carry the weight of everything that was coming.

That night, after Addie was asleep and the dishes were drying in the rack, Harper sat on the couch with Alyssa, his body angled toward her, one leg bouncing unconsciously.

He told her everything. Well, almost everything. The broad strokes.

He talked about meeting Maguire, the jurisdictional tug-of-war, the strange circumstances surrounding the yacht, and how the trail led to a man named Asher Kincaid.

"This guy... Kincaid," Harper said, leaning back with a sigh, "he's a snake. I know exactly the type. I grew up with guys like him, always preaching obedience while masking control. Hungry for power, dressed up as spiritual guidance."

Alyssa tucked her legs under herself on the couch. "The kind that uses God like a leash."

"Exactly."

She studied him for a moment. "What about the couple?"

Harper rubbed a hand over his jaw. "Far as I can tell, they were happy. Solid. Daniel Rainier, he was a Coast Guard JAG officer, worked on the Blackwake stuff around the same time I did, then transferred out recently. Sharp guy. He and his wife, Malia, bought that yacht, fixed it up with their own hands. They called it *The Halcyon Way.*"

Alyssa raised an eyebrow. "Peaceful path. Sounds like they were looking for calm."

"They finally got pregnant," Harper said, his voice softening. "Took a month off. Cruised the San Juans. A babymoon."

Alyssa's hand instinctively settled over her own belly. "God..."

"I went to see Malia's parents today. The Kaluas. Good people. Her mom, Leina—" He stopped, swallowing once. "She showed me a picture. Malia and Daniel holding their sonogram. Big grins. So proud. So damn *full* of life."

He looked down, jaw flexing. "And now they're just... gone."

Alyssa's gaze didn't leave his face. "You're in this, aren't you?"

He didn't answer right away. He reached across the couch and laid his palm gently on her belly.

"Lyss," he said, voice barely above a whisper. "They were expecting their first. Building their family. Living quiet, good lives. I can't shake the feeling—"

"That it could've been us," Alyssa said softly.

He nodded, his hand still on her stomach. "I just keep seeing their faces."

Alyssa was quiet for a moment. Then she reached up and touched the side of his face, thumb grazing his cheek.

"Babe, I get it. You need to see this through."

"You sure?" he asked, his hand finding hers.

She nodded. "I can put up with this rental house a little longer. But I want you back when it's done. Really back."

"I will be," he promised.

"I know," she said, eyes steady. "But be careful. I don't want Addie asking why Daddy's not home again."

That one hit deep. Harper closed his eyes briefly and kissed her knuckles.

"I won't let this eat me, I swear. But I have to do it."

"Then go find the truth," Alyssa said. "And come home."

Later that night, the house was quiet.

Alyssa's back pressed lightly against Harper's chest as they lay beneath the thin sheets. His hand rested on the curve of her belly, fingers tracing idle patterns he didn't realize he was making. Her breathing was slow, steady—until his hand shifted lower, brushing gently along the curve of her hip. He felt her inhale, felt the slight arch of her back as she pressed back into him, responding without words.

His fingers found the edge of her shirt, slipped beneath it, exploring familiar skin with quiet reverence. She turned her head slightly, and he kissed the curve of her neck, slow and lingering. Her body moved in time with his, a rhythm built from years of trust, of knowing each other's needs without needing to ask.

There was a quiet urgency to their touch, like they both sensed how fleeting and fragile peace could be. The kind of intimacy that wasn't about escape, it was about anchoring. About saying *I'm still here.* About choosing each other again, even with the world pressing in.

Clothes slipped away, soft and unhurried. They stayed close, Harper holding her as they moved together, every motion deliberate and grounded in something deeper than desire. It wasn't fast. It wasn't wild. It was a promise. A reminder.

They didn't speak. They didn't need to. Only the soft shuffle of sheets, the warmth of skin against skin, and the steady return to breath as they finally stilled, wrapped in something that felt, just for a moment, like safety.

Afterward, Harper held her close, his heartbeat slowing as sleep began to take him.

But rest didn't last long.

The dream came slowly at first—shadows flickering across a hallway, the smell of cordite in the air, the copper sting of blood in his nose.

He was back in Blackridge.

The station walls closed in around him, familiar and wrong. He heard shouting. Gunfire. Felt the bone-deep weight of loss before he saw it. The distorted echo of boots slammed on tile. Somewhere, someone was screaming for help. A voice he couldn't place. Maybe it was his own.

Then he saw him.

Sergeant Foster lay on the ground, blood pooling under his vest, mouth open like he'd died mid-sentence. His eyes stared past Harper, wide and still.

Harper tried to reach him, but a thunderclap of a gunshot froze him in place.

Dunham, his former Sergeant, stepped out of the smoke, pistol raised. His eyes were hollow. No conscience behind them. Only purpose. The same kind that had let him traffic children from behind a badge. Smoke coiled from the barrel of his gun and seemed to fill the hallway like a living thing, thick and suffocating.

Harper raised his pistol towards Dunham and pulled the trigger. *Click.* The gun wouldn't fire. Harper looked at it in panic, seeing the bullet he fired slide out of the barrel and drop to the floor like it was coated in molasses. Dunham's laugh echoed through the dark fog. Harper aimed and fired again.

Click.

The slide locked. Useless.

Dunham smiled.

His laughter echoed through the dark, twisted corridor as Harper ran, his heart pounding, his lungs burning. The hallway stretched on forever, doors slamming shut before he could reach them, one after another. He could hear their cries behind the closed doors. Women. Children. He knew the awfulness of what was occurring behind the doors at the hands of evil men. But he was too late to save them. Always too late.

He turned a corner and saw the Rainiers' yacht floating in the fog, impossibly adrift in the middle of a dimly lit corridor. Malia stood on the bow, soaked, screaming his name. Screaming for help. Her voice fractured the silence like glass.

He ran toward her, but the yacht pulled away, fading into the mist. He ran faster, catching glimpses of the yacht, bringing it back into partial view. Malia was still standing on the bow, reaching for him. But it was no longer Malia. Alyssa now stood in her place, pregnant, reaching for him with fear in her eyes.

"Jake," she cried out. "Please help me..."

He ran faster still, trying to reach her.

The hallway tilted. She was falling. And then he was falling too.

He woke with a gasp, sitting up in bed. The bedroom was dark and still. The fan hummed softly in the corner. Beside him, Alyssa slept, her breathing rhythmic. Peaceful.

Harper put his elbows on his knees, palms pressed to his face. Sweat clung to his bare chest, heart thudding like he was still running.

He looked over at her. Then down to her stomach. He let out a breath and rubbed his eyes.

This wasn't just another case. It never had been.

CHAPTER
SEVEN

September 11.

The next morning, Harper stood in the backyard with his phone pressed to his ear, the morning air still cool against his skin. Birds called lazily from the trees lining the fence, and somewhere down the block a sprinkler hissed to life.

"SSA Easton," came the voice on the other end, clipped and alert.

"It's Harper," he said. "I wanted to give you an update."

He laid it out, the yacht, the missing couple, the eerie cleanliness of the scene, and the bill of sale tied to a local family pastor named Asher Kincaid. He talked about meeting Maguire, the jurisdictional tug-of-war, and the early signs pointing toward foul play.

There was a pause. Then:

"This guy, Kincaid, he seem good for it?" Easton asked.

Harper rubbed the back of his neck. "He's something. Smooth. Charismatic. The kind of man who's always five seconds ahead of the truth. And something's not adding up here, boss."

"And jurisdiction?"

"Still unclear. Seattle PD's officially involved. Maguire's on it. But the victims—with Daniel Rainier being a Coast Guard officer, active duty, and the boat likely used in the commission of a double homicide, this falls under CGIS."

"Right. Sounds like it's ours. And also Seattle PD's. Which means headaches."

"Yep," Harper said.

Another beat of silence.

"What about a connection to Blackwake?" Easton asked.

"I checked with Cross. So far, we're not finding any. But he's going to ask around, just in case."

"And I'm guessing," Easton said, "you're about to ask me for it."

Harper chuckled. "You know me too well."

"Only because I've cleaned up after you before. What about Alyssa and the baby?"

Harper's voice softened. "Boss... that's why I *have* to do this. Not only because of what we went through back east, but Malia Rainier was five months pregnant. She and Daniel were expecting their first. This wasn't just a missing persons case. This was a family that never made it home."

Easton was quiet for a long moment.

"And Alyssa's good with this?"

"We talked it over last night. She knows what this is for. We're in. I just need your sign-off to extend my orders."

"I figured this was coming," Easton said. "Seattle PD called over, let us know they were assigning a detective and looping in CGIS. When I didn't hear from you all day, I knew you were already buried in it."

"You know I wouldn't be coming to you if it wasn't the real thing," Harper said.

"I do. And frankly, I'm glad you did." Easton's tone shifted, more pragmatic now. "We're short right now. I've got one agent on temporary duty out of district, one's on medical leave, and the rest are stretched thin across five active cases. If this had come up two weeks ago, we might've had someone to hand it to. Right now?" He paused. "You're it."

"I can handle it."

"I know you can," Easton said. "Stonehaven proved that. You've got a homicide detective's brain and a Coastie's gut. Honestly, pairing you with Seattle PD on this one's probably the best we could do."

A pause.

"Orders are already cut. All you have to do is accept. Open-ended. You'll stay on until this case is closed. But I may need to loop you in on other consults along the way, but this'll be your primary."

Harper exhaled. The commitment settled over him like a weight, but also, strangely, like a clarity. The turning point. The quiet, steady shift from borrowed time to committed duty.

"Appreciate it," he said. "If you can get me access to the AIS tracking logs, I want to pin down the yacht's movement. Nail the timeline."

"Already ahead of you," Easton replied. "I had IT scrape the data as soon as Crenshaw called it in. Check your email."

Harper put the phone on speaker, tapped through his inbox, and opened the file marked *AIS—Halcyon Way*. A list of time-stamped entries appeared, each ping tied to a GPS coordinate.

September 9, 08:07 – Arrival at the Shilshole Point Marina.
September 9, 15:43 – Departure, heading west into Puget

Sound.

September 9, 23:19 – Returned to Elliott Bay.

After that, nothing. No movement. No ping. No return to the dock.

Harper stared at the final entry.

"Boat came back late," he said. "But not to the slip. Just floated offshore until morning."

"You think they were already gone?" Easton asked.

Harper nodded into the phone. "Or someone else brought it back. Either way... they didn't make it home."

Easton was quiet for a long moment.

"Alright Harper. Find the LT and his wife. Bring them home, or bring their story home."

"You've got it, boss."

●●●●●

Later that morning, they met again at The Shanty. Same table, same briny air, same scent of burnt espresso clinging to the awning.

Harper arrived first this time, already nursing a black coffee, eyes shaded behind his sunglasses. Maguire appeared a minute later, a paper bag in hand and something tired in his posture.

"Brought scones," he said, setting the bag down. "Because what this case needed was more flaky layers."

Harper gave him a nod. "Appreciated."

Maguire slid into the seat across from him, pulled out a notebook, and set it down. "Broker's a ghost. No registered LLC, no business license in the county. If Trevor Oliver exists, it's under a different name."

Harper nodded slowly. "Figured. And Kincaid?"

"Clean," Maguire said. "Ran him through NCIC, state databases, even did a quick check on local warrants. Nada. Couple parking tickets from his undergrad days, but nothing since."

"Where did he go to school?"

"Northwest University in Kirkland. Private Christian college. Majored in 'Youth, Children, and Family Services.' Masters in Ministry Leadership and Theology." He flipped his notebook closed. "Straight-line pastoral track."

Harper leaned back, tapping his cup. "So, no gaps. No sudden disappearances. No name changes?"

"Not that I found," Maguire said. "Graduated clean, started as a Youth Pastor at Living Water, worked his way up."

Harper rolled his eyes. "Youth Pastor. That tracks. All that oily charm."

Maguire chuckled, but there was an edge behind it. "I'll say this much. If he's hiding something, he's done a damn good job keeping it off paper."

Harper nodded slowly, then let the thought go. For now.

"What about you?" Maguire asked, tearing a corner off a scone. "How did it go with the parents?"

Harper exhaled through his nose, like the air carried weight. "Hard. The Kaluas live in Snoqualmie. Picture-perfect house, garden flag, the works. They were hoping the Rainiers had just extended their trip."

Maguire's face tightened slightly.

"Malia was five months pregnant," Harper said. "First baby. They'd been trying for a while."

Maguire sat back, silent.

J.K. WOLFE

"Daniel's folks passed a while back," Harper added. "East Coast. But I reached out to some of his friends back east. They confirmed the same, that he'd been working nonstop, the boat was their escape. Said he was excited to be a dad. The kind who *wanted* it. Wanted the whole thing."

"Christ," Maguire muttered, shaking his head.

Harper looked out over the water. "He was a worker. Quiet type, sharp. They said he'd never half-assed anything in his life."

They sat in silence for a beat, the distant clang of a halyard tapping metal in the breeze.

"I called Easton this morning," Harper said. "Told him I want to stay on. He cut the orders. I'm in this, officially."

Maguire raised an eyebrow. "That mean I get to keep you as a partner?"

"For better or worse," Harper said, sipping his coffee.

"Long as you're not expecting me to share my lunch or ride shotgun in a Crown Vic, we'll get along fine."

Harper smirked faintly. "I think I can manage that."

Maguire picked at the scone again, more serious now. "So, what's our next move?"

"We keep pulling," Harper said. "The yacht's AIS data came in this morning. I got the timestamps from Easton."

Maguire looked up.

"September ninth," Harper said. "They docked at Shilshole Marina at 08:07. Departed around 15:43. Then came back into Elliott Bay just before midnight–23:19. But here's the thing: they never docked again. No slip. No ping. Just sat offshore."

Maguire frowned. "And then nothing?"

Harper nodded. "Nothing after that. Boat was dead in the water until the patrol found it the next morning."

Maguire leaned back, chewing that over. "So, either they went missing out there...or someone else brought the boat back."

"Exactly." Harper stared past him, toward the water. "If someone killed them at sea, it'd explain the lack of evidence. Tide, current, deep channels. You lose a body out there, odds are you don't get it back."

"And whoever brought the boat back didn't bother tying up."

"Maybe didn't know how. Or didn't want to be seen."

They sat with that for a long moment.

Maguire broke the silence. "You still thinking Kincaid?"

Harper's gaze stayed on the horizon. "I think we hold him in the wings. He's clean on paper, but this whole thing stinks."

Maguire gave a slow nod. "So, who do we look at next?"

Harper reached for his tablet. "The AIS data puts them at the Marina for a bit. Time to find out who might've seen *The Halcyon Way* when it came back. And who was on board."

Maguire smiled. "Let's go shake the docks."

CHAPTER
EIGHT

The Shilshole Point Marina stretched out beneath a gauzy gray sky, gulls wheeling above the water like scraps of thought. Slender masts rocked gently in their slips, and the tang of salt and diesel clung to the early afternoon air.

Harper stepped out of the sedan, scanning the rows of boats and small weather-worn buildings ahead. A modest office with a *Harbormaster* sign hung crookedly above the door sat beside a stack of empty crab traps and a faded soda machine.

"Quaint," he said.

"You sure this is where they kept it?" Maguire asked, adjusting his coat collar.

"Slip forty-two. Month-to-month rental. Long-term. It's theirs" Harper nodded, already walking.

Inside the office, it smelled like engine grease, salt, and reheated coffee. A rusted bell above the door gave a reluctant jingle as they stepped in.

Behind the counter stood a wiry man with sun-worn brown skin, dark eyes, and a Seahawks cap pulled low over neatly trimmed black hair. His navy windbreaker looked a decade old but clean. His name tag read *R. Calderón.*

"Good morning, señor," the man greeted them, his voice wrapped in a soft but persistent Mexican accent, his English fluent, but with vowels still shaped by childhood in another country. "What can I do for you?"

"Morning," Harper said, showing his badge. "Special Agent Harper, Coast Guard Investigative Service. This is Detective Maguire, Seattle PD."

Calderón straightened, eyes narrowing slightly. "Something wrong?"

Harper cut to the chase. "We're investigating a boat docked here. *The Halcyon Way*. Belonged to Daniel and Malia Rainier."

Calderón blinked. "Sí... yes. I remember them."

"You sure?" Maguire asked. "It's been a few days."

"Of course I'm sure." His gaze lingered too long. "They were regulars. Kept to themselves. Polite. Malia..." He smiled faintly, wistful. "She had this kindness. Real sweetness to her. The kind you don't forget."

Harper narrowed his eyes slightly. "When's the last time you saw them?"

Calderón leaned against the counter, thinking. "Two, maybe three days ago. They came back in the morning. I remember, because Malia had her hair different, cut short, dyed red. Spiky, like fire. Surprised me. She laughed, said it was her 'new mom look.' Said she'd gotten it cut up somewhere up in the San Juans during the trip."

"What were they wearing?" Harper asked.

He didn't hesitate. "Jeans. Light blue blouse. Belly just starting to show." His eyes glazed a little. "She looked beautiful, you know? Pregnancy, it suits some women. She had that glow."

"And Daniel?" Harper asked.

The softness in Calderón's face disappeared. His mouth flattened. "Cargo pants. Windbreaker. Didn't say much. Kept looking around like he was worried about the boat more than his wife." He shrugged. "Guess some men don't know what they have."

Harper's brow ticked upward.

Calderón continued, too casually. "I even joked with Malia once, told her if she ever got tired of the boy, Latin lovers got rhythm. She laughed." He chuckled, low and to himself, but didn't meet their eyes.

Maguire's face darkened slightly, but he kept his tone even. "Anyone else around that morning? Strangers? Friends?"

"No, just them. I helped tie off the lines like usual. We talked for a bit. She thanked me. Always polite. He barely looked at me."

"Any sign of distress?" Maguire asked.

"No, no. She looked happy. Tired, maybe. But happy."

"You see anyone with them? Friends? Strangers?"

"No, just the two of them. Docked mid-morning. I said hi, helped tie them off."

"You keep surveillance footage here?" Maguire asked, shifting the tone.

His shoulders tensed. "Normally. But...not that day."

"Why not?"

He sighed. "Someone cut the wires. The tech guy thinks it was someone looking for copper, but there's no copper in those cables. Just coax."

Harper and Maguire exchanged a look.

"They cut the wires, didn't take anything?" Harper asked.

"Exactly. Cameras down, nothing else touched."

"No security log either?" Maguire asked.

Calderón grimaced. "We have a sign-in book, but I didn't get them to sign. I knew them. Regulars. It was a busy morning, and..." He trailed off.

Maguire's eyes sharpened. "You're saying the last people to see them alive weren't logged, and there's no footage because the wires just *happened* to get cut?"

Calderón held up his hands. "I didn't know they were missing. If I had, I would've—"

"We're not blaming you," Harper said evenly, though he didn't quite mean it. "But this is a missing person investigation now, and everything matters."

Calderón nodded slowly. "Of course. You think... they're dead?"

Harper didn't answer the question. "You see anyone hanging around lately? Anyone asking about them?"

He shook his head. "No one I didn't recognize. Just Malia and Daniel. I said hi. She smiled. That was the last time I saw her."

Harper pulled out the photo of Malia and Daniel holding the sonogram. Malia's long dark hair shone in the light, a plumeria tucked behind her ear.

Calderón stared at it, lips pressing into a thin line. "Sí. That's her. The hair's different in the photo, but..." He tapped the image. "The smile. You don't forget a smile like that."

Harper slid over his card. "If anything comes back to you, give us a call. Even something small."

He took the card gently, his thumb lingering on the edge. "I hope you find them, Agent. She... she didn't deserve anything bad."

Harper nodded. "I didn't catch your first name, Mr. Calderón?"

"It's Rafael," he responded.

"Thanks, Rafael. We'll be in touch."

Outside, the wind had picked up. Harper tucked his coat tighter as they made their way down the dock.

Maguire gave a low whistle. "Our boy's got a crush."

Harper didn't smile. "He remembers the blouse, the hair, the way she *glowed*. But no logs. No cameras. And his wires get cut the same day she disappears."

"Yeah," Maguire said, glancing back at the office window. "He's either a poetic romantic..."

"Or lying through his teeth," Harper finished.

They headed to the car in silence.

Still, as they walked back to the car, Calderón's words clung to Harper's mind, slick and unnatural. Something about the way he spoke about Malia Rainier left a film Harper couldn't wash off, like oil on water, spreading wider the longer he thought about it.

•••••

Back at Maguire's desk in the Seattle Police Department's Criminal Investigations Division, the familiar scent of burnt coffee and too many bodies in too small a space hung in the air. His workstation was tucked between a pair of gray metal filing cabinets and a half-dead ficus that hadn't seen sunlight since the Obama administration.

Harper stood beside him as Maguire typed Calderón's name into the system. The background check took only seconds to start populating.

"Rafael Calderón," Maguire read. "Born 1992, Cuernavaca, Mexico. Moved to the U.S. with his parents when he was eight.

Grew up in south Seattle. Graduated Rainier Beach High. No military. No felonies."

He clicked through the tabs. "Couple speeding tickets. One DUI about five years ago. Went through diversion. Completed the whole program, no violations."

"Anything more recent?" Harper asked.

Maguire narrowed his eyes. "Hold on..."

Another tab blinked open. Maguire leaned in.

"Well, well," he said. "Temporary restraining order. Issued three years ago. Woman in his apartment complex filed it after he allegedly followed her home from work... more than once."

Harper raised an eyebrow. "Did it stick?"

"Not long. She moved out before the court date. Case was dropped. But she described him in the affidavit as *fixated*. Said he watched her from his balcony, waited in the laundry room. Classic stalking behavior."

Harper frowned, arms crossed. "Did she press charges?"

"Nope. Said she just wanted to feel safe. Said he never touched her. Just... lingered."

Harper exhaled slowly through his nose. "Jesus."

Maguire shook his head. "No follow-up reports. Nothing criminal filed. But it paints a picture."

"Yeah. A guy who gets obsessive. Charming on the surface, but..."

Maguire finished the thought: "Entitled underneath."

A pause passed as they both considered the implications.

"Any known connection to Malia?" Harper asked, straightening.

"No criminal reports. No calls. No complaints." Maguire scrolled through her profile, images flickering past. "He follows her on one of those photo-sharing apps. Nothing mutual though. She never followed him back."

Harper's jaw tightened. "So, he was watching. And given how he spoke about her..."

"Guy remembered what she wore four days ago," Maguire said, glancing over. "Jeans, blouse, red hair, pregnant glow... It's a little much for a dock worker who tied off their lines once or twice."

"And Daniel?" Harper asked. "You catch how fast he brushed him off?"

"Yeah. Barely talked about him. Cold. Like Daniel didn't belong."

"Or like Daniel was in the way."

Maguire gave a half-nod. "You thinking what I'm thinking?"

Harper nodded slowly. "That's enough to shift gears. Kincaid can simmer a bit while we chase this down."

"Yeah," Maguire agreed. "Creeps like this don't always escalate, but when they do..."

"It gets dark, fast." Harper tapped the edge of the tablet. "Kincaid's definitely still a question mark, but this guy? We'd be idiots not to press in."

Harper opened the case file on his tablet and pulled up Malia's social media account again. "Let's see who else she was close with..."

After a few minutes of scrolling, Harper stopped. "Sadie Cress. Tagged in a bunch of posts. Looks like they were roommates in college. Still close. She commented on that sonogram post a couple weeks ago."

Maguire leaned in. "Think she'll give us a better read on Malia's state of mind? Maybe verify that haircut story?"

"That's the idea."

Harper tapped the screen, darkening it, and slid the tablet under his arm. "Let's go see what Sadie knows."

CHAPTER
NINE

The afternoon sun glinted off the windshield as Maguire merged onto I-5, downtown Seattle rising like a jagged crown in the distance. Traffic was steady but manageable, the hum of the engine filling the quiet between them.

They were headed toward a high-rise near Belltown, one of the newer apartment towers overlooking the Sound. According to the lease records, Sadie Cress and her husband had lived there for the last year. Malia had tagged her in a dozen posts over the last few months—coffee dates, baby prep, a weekend trip to Port Townsend.

Harper sat in the passenger seat, thumbing through the last of Malia's social media posts on his phone. He didn't say much at first, just scanned with a practiced eye, looking for patterns, inconsistencies, anything that might be off.

Maguire adjusted the volume on the radio, just low enough to break the silence, then glanced over.

"You always this quiet on a drive, Coastie," he said, half a smirk playing at the corner of his mouth, "or are you still trying to figure out if I'm a heretic or just a pain in the ass?"

Harper looked up, eyebrow raised, a lopsided smile tugging the corner of his mouth.

And just like that, the ice cracked and another sliver of space carved open between them, ripe for something real.

Harper smirked, slipping his phone into the breast pocket of his jacket.

"Still weighing the odds," he said. "Could go either way."

Maguire gave a quiet chuckle and made a left onto Alaskan Way, the high-rises of Belltown climbing ahead of them like glassy cliffs.

"She lived close to the Rainiers?" Harper asked.

"From what I gathered, yeah," Maguire said. "They were tight. Sadie was Malia's maid of honor a couple years back. I called her this morning, gave her a heads-up we might be stopping by."

"How'd she take it?"

"Shocked. Shaken. She said she hasn't been able to sleep since Malia's mom called. Said Daniel was like a big brother to her husband, Kyle."

They parked on the street near the garage beneath the tower. As they got out, Harper glanced up at the balconies lining the concrete structure. Potted plants, wind chimes, and a child's scooter leaned up against a glass railing three stories up.

Elevator doors opened with a dull chime, and they stepped into the mirrored car. Maguire hit the button for the 17th floor.

"You want me to take point?" he asked.

Harper shrugged. "Let's just see how she is. Read the room."

The hallway on the 17th floor was tastefully bland, with neutral carpeting, muted light fixtures, and numbered doors with minimalist brass hardware. They found 1712 halfway down. Maguire knocked twice, firm but not aggressive.

A few seconds later, the door opened to reveal a woman in her early thirties, soft around the edges, dark brown hair in a low ponytail. She wore no makeup, a hoodie and leggings. Her eyes were red-rimmed, as if sleep and tears had been taking turns.

"Sadie Cress?" Harper asked gently.

"Yeah. Detectives?" she said, voice hoarse but steady.

"That's right. I'm Detective Maguire, this is Special Agent Harper. Thanks for agreeing to speak with us."

She stepped aside, motioning them in. "Sorry for the mess. I've been...it's been a lot."

The apartment was clean, but lived-in. A blanket was draped over the arm of the couch. A half-full mug of tea sat cooling on the coffee table. Dog toys were scattered near the patio door, and a corgi mix lifted its head from a nearby dog bed, sniffed once, then let out a sleepy huff before curling back into its nest. Sadie shifted her weight from foot to foot, tugging the hem of her hoodie down over her stomach as though the fabric might shield her from their scrutiny.

"Can I get you anything? Water? Coffee?"

"We're okay, thank you," Harper said.

Sadie hesitated, eyes flicking between them. She needed something to do, some sliver of agency to hold onto.

"Are you sure?" she asked again.

Harper saw it in her expression, the way grief and worry clawed for usefulness. He gave a small, measured nod. "On second thought, coffee would be great."

"Same here," Maguire added. "Thanks."

"Cream? Sugar?"

"A little of both," Harper said.

"Black," Maguire added.

Sadie disappeared into the kitchen. The quiet clink of ceramic and the gurgle of a coffee pot filled the brief silence. When she returned, she handed them each a mug and gestured toward the couches.

They took their seats while she settled into an armchair across from them. She lowered herself into the chair, curling into the cushions. She held her own tea close, cradled against her middle like it was the only thing holding her together.

"Sadie," Harper began gently, "do you know if Malia and Daniel were planning to sell their boat?"

She nodded. "Yeah. Malia told me they were going to list it after this trip. Said it was time—they wanted to start saving for a bigger house. With the baby on the way, she said they were even talking about a second someday. She joked that she wanted a backyard big enough for a swing set before the first kid could walk. That was Malia, always planning. Always dreaming ahead."

Harper jotted a quick note. "Did they have any plans to leave town after this trip?"

Sadie shook her head. "No. This was the last hurrah before nesting. They were coming home to settle in. Malia called it her 'season of roots.' She told me she was ready to slow down, ready to make a home instead of chasing horizons."

She stifled a sob, covering her mouth with her hands. "I still can't believe this is real," she said quietly. "Malia texted me when they left Friday Harbor. That was the last time."

Harper nodded. "We're doing everything we can to find them. Part of that is understanding who they were, what their lives looked like in the days before they disappeared. You and Malia were close?"

"Since college," Sadie said, nodding slowly. "She was... she was like a sister."

"Where'd you go to school?" Harper asked.

"University of Washington."

"Huskies," Maguire said, flashing a half-smile.

"Did you go?" she asked.

"Naval Academy," Maguire replied, showing a USNA class ring on his right hand.

"Were you roommates?" Harper asked.

"Sorority sisters. Alpha Delta Pi."

Harper said nothing and took a sip of the coffee. It was strong and just slightly over-sweetened. He didn't mind.

"We met during pledge week," Sadie continued, voice warming slightly. "She was quirky, but grounded. We clicked right away. Academics were important to both of us, but I had a hard time balancing things back then, studying, social stuff, figuring out who I was. Malia helped me with all of it. She had this way of pulling you into life when you were hiding from it. Even when she was scared, she didn't show it. She carried her fears quietly, but she never let them stop her from moving forward."

She paused to take a sip of her tea, then stared into the middle distance as the memory surfaced.

"She made it all look effortless. People gravitated to her. She had this quiet confidence... like she already knew who she was. She didn't have to prove it to anyone."

The silence stretched, easy now, letting the warmth of recollection ease the tension.

"I remember this one time, finals week. We were both in the same modern history class. I'd been up all night, cramming, pages of handwritten notes, color-coded flashcards, full panic mode. We grabbed coffee an hour before the test. She asked to see my notes, flipped through them for maybe forty-five minutes... and then aced the exam. A-plus." Sadie laughed softly, her shoulders shaking, the hoodie stretching a little across her frame, her eyes misty. "I got an A-minus. She barely even studied. Just... photographic memory or something."

Harper and Maguire let the moment breathe.

"I had a baby shower planned for her next month," Sadie said suddenly. "I'd already bought her gift. A handmade blanket with their last names. It shipped yesterday. She texted me just last week about paint colors for the nursery. She was so excited. She wanted something bright, cheerful, not the boring neutrals everyone was doing. Said her baby deserved a room full of sunlight."

Harper leaned in slightly, his tone gentle. "Sadie, we were hoping you might help us access some of her private social media accounts. Sometimes friends and family have insight that can help us see things others miss."

Sadie nodded and sniffed, wiping her nose with the sleeve of her hoodie. "Yeah. Yeah, of course. We followed each other on one platform. She wasn't huge on social media, but she posted stuff here."

She pulled out a tablet from under the coffee table and began typing in her password. As the home screen lit up, Harper glanced at a nearby shelf and saw photos of Malia and Sadie smiling at weddings, baby showers, birthday dinners. One showed Malia and Daniel in front of their yacht, windswept and happy, arms wrapped tight around each other. Malia wore a white floral dress and a fresh lei, her long black hair caught in the breeze.

Sadie handed the tablet over. "Here. I'll unlock whatever you need."

Harper began swiping through the feed. Because Sadie was listed as one of Malia's closest "friends," he now had access to more than before: private albums, tagged locations, and comment threads hidden behind privacy settings.

Malia's world unfolded in soft-lit snapshots. A windswept marina in the San Juans, mason jars of decaf lattes with seafoam hearts, her hands cradling the curve of her belly while Daniel kissed her temple. Moments that felt curated, but real. Tender. Intimate.

Harper scanned each post with practiced efficiency, looking at dates, timestamps, tagged accounts, and location data. His finger paused over a series of vacation shots from the week before they vanished. Malia on the deck of *The Halcyon Way*, wind tugging at her sunhat. Daniel beside her, grinning, hand on the helm.

Then came the comments.

Most were the usual well-wishes, friends gushing about how radiant she looked, relatives asking about nursery plans.

But sprinkled in between, he noticed a familiar name.

Rafael Calderón.

The first few comments were innocuous.

Hope you two are having the best trip!

Sunshine looks good on, Malia.

That smile—man, I miss seeing that around the marina.

Then, a shift.

Harper's brow furrowed as the tone darkened.

Bet Daniel doesn't appreciate you the way you deserve.

Some guys don't know how lucky they are until it's too late.

If it were me... well, let's just say Latin lovers have rhythm. Satisfaction guaranteed, in AND out of the bedroom. ;)

Maguire, reading over his shoulder, gave a low whistle. "That escalated."

Harper turned to Sadie. "Did Malia ever mention anything about these comments?"

Sadie leaned in, eyes narrowing as she scanned them. "Yeah, I remember those. She told me the dock guy—Rafael—had a thing for her. Said it started innocent, but it got weird fast." She held out a hand. "May I?"

Harper passed her the tablet. Sadie swiped through a few settings, then turned the screen back to them.

"Looks like she blocked him. See? Last comment was September 8."

Harper checked the timestamp. Two days before the yacht was found drifting. One day before the AIS data placed *The Halcyon Way* at the Shilshole Point Marina.

"Looks like we'll need a warrant to dig further," Maguire said.

Sadie hesitated. "You might not need one. I mean... I know her passwords. They've been the same since college." She took the notebook Harper offered and scribbled down Malia's email and password.

"Any chance you know Daniel's?" Harper asked.

"No, sorry. He was a little more private. I don't even think he had a Facebook."

"That's okay," Harper said. "You've been a big help." He paused, then added, "One more thing—did Malia mention getting a haircut?"

Sadie smiled faintly. "Oh, yeah. She was excited about it. Said she wanted a fresh start before the baby came. Sent me a picture."

She shifted forward in the chair, leggings pulling at the knees as she dug her phone out of her pocket and held it out.

Malia with short, spiky red hair, beaming in a bathroom mirror.

"Can you send that to me?" Harper asked.

"Sure thing. What's your number?"

He rattled it off. A moment later, his phone buzzed.

"Thanks again for your time," Maguire said, rising. He handed her his card. "If you think of anything else, don't hesitate."

Sadie stood with them. "Of course. And if... when you find them, will you let me know?" Her hands twisted together, fingers worrying the fabric of the hoodie. For a moment she looked smaller than she was, folded in on herself with worry.

Harper nodded. "You have my word."

•••••

They wound through downtown traffic in silence at first, the hum of the engine filling the quiet space between them. The city pressed in all around—high-rises wrapped in mirrored glass, construction cranes frozen mid-swing, pedestrians bundled against the chill.

Maguire unscrewed the lid of a stainless-steel travel mug he'd left in the cup holder. The aroma of lukewarm coffee wafted out. "So," he said, taking a sip, "what's our next move?"

Harper kept his gaze on the road. "We've got a few threads to pull. I'll file for a subpoena on Malia's social media. Even with the password, we need to do it right. Federal administrative subpoena'll be faster than a full warrant."

"Copy that." Maguire shifted in his seat. "I'll tap a few people in White Collar. See if anyone knows our mystery broker. A guy like that doesn't stay invisible unless he's damn good. Or someone's keeping him that way."

"And Calderón," Harper added. "That guy's giving me the creeps. Stalking cases turn fast. One minute it's bad jokes and flattery, and the next, it's restraining orders and blood on the pavement."

Maguire didn't ask, but Harper's voice had shifted, flattened, like someone touching a scar. Maguire didn't press. Some silences weren't meant to be filled.

They pulled into the SPD parking garage, the concrete gloom swallowing the car. Maguire eased into a space beside Harper's vehicle and killed the engine.

"You good?" he asked.

"We're moving forward," Harper replied, opening the door. "Let's keep it that way."

They got out and went their separate ways, the weight of the Rainiers trailing like a shadow behind them.

CHAPTER
TEN

As Harper pulled away from Seattle PD, the late afternoon sun fractured across his windshield, casting shards of gold through the glass. The fifteen-minute drive to Coast Guard Base Seattle gave him just enough time to think, which lately felt like both a luxury and a curse.

He kept one hand on the wheel, the other draped casually over the gearshift as the city blurred past. His thoughts circled back to Calderón and the too vivid recollection of Malia's outfit, her smile, the spiky red haircut. The way his voice softened when he talked about her. And how it cooled, ever so slightly, when Daniel's name came up. Not to mention the social media comments they'd seen.

The timeline matched the AIS data—*The Halcyon Way* had docked at Shilshole Point Marina just after 8:00 a.m. on September 9, then left again that afternoon. According to the logs, it never returned to the slip. Just drifted back into Elliott Bay close to midnight.

But something gnawed at him. So far, Rafael Calderón was the only person to place the Rainiers at the marina that morning. No one else—no nearby slip renters, no harbor staff, no dockside cameras—had confirmed seeing them in person. Just him.

It wasn't overt. Not enough to file charges. But it had a familiar stink. The kind Harper had seen before, the obsessive need to insert yourself into someone's life. The quiet entitlement that curdled into something darker when the object of affection didn't reciprocate.

Stalking cases were always hard to pin down. Full of near-misses, plausible deniability, and gaps the law couldn't quite stretch across. And sometimes...sometimes, it didn't end in court dates or restraining orders.

Sometimes, it ended in blood.

His jaw tightened.

He'd seen it firsthand, years ago, when he was still in uniform. A woman had come into the station three times in one week, begging someone to take her ex seriously. There was a ring of desperation in her voice that clung to Harper even now, like smoke in his lungs.

He hadn't been able to do enough then. Not in time.

•••••

Then.

The call seemed routine. A welfare check just outside the city limits, county's jurisdiction, but the Sheriff's Office was slammed, so they asked Stonehaven PD for mutual aid. It happened all the time. Patrol would respond, calm things down, hold the scene until a deputy arrived.

Simple. Triage work.

It was early, around 0700, when Officers Cooper and Harper rolled out. The call was for a disturbance at a small commercial business. A woman named Faith had locked herself inside and called 911. Her boyfriend was outside, yelling.

As they drove, dispatch updates came steady through the radio.

"Caller states the male, Mason, is at the door, pounding, yelling. She fled their apartment this morning and went straight to work. Her supervisor locked the front entrance. Male followed her and is demanding to be let in. Mason is reported to be a white male, 28 years old, wearing jeans and a hoodie."

Harper glanced toward Cooper's unit in the next lane. Both cruisers moved faster now, still no lights, but urgency building.

"Update for Stonehaven units: Reporting party states there was a physical altercation earlier this morning. A firearm may have been involved, unknown if the male is currently armed."

Harper clenched his jaw. His foot pressed the gas a little harder. This was no longer just a welfare check.

Another burst from dispatch. "Caller now states male is attempting to break in. Screaming and glass breaking heard in the background. Line is open. Caller not responding."

Harper snapped on the lights. Ahead, Cooper's bar flared to life in sync.

They rounded the corner, tires chirping against the blacktop, and rolled up fast on the scene. The front of the business came into view, glass door shattered, a jagged maw where the entry used to be. Slivers of safety glass sparkled on the pavement like ice. No one in sight.

Harper threw the cruiser into park and stepped out, drawing his sidearm in one smooth motion. Cooper was already out of his car, weapon raised, eyes scanning.

They moved fast, falling into rhythm. Without speaking, they stacked beside the broken doorway, Cooper taking the lead, Harper covering.

"Stonehaven PD!" Harper called out, voice firm but clear. "If anyone's inside, make yourself known!"

Silence.

Cooper gave Harper a nod. *Ready.*

Harper reached for the door, but it barely budged. Cracked glass jammed the bottom track. He gave it a hard kick, scattering the debris, then yanked the handle again. This time, the door groaned open, catching at an awkward angle.

Inside, darkness. The overhead fluorescents were off, or broken. A narrow hallway stretched ahead, the floor littered with more shards of glass. On the right, Harper could just make out the edge of an office desk and overturned chair.

"Police!" Harper called again. "Anyone in here, announce yourself!"

Still nothing.

They entered. Harper took point, stepping carefully over the debris. Cooper followed, close behind, steady, muzzle up, watching their six.

Glass crunched under Harper's boots as he moved down the short hall. The air smelled of dust and something sharper, metallic. Blood.

He angled toward the open space to the right, slicing the corner of the room as he cleared it. There was a cheap metal desk, papers strewn like fallen leaves. Behind it—

A body.

"Stonehaven PD! Show me your hands!"

The figure did not move.

Harper repeated the command.

The figure remained still. Harper continued to move cautiously forward, watching both the figure on the ground while sweeping his eyes, and pistol, back and forth in the room to make sure no one was going to jump out at them. Harper scanned the rest of the room quickly. No other visible threats. Just a hallway leading deeper into the building.

"Cover the hallway. I've got the person down," Harper said to Cooper.

"Copy," Cooper said, pointing his pistol to the hallway in the back.

Harper advanced slowly, weapon still trained. The figure was slumped on its side, a middle-aged man in jeans and a faded work shirt, soaked with blood. One arm stretched out unnaturally in front of him; the other was curled against his torso, fingers still clutched loosely as if reaching for something long gone.

He knelt beside the man. No weapon in hand. No signs of breath. Blood pooled beneath his mouth and neck, glistening where it hadn't dried.

He pressed two fingers to the carotid. Nothing.

"We've got one down," he said into the mic clipped to his vest. "Male, mid-fifties, multiple stab wounds. No pulse."

He stood and nodded to Cooper. Together, they moved toward the back hall, boots quiet now on worn carpet. They moved toward the next door.

Another office. Smaller. Lights off, door slightly ajar.

Harper edged the door open.

Inside, a small figure lay curled on the floor, knees drawn up, arms tucked tight. A woman. Blood soaked her shirt, slashes and punctures covering her torso. She wasn't moving.

Standing behind her, knife in hand, was a man in his thirties. Blood on his hoodie. Mason.

"Drop the fucking knife!" Harper shouted, leveling his weapon. "Drop it! Drop it right fucking now!"

Cooper moved in beside him, both of them in the doorway, guns raised.

Mason didn't flinch. His eyes were wild, distant.

"Faith was *mine*," he said quietly, venom in his voice. "If I couldn't have her..."

"Don't do it!" Cooper barked. "Don't you fucking do it!"

In one fluid motion, Mason drew the knife across his own throat.

Blood sprayed. He staggered, collapsed to the floor, twitching violently.

Harper rushed in, kicked the blade clear, and dropped to his knees beside the woman. Faith.

He turned her gently onto her back.

Multiple stab wounds. Deep. Angry. Her eyes were open, glazed. Staring at nothing.

No pulse.

"Come on," Harper muttered. He started compressions. *One, two, three...*

Cooper's voice roared in the background. "Suspect down! Victim down! We need medics now!"

It didn't matter.

Faith was already gone.

Mason joined her in the silence soon after.

•••••

Now.

Harper blinked hard, forcing his grip to loosen on the steering wheel. The past receded like a riptide, dragging its salt and

98

iron memories with it. He exhaled slowly, steadying himself as the gates of Base Seattle came into view.

He flashed his credentials at the guard shack and rolled through without a word. The low-slung buildings of the Coast Guard base stretched ahead, familiar in their dull uniformity. Harper found a spot near the administrative building and killed the engine.

He sat for a moment in the quiet, the ticking of the engine cooling filling the silence. Mason's face still hovered behind his eyes—that wild stare, the final spray of blood.

Faith was mine.

Harper shoved the door open and stepped out into the chill.

Inside, the hum of fluorescent lights and printers felt almost sterile. Detached. He made his way to the CGIS unit office, knocked once, and let himself in.

SSA Easton looked up from a stack of reports. "Harper. Didn't expect you back so soon."

"I need an administrative subpoena," Harper said, voice low and even. "Malia Rainier's social media accounts. I've got her login already, but I want to do this right. Cover the bases."

Easton gave a small nod. "Give me the names and associated emails."

Harper handed over a slip of paper from his notebook.

Easton read it over. "You think there's something there?"

"I don't think," Harper said. "I *know* there's something. Just don't know what yet."

Easton gave him a look—sharp, calculating—but said nothing. He stood, stepped out of the office, and closed the door behind him.

Harper remained by the desk, arms folded, eyes on the Coast Guard crest hanging crooked on the far wall. A dull ache had settled behind his temples.

Five minutes later, Easton returned and handed him the signed form.

"Here you go," he said dryly.

Harper managed a faint smile. "Appreciate it."

"Keep me posted."

Harper gave a nod, tucked the subpoena into his folder, and turned to leave. The halls felt narrower now. The work heavier. But the path was clear.

She was mine.

Mason's words echoed in his mind, but now, he heard Calderón's voice.

CHAPTER
ELEVEN

H arper sat down at his desk and fired up his laptop. He navigated to Malia's social media profile and logged in with the credentials Sadie had given him. The interface loaded slowly, familiar but sterile in its brightness.

He pulled up the same photos he'd seen through Sadie's account, the ones with Calderón's lewd comments buried beneath layers of sunshine and smiles. They still made his skin crawl.

In her drafts folder, a single video stood out. Unposted. Untitled. Almost like she hadn't had time to finish it.

He clicked it.

The screen lit up with fragments of joy, a montage Malia had been stitching together. Moments from their babymoon, put together with care. A montage Malia had been stitching together with the quiet devotion of someone preserving a future she believed was certain. Malia and Daniel seated at a beachfront dinner table, candles flickering between them, her hand resting protectively on her stomach. Another clip: Malia laughing, arm outstretched, filming as they walked hand-in-hand along the shoreline. The wind teased her dress and swept her freshly cut hair across her cheek.

Then, a still frame.

Malia stood beside a Locks of Love poster, smiling wide. In one hand she held a zippered bag containing a bundle of raven hair.

Her other hand brushed her new red and spiky cut with a mix of pride and apprehension, like someone on the cusp of change.

Harper stared at the photo for a long moment, absorbing the light in her eyes, the quiet hope in her body language, the way her shoulders leaned forward like she was stepping into a new life. He glanced beneath the image.

"Ay ay ay mamacita!! That hair is fuego. Let me show you just how en fuego you make me when you get down south! ;)"

His lip curled in disgust.

He navigated over to her direct messages, then into the message requests, where messages from people she didn't follow lived in quiet, digital purgatory.

There it was. Calderón's profile, pinned near the top. Dozens of unread messages.

Harper clicked.

The first was dated nearly two weeks earlier, the day Malia and Daniel left on their trip.

Hope you have the best time. The San Juans are magical this time of year. Try to relax, okay? You deserve that and more.

Innocent enough. Maybe even kind.

The next came a day later:

Miss that smile already. The docks are quiet without you.

Then:

Still can't believe you went with him. You know you can talk to me, right? I'm always here. Always have been. You don't have to pretend he makes you happy.

Harper scrolled, frowning.

You and me, we're meant to be. You just forgot for a while. He doesn't see you the way I do. Doesn't worship you. You deserve worship, mi amor.

The messages grew longer. More desperate. Like a man writing in the middle of the night with nobody to stop him.

I know you're not just ignoring me. He's watching your phone, isn't he? Bastard probably reads everything. Makes you feel small. Weak. You're not weak, Malia. You're mine. You've always been mine.

Harper exhaled through his nose, shoulders stiff.

Sometimes I think about what it'd be like if you stayed after mooring the boat. Just one night. I'd cook for you. Draw a bath. Rub your feet. Then I'd make you feel everything he's forgotten. Slow. Deep. The way a real man takes care of whats his.

The messages grew longer. Needier.

That dress you wore last week, Dios mío. I could barely focus. I know you saw me. You wanted me to look, didn't you? My dirty little marina queen. You tease me like that and expect me to just smile and nod?

Had a dream about you. We were on your boat, and he was gone. You called to me. Begged me. We made love under the stars. It was perfect. Real. You felt safe.

I woke up so fucking hard it hurt. Still hurts. I need you, Malia. You feel it too. Don't lie to yourself.

I'm going to think of you tonight when I come.

By now, the messages were flooding in hourly. Paragraphs at a time. Misspelled words. Jarring leaps from affection to rage.

He's keping you from me. I can see it. You never smile the same when hes around. I'd giv you the world. I don't care about the baby, it's not his anymore. Not really.

You think he'll stay when your body changes? When the glow fades? I'll love you through it all. Every stretch mark. Every tear. Ill kiss you while you still bleed and tell you you're still the most beautiful woman alive.

Counting down the days until it's you in my bed, mi amor.

Harper let out a low whistle. "Christ. This guy's delusional," he said aloud.

His throat tightened. Alyssa was six months along, glowing in ways that left him humbled. The thought of someone twisting that into fetish and possession churned his stomach.

Then came the last message.

September 8. The day before they were last seen.

Harper hesitated, then tapped it open. The system loaded the message slowly, as if resisting.

The text was a wall, unhinged and raw. A manifesto of obsession.

You can't keep pretending anymore. You want it. You want ME. You want what I do to you in my dreams. On your knees. Begging. Crying. Screaming my name as we fuck until your voice breaks. You think I havent seen the way you look at me? Don't lie. You want to be my lil slut.

Im going to tie you to that boat and take you every way you need. Id taste every inch. Own every inch. You were made for this. For me. Not him.

Your going to bed me for my cock. Gag on it, loving it. Im going to fuck you until your legs shake, til you cant scream anymore. and youll beg me for more still. my lil cumslut

He'd seen words like these before, scrawled on letters, whispered into voicemails. Once, in Stonehaven, it had ended with a man bleeding out on a kitchen floor. Stalking never stayed just words.

Harper shut his eyes a moment, forcing the bile down. For half a second, he pictured Alyssa's face on the screen, her smile dissected by some stranger's obsession. He opened them quick, jaw clenched hard enough to ache.

Then the final photo. Something told him this last one would be the worst one yet.

Harper flared his nostrils as the unsolicited image loaded, a vulgar, close-up shot of Rafael, nude, erect, and leering at the camera, sent without shame. Without hesitation.

And beneath that, the final line:

Hes just in the way now. You know that. I know that. Everyone knows that. If you want me to fix it, say nuthing. Let me be the one. I'll raise the baby like its my own. You'll be safe. You'll be mine. You never have to see that smug prick again.

Harper slowly backed out of the message thread, eyes burning from the glow, stomach tight.

He leaned back in his chair, jaw set, staring at the ceiling, willing the bile in his throat to settle.

"Holy shit. He thought they were in a relationship," he said to no one. "Thought she wanted Daniel gone."

The silence that followed was thick. Oppressive. A quiet that hummed with the possibility of violence.

Harper pulled out his phone and dialed Maguire.

"Hey, Coastie. What's up?" Maguire answered, his voice casual.

"I got the subpoena," Harper said. "You'll never guess what I found from our friend at the docks."

He laid it out, every message, every escalation, the obscene photo, the offer to remove Daniel, all of it.

There was a pause on the other end of the line. Then Maguire gave a low whistle.

"Well, fuck me," he said. "Sounds like our boy had more than a crush."

"He was living in a fantasy," Harper replied. "Completely unhinged. Thought she was his. Thought the baby would be his, like he'd knock off her husband and adopt the kid."

"You think he actually killed them?"

"I don't know," Harper said, glancing back at the screen. "But I know this, he definitely wanted to. And he's delusional enough to think she wanted him to."

Maguire exhaled. "We need to hit his place. Today."

"No shit. Before he runs," Harper said. "Can you talk to the judge, get us the warrant? I'll be back at SPD in twenty."

"You've got it," Maguire said.

There was another pause.

"You sound rattled," Maguire said quietly.

"I'm fine," Harper replied, too fast. "Let's go see our little red flag."

CHAPTER
TWELVE

Harper glanced at the dash clock as the streets of Seattle blurred past, the sedan's blue lights reflected in windshields and windows alike. *6:05 p.m.*

He hit the call button. Alyssa picked up on the second ring.

"Hey love," she said, her voice warm through the car's speakers.

"Hey babe. Gonna be a late one," Harper said. "We've got to hit a house."

"Okay. Be safe, alright?"

"Always. Love you."

"Love you too."

He ended the call just as he pulled into the lot at Seattle PD. Maguire was already outside, leaning against the trunk of his own car, a manila envelope in hand.

"Got the warrant," Maguire said.

Harper stepped out, leaving the car running. "That was fast."

"Judge didn't need much convincing after I dropped a few of those gems Calderón posted. Threw in the part about Malia being pregnant. You could almost hear the shift in his face."

"Perfect," Harper said, already sliding back behind the wheel. "I'll drive."

Maguire circled to the passenger side and climbed in.

"I've got a few uniforms staged a block away," he said. "Calderón should be home shortly, if he isn't there already."

Harper was already in drive, turning back onto the street. "What's the play?"

"Quiet entry. No lights, no sirens. Knock and talk first. If he opens up, we show the warrant and go from there."

"Low key. I like it."

"But if he ducks or tries anything stupid, SWAT's on standby. With the Rainiers still missing, we've got exigency all day long."

The sun was dipping behind the buildings, leaving Seattle draped in that soft, bluish dusk that gave everything a deceptive calm. Harper steered them west, cutting through downtown with clinical efficiency, his eyes flicking between mirror, traffic, and the ETA on the GPS display.

Maguire rode in silence for a stretch, flipping through a slim notepad. "Calderón rents a one-bedroom near the marina. Second floor, faces the water."

"Figures," Harper said, his voice low. "People like that always want the view."

"You'd think someone obsessed with control would pick a bunker," Maguire said. "But no. Gotta see their reflection in the glass."

Harper smirked faintly. "Or he wanted to be able to troll for new victims. Watch them from his window."

Maguire nodded but said nothing. The air in the car had shifted, calm but coiled tight. A storm just waiting for the right spark.

They turned off the main drag, heading back towards the waterfront. A line of sailboat masts tilted gently in the breeze like quiet sentinels. The apartment buildings here were mid-range modern, with steel railings, smoked glass balconies, and curated plants in concrete planters.

Harper tapped the brakes, easing them around the corner. "There," Maguire said, pointing to a narrow three-story unit near the edge of the lot. "Second one from the end."

Harper let the car roll to a stop half a block away, engine idling as he watched the windows for movement.

"Uniforms are just south of here," Maguire said, checking his phone. "They'll hold unless we call it."

"Good." Harper killed the engine.

For a moment, neither of them moved. Just the quiet creak of cooling metal and the distant groan of boat lines straining against their cleats.

"Ready?" Maguire asked.

Harper nodded once. "Let's roll."

As they stepped out, they shrugged into their bullet-resistant vests with practiced precision—Maguire's with SEATTLE POLICE emblazoned in bold white lettering across the back, Harper's reading FEDERAL AGENT on the back with CGIS over the chest. They walked the half block, then started up the stairs, shoes quiet on the concrete steps.

The sleek and modern apartment complex was built in a minimalist style, with a concrete, winding stairwell. They rounded the corner and stopped in front of Apartment 2B, Calderón's unit. Harper took position to the left of the door, Maguire to the right, both staying just outside the fatal funnel. They exchanged a glance, Maguire giving a small nod.

Harper raised his fist and knocked.

RAP RAP RAP.

Silence.

He reached out again, louder this time.

RAP RAP RAP.

Still nothing.

Harper took a breath, leaning in to knock a third time—and froze.

A soft, mechanical *click* sounded from inside the apartment. Not loud, but unmistakable. The hair on his neck stood on end, goosebumps shivering down his arms as he recognized the sound for what it was: A round being chambered.

"GET DOWN!" Harper shouted.

Time slowed. The door exploded outward, cheap wood splintering as bullets ripped through it, the sound shattering the quiet evening. Harper dove backward, landing hard on his back, pain shooting up his spine as his hand went to his holster. He drew his Glock, muzzle tracking upward to the door as he slid behind the wall as cover.

Maguire rolled right, slamming his back against the wall of the alcove. "Shots fired! Shots fired at police!" he shouted into his radio. "We're taking fire! Move in!"

More rounds punched through the drywall, tearing into the railing across from them. A flowerpot exploded in a burst of ceramic and dirt. Harper crawled behind the concrete stairwell landing, heart hammering, taking shallow breaths, adrenaline burning hot. He could see muzzle flashes inside the apartment through the holes in the door. One shooter, moving fast.

He locked eyes with Maguire. *Ambush.*

They were pinned.

Boots pounded behind them as uniformed officers tried to push up the stairs, but the moment one stepped into view, gunfire cracked again. Bullets stitched the concrete, slamming into the lead officer's leg.

"AHH–!" the cop screamed, crumpling backward. He tumbled down the steps, limb flailing, blood trailing behind him.

"OFFICER DOWN! OFFICER DOWN!" another officer shouted into his mic, crouching behind the railing.

Maguire's voice was sharp, controlled. "Suspect firing from inside apartment, second floor. We are pinned. Request SWAT entry now. Repeat, urgent, need tactical response."

Then, without warning, the gunfire stopped. The sudden silence rang in Harper's ears as he crouched low behind the wall. He didn't move. Didn't breathe. *Is it over? Or is he just waiting for us to move?*

Harper reached down, yanked off one of his Chuck Taylors, and slowly extended it past the edge of the wall, raising it just above head height like a test balloon. The moment it cleared cover—

CRACK CRACK CRACK!

The shoe exploded in his hand, rubber and canvas ripped apart mid-air.

"FUCK!" Harper yanked his hand back, heart pounding. The shredded remains of his Converse landed on the stairwell behind him.

"He's still got rounds," Maguire said, breathless. "And he's not done."

Harper glanced over the railing toward the parking lot. Red and blue lights strobed through the trees. Sirens. SWAT was coming, but not fast enough. He ducked low again, wiped the sweat from his brow, and tightened his grip on the Glock.

"You good?" Maguire called out.

Harper gave a single nod. "I've got enough left in the tank."

Another round tore through the doorframe, wood fragments and dust filling the air like shrapnel. Then—movement.

Harper saw it from the corner of his eye: a young woman stepped out of a neighboring apartment. Leggings, athletic shirt, and earbuds in her ears. She froze mid-step, her eyes locked on Harper's. A heartbeat of silence, and then a sharp report split the air.

She screamed and crumped, earbuds scattering across the walkway.

"Shit! Civilian hit!" Harper yelled, ducking even lower. The woman was whimpering, holding her thigh as blood pooled fast beneath her.

Maguire popped off two quick shots through the hole in the door as Harper pressed himself flat to the concrete. "We're sitting ducks!" Maguire shouted over the echo of shots. "We wait here, she bleeds out!"

"I'm going!" Harper yelled back. "There's no apartments behind his—backdrop's clear!"

Maguire didn't argue. "On your go!"

Harper inhaled once, then launched forward, sprinting low across the landing. More gunfire ripped overhead, chewing chunks from the stucco behind him. Maguire kept the pressure on, firing controlled two round bursts toward the muzzle flashes inside the apartment.

Harper reached the woman and dropped behind her. "I've got you," he said, sliding his arms under her and dragging her back out of the line of fire.

He crouched over her. Blood soaked the concrete, entry high on the thigh. Not spurting, but bad.

"I—my name's Becca," she gasped. "Just moved in—law school—I didn't know—music too loud—"

"Stay with me, Becca," Harper said, ripping open his pocket trauma kit. "You're going to be okay."

The iron tang of her pooled blood and the acrid smell of the gunfire filled his nostrils. He yanked the tourniquet tight just above the wound, cinching it hard. She screamed, bucked, but didn't pass out.

"Good," he said. "You're tough."

She looked at his vest. "CGIS?"

"Coast Guard Investigative Service."

"Didn't know you guys did this sort of thing."

"Me neither," he said, flashing a grim smile.

He looked back toward Maguire. "You good?"

"I'm good!" Maguire called back.

Harper turned back to the woman. "Becca, you're going to be okay. I need you to stay right here. I have to end this so we can get you help, okay?"

She whimpered. "Please, don't go..."

"You're brave. You've got this. Just keep breathing through the pain, okay? You've got this. Say it with me: 'I've got this.'"

Becca nodded and repeated it, voice trembling. Her face was pale, her eyes wide with fear.

She'll make it if we can get her help. Just need to stop this now.

Harper looked back at Maguire. "Moving!" he shouted.

"Covering!"

Maguire fired another two shots into the hole in the door as Harper sprinted back to his previous position, sliding down as more rounds smacked the wall behind him.

"How far out's SWAT?" he asked.

"Five minutes," Maguire answered, putting a fresh magazine into his pistol.

"Too long," Harper said. "She can't wait that long."

"What are you thinking?" Maguire asked, eyes flicking between Harper and the door.

"I can get in her apartment, use the fire escape. Come in through the rear."

"Too exposed."

"So is this." Harper nodded toward Becca. "Even quicker, I hop patio to patio. If you hear glass break, that's your cue. Stop shooting."

Maguire hesitated, then nodded. "I'll keep him busy. Don't be a hero, puddle pirate."

"Wouldn't dream of it, Squid," Harper flashed a grin, a confidence he didn't feel. "On three."

Three. Two. One.

Harper broke cover and ran back to Becca's door as Maguire laid down suppressing fire. Concrete chipped behind him, but he made it.

"Becca, I need your keys. I'm going through your unit to flank him."

Becca nodded, her face a mask of pain and ashen. She dug into the waistband of her leggings and handed them over, hand slick with blood. Harper low-crawled to her door, unlocked it, and pushed inside. Modern, tidy, not cluttered. He moved straight through to the balcony and slid open the door.

Evening air hit him. He kicked off his remaining shoe and socks and stepped barefoot onto the cool concrete and looked across.

Two units down. Between them were narrow gaps of concrete, steel, and open air. Just enough clearance.

He took a steadying breath and climbed the rail. The drop below was a clean fifteen feet to pavement. No room for mistakes. He crouched, then leapt and landed hard, bare feet hitting the concrete with a dull thud. No time to hesitate. Another leap over the next patio. He was now behind Calderón's.

Harper dropped into a low crouch beside the glass door, heart thudding. The balcony was bare except for a small table and a dead potted plant. Gunfire inside, one round. He heard Maguire return it.

He grabbed the ceramic pot, stood, and hurled it through the glass. The sliding door exploded inward in a violent crash, shards scattering across laminate flooring. Another shot rang out from inside. Harper dropped to a crouch, pistol raised, waiting.

Silence.

He held his breath. Still nothing.

Harper stayed frozen for a second longer, then crept forward. He eased forward and pressed up against the open doorway, his Glock trained on the dark emptiness inside. The only sound now was the wind brushing through the trees and sirens converging.

Harper didn't trust the silence. He moved quietly and sidestepped shards of broken glass, careful not to step on them with his bare feet. He silently moved through the dark kitchen, clearing it, pistol raised. He could feel his heartbeat thudding in his ears, the silence eerie.

He moved past the kitchen to the hallway, consciously keeping his breath controlled. Up ahead, he could see the pockmarked door, large holes blown through from the exchanged gunfire. On the floor, a figure lay on the ground.

Harper pulled out a small penlight from his pocket and shone it on the figure. Calderón. Or what was left of him.

The man was sprawled on the floor in a grotesque angle, his legs crumpled forward, head bent sharply back. An AK-style rifle lay next to his right hand. The contortion seemed more severe than it was, Harper realized, because the top half of his skull was gone. He swept his light back, seeing blood, brain matter and pieces of bone painting the wall behind the body.

The last shot Harper had heard had been *the* last shot. It had been Calderón ending the standoff. And himself.

Goddammit. They'd just lost their only lead.

"He's down!" Harper shouted, holstering his pistol. He crossed the room and unlocked the front door, stepping back to let Maguire in.

"Fuck," Maguire muttered, lowering his weapon as he took in the scene.

Harper didn't pause. He sprinted back to the walkway. Becca was still lying there, conscious, barely.

"Stay with me, Becca. It's over. I've got you,"

He scooped her into his arms. Her skin was cold. Shock was setting in fast. Her brown eyes fluttered open, heavy-lidded, fighting sleep as she searched his face. He didn't slow down, taking the stairs two at a time, legs burning.

"Medic!" he shouted, breaking into the open as red and blue lights spun through the night. "She needs help now!

116

A pair of medics rushed to meet him. He handed her off, as they loaded her into the waiting ambulance. The doors slammed shut and the sirens wailed to life.

Harper stood there for a moment, breathing hard, hands blood-slicked and trembling. He turned back toward the apartment. Toward the shattered door, the broken glass, and the echo of gunfire still ringing in his ears.

What in the ever-loving fuck just happened?

CHAPTER
THIRTEEN

Maguire was waiting for Harper when he got back up to the landing. Harper had pulled a spare pair of work boots from the trunk, an old, steel-toed set stained from past searches. It was part of his kit for messier search warrants.

"You're going to want to see this," Maguire said.

Maguire didn't say another word as he led the way back inside. Harper followed wordlessly as he put on blue nitrile gloves. They stepped around Calderón's body, its twisted, motionless form a reminder of the destruction they had just lived through. Forensics would have their hands full. But Harper could already feel it. Something else was festering here. Something dark.

They turned down a narrow hallway. One door stood open, just off the entryway.

Harper stepped inside—and froze.

The entire far wall was covered in shelves. Homemade, from rough lumber with uneven cuts, stained dark like someone had tried to make it match the furniture but didn't care enough to get it right. The shelves stretched nearby from floor to ceiling. And every inch of them was filled.

Photographs.

At first glance, it looked like a personal collection, some warped obsessive fan tribute. But as Harper stepped closer, the sickness of it sank in.

Malia's face was everywhere.

Dozens—no, hundreds—of images. Some were clearly pulled from her public social media: vacation photos, candid group shots, professional headshots, selfies. But others were unmistakably personal, intimate moments snapped from the shadows. One image caught Harper's eye: Malia in her kitchen, reaching for a coffee mug, still in her robe. Another showed her brushing her hair, the image distorted by a pane of glass. The angle was wrong, too high and too close. He realized with a chill that Calderón had taken it through the Rainers' condo window, likely with a telephoto lens.

"This definitely wasn't from social media," Maguire said softly, pointing to one of the creepier shots.

Harper looked at the image he had pointed out. It was Malia, drinking from a mug. She was in a lacy, sheer blue bra and panties. The image was zoomed, the detail startlingly clear. In the blurry foreground, partially drawn blinds could be seen.

"He used an expensive lens. She thought she was in the privacy of her own house," Harper said.

"He was watching them," Maguire said. "From the marina. From the condo."

Below the photos were items, physical keepsakes arranged with unsettling reverence. A hairbrush with strands of dark hair still tangled in the bristles. A violet hair tie. Clipped locks of hair in a Ziplock bag. A printed receipt from a grocery store near their building. Handwritten notes detailing her routine. Times she left for work. When she came home. Whether she was alone.

Then Harper saw it, tucked into the lower shelf, barely visible under the clutter. A small jewelry box. Inside, nestled like a trophy, was a pair of lace underwear. The same blue panties seen in the zoomed in photograph. Faint stains marked the fabric.

Harper didn't speak. He didn't need to.

His eyes continued to sweep, and found a cluster of framed photos showing Malia and Daniel together. Her smiling, radiant face glowing with affection. But in each one, Daniel's face had been violently scratched out. Deep gouges cut across the paper. Some were torn completely through. The damage wasn't random, it was surgical and rage-fueled.

A notebook sat next to the shredded photos. A thick, leather-bound journal. Maguire opened it, flipping carefully through the pages with his gloved hands.

"Jesus Christ," he said.

Inside were fantasies, pages of them. Obsessive, unfiltered, delusional. Calderón had written as if Malia already loved him, as if Daniel was the only thing standing in their way. Some of the entries read like diary pages from a parallel reality where they were together. Others read like scripts from a violent pornographic fever dream.

Near the back were plans. Detailed ones.

"He knew Daniel's habits," Maguire said. "Wrote it all down. Said Daniel always came alone to the yacht after a trip. Cleaned it himself. Calderón planned to show up, pretend to patch things up, offer to help. Then he'd shoot him with a suppressed .22. Hide the body on his own boat. Dump him somewhere deep off Bainbridge."

"He disabled the cameras himself," Harper added, voice tight. "He wanted the murder to be clean. No video, and no struggle."

Then Maguire froze.

"Harper," he said, pointing to the corner of the room. "You seeing what I'm seeing?"

At first, Harper thought it was just a pile of clothes on the bed. But as he stepped around the side, he saw the shape of it—and recoiled.

It was a sex doll. Life-sized and anatomically correct. Propped up in the bed like a sleeping lover. Its limbs arranged under the sheets. The figure wore one of Malia's old dresses, wrinkled and stretched to fit. The face had been custom printed. Malia. Or at least a grotesque approximation of her.

The craftsmanship was high-end, thousands of dollars easily. Silicone skin, insertable features. The hair matched. Even the eyes had been colored to match her hazel-green irises exactly.

Harper stepped closer.

The doll's wrists were bound with boat line, tight and deliberate, knotted with practiced precision with a sailor's square knot. He pulled the sheets back, and saw the same type of line around the ankles, then linked from wrists to feet to a loose noose around the neck. The configuration was unmistakable.

"A hogtie," Maguire said grimly. "Designed to tighten the more the body struggles."

"He was rehearsing," Harper said.

Maguire looked away first. He exhaled through his nose and muttered, "this guy was gone. Full-on delusional. Fantasy took over reality completely."

Harper didn't answer. His stomach churned. He could still smell her perfume on the clothes, clinging to the doll like some final insult. He stepped back, eyes sweeping over the madness one last time. The wall of images. The journal of fantasies. The desecrated photos. The tied-up doll in the bed.

It wasn't just obsession. This was possession.

Harper rolled his shoulders to ease the tension. His muscles there felt like cables, drawn tight.

"I'll get CSU in here. Carefully. No one will touch a damn thing unless you say so," Maguire said.

He paused, then added, "You're gonna have to oversee it. Force Investigation Team and OPA is gonna swarm this place once they get the report."

Harper glanced at him.

"Office of Police Accountability," Maguire clarified. "Seattle's version of IAD. FIT and OPA will put me on a shelf until the shooting clears. You'll be solo until then."

Harper nodded. He understood the drill, and the weight it came with. He'd been through it himself, twice last year.

Behind them, the room stood silent. But the weight of what Calderón had built, the shrine, the plan, the grotesque mimicry, hung in the air like rot.

Whatever lines Calderón had once walked, he'd long since crossed them. This wasn't just a stalker. This was a man who'd built a world where Malia was already his. And would kill anyone who got in the way.

Maguire gave a low whistle. "Jesus. And here we were chasing down paperwork and shady pastors like this was some kind of real estate scam."

Harper nodded slowly, still staring at the wall of photographs. "No. This...this was never about money. Or fraud. It was about her, all along."

For a moment, the theory hardened between them like concrete. Calderón hadn't just fantasized about taking Daniel out, he'd planned it. He knew their routines. He had the tools. He had motive, obsession, and now he was dead.

"Hell of a thing," Maguire said. "We might've just closed this case."

•••••

Maguire was leaning against the apartment's outer wall when Harper stepped out. The CSU van had just arrived, along with a pair of unmarked sedans that signaled the Office of Police Accountability was officially on scene.

"Game time," Maguire said under his breath.

A man in his mid-forties stepped out of one of the sedans, wearing a navy blazer over a charcoal button-down, no tie. His sunglasses stayed on despite the fading light. His hair was parted so sharply it looked like he measured the angle. He glanced around like a man already smelling bullshit. Harper could've sworn he saw the man's eye twitch.

"Detective Maguire," the man said, stepping forward. "Sergeant Russell Danning, Special Investigator, OPA. You're being relieved of duty pending administrative review of the use-of-force incident. Badge and weapon, please."

Maguire didn't argue. He took a slow breath and handed both over. "This was a justified shooting, Danning," he said calmly.

"That's for us to determine," Danning replied with a smile that showed entirely too many teeth. "Why don't you go home and get some rest. We'll call you."

Maguire gave a tight nod and walked past Harper without a word. Harper watched him go, then turned back to Danning. He'd sized the man up immediately. He knew the type.

"I never fired my weapon," Harper said. "So my command won't be putting me on leave. I'll continue to work the case until Detective Maguire is cleared. You'll conduct your review, but I'll need all ballistic and forensic data related to the shooting when your team's done. My investigation remains active."

Danning raised an eyebrow. "And what investigation would that be?"

Harper stepped closer. "A federal investigation into a suspected double homicide involving two missing persons. This scene may be collateral, but I expect your full cooperation."

Danning's smile thinned. "We'll share what's appropriate."

"No," Harper said, voice hardening. "You'll share *everything*. I'm not some patrol officer you can push around. Don't play jurisdictional games with me, especially when you *know* damn well this was a good shoot. Maguire saved my life. He's not the trophy you're looking for."

Danning's mouth twitched. "I wasn't aware I was looking for one."

"Yeah, you were," Harper said. "You walked in like a man already writing the report. But let me make one thing clear—you're not pinning anything on him just because it makes a good headline."

Before Danning could reply, one of his investigators stepped out from the bedroom, holding up Calderón's cell phone in an evidence bag.

"We'll take custody of the phone," the woman said.

"No, you won't," Harper replied, stepping forward. "That's coming with me."

Danning stepped in front of her. "This is an active OPA scene and part of a critical use-of-force review. That phone is material to our investigation, Agent Harper."

125

"It's also material to mine," Harper said, holding his ground. "We're working a federal case involving a missing pregnant woman and a U.S. Coast Guard officer, both who are presumed dead. This suspect just shot at a federal agent. That puts me in charge. That phone is part of a broader homicide case."

Danning's voice turned cold. "This isn't your fiefdom. I don't care what federal alphabet soup you came out of, this is a police accountability matter. Our jurisdiction. You're pushing it, Agent."

Harper took a step closer, dropping his voice just enough to draw Danning in. "That's *Special Agent* Harper, Sergeant. And you're posturing. You want to see pushing it? You want to flex jurisdiction?" Harper leaned closer. "Fine. But let me give you a little warning, Sergeant. You start stonewalling a federal homicide investigation involving a commissioned military officer, and you're going to find yourself reassigned to desk duty in a heartbeat. You really want to piss off the United States Coast Guard right now? Because I promise, they bite harder than your office does."

Danning's mouth tightened. "OPA has standing—"

"Not over a federal homicide case you don't. This isn't your trophy, Danning. And neither is Maguire," Harper said, his tone razor-sharp. "I know your type. You're here to build a win, not find the truth. But you picked the wrong scene. This is a federal investigation. The Supremacy Clause gives my case priority. I could take over this entire fucking case, including your ballistics and your shoot review. Be grateful I'm in a sharing mood. Take your scene photos. Interview your witnesses. But that phone? It's mine. And anything else relevant to my case walks with me. But don't get in my way. Are. We. Clear?"

The two men locked eyes. Danning flexed his jaw so hard Harper thought he might chip a tooth. A vein pulsed at his temple.

The eye twitch returned. But finally, he gave a tight nod. "Fine. Just don't contaminate the chain of custody or I'll have your badge next."

Harper gave him a dry look. "Not yours to take, Sergeant. Next time, leave your fucking ego in the car."

Danning didn't reply.

Harper turned and walked out, phone in hand. He was already thinking ahead.

CHAPTER
FOURTEEN

Harper first called Alyssa on his way back to the office. He'd learned long ago it was better for her to hear from him than from the news after a critical incident.

She picked up immediately.

"Hey," she said, her voice low and alert.

"I'm okay," he said quickly. "Wanted you to hear that first."

There was a pause, the kind that let him hear her breath steadying. "Was it the guy from the marina?"

"Yeah," Harper said. "Raided his place with SPD. Things escalated." He hesitated. "He's dead. Took his own life after opening fire on us. I didn't shoot, but Maguire did."

"Oh my God," she whispered. "Are you okay? You weren't hit?"

"No, I'm good. I got a civilian out, she's stable. Medics got to her in time."

"Jesus, Jake."

"I know."

Another beat of silence.

"I hate these calls," she whispered into the phone.

"Me too."

"But I'm glad you're safe. Thanks for letting me know."

He felt the warmth of that land softly in his chest. "I'll be home later, after I drop off some evidence. Just wanted you to know."

"Okay. Be safe, Jake. I need you to come home to us. I love you."

"I love you, too."

He ended the call and immediately dialed SSA Easton.

"Tell me you're calling to say this guy offed himself before you could," Easton answered dryly.

Harper snorted. "Close. But I need a heads-up. OPA's on scene. Investigator named Danning, came in trying to swing his weight around."

Easton's tone shifted. "Danning? He's a climber. Likes to leak things to reporters and frame it as transparency."

"Figured. He relieved Maguire, tried to take some of the evidence from me, including the suspect's phone. He threw jurisdiction in my face, I threw it back. Federal case, Supremacy Clause, the works."

"Did you keep the phone?"

"Yeah, took it right in front of him. I'm on my way in with it right now."

There was a short pause. "Good. I'll make some calls. Danning's political, but he knows where the real lines are drawn. I'll make sure he remembers which side of them he's on before he even thinks of leaking this."

"Appreciate that."

Easton's voice hardened. "From everything I've heard, Maguire's a good cop. You did right standing your ground. I won't let Danning scalp him for a press release."

Harper exhaled slowly. "Thanks, sir."

"Keep moving. You've still got a case to solve. I've got your back."

Harper hung up, the lines of tension still tight across his shoulders, but now there was something bracing underneath them. Support. And the space to finish what he'd started.

•••••

After dropping the phone off with Francis, the on-call digital technician, who looked like an overcaffeinated kid in a CGIS hoodie and promised to have a full data pull by morning, Harper signed the log, handed over the chain-of-custody form, and made his way out into the night.

By the time he pulled into the driveway, it was just after 11 p.m. The porch light was on, casting a warm glow against the siding. Inside, the house was quiet, still, the kind of silence that only came when everyone was asleep.

He stepped carefully inside, locking the door behind him. Boots off. Gun and badge stowed in the safe at the top of the entryway closet. The hum of the refrigerator was the only sound.

Alyssa and Addie were already in bed. Harper padded softly down the hall and into his daughter's room. Her nightlight cast gentle constellations across the ceiling. Addie was curled on her side, one small hand tucked beneath her cheek. He knelt beside her bed and kissed the crown of her head. Her blond curls still smelled faintly of strawberry shampoo and bath soap. He lingered for a second longer than usual. Just enough.

Back in the master bath, he stripped down and stepped into the shower. The water was hot, almost scalding, and he let it hit his shoulders and back like a kind of penance. He scrubbed harder than necessary, rinsing away the grit, the grime, and the psychic residue of the day. The blood on his pants. The glass. The smell of that goddamn hallway where Calderón had blown his head off. Visions of the sex doll with Malia's face danced in front of his face every time he blinked.

Afterward, Harper sat on the edge of the tub, toweling off. Under the bathroom light, he saw the soles of his feet. They were angry red with embedded shards of glass from the sliding glass door he'd shattered. He winced as he dug them out with a pair of tweezers and sterilized the cuts with rubbing alcohol, then wrapped them with gauze and medical tape. Field fix. Nothing fancy. The cuts were small and wouldn't require stitches, but he'd be limping a bit tomorrow.

Alyssa stirred when he slipped under the covers.

"Mmm," she murmured, half-awake. Her hand found his under the sheets. "You're home."

"I'm here," he whispered.

She nuzzled into his shoulder, eyes still closed. "Love you."

"I love you too." Harper pressed a kiss to her temple.

She was asleep again in seconds.

Harper lay there in the dark, staring at the ceiling, letting his breathing sync with hers. The house was quiet. Safe. But his mind hadn't followed him home. It was still in that apartment, staring at a wall of madness and a lifeless body with no skull.

Eventually, exhaustion won out. His eyes closed. But his sleep was thin and troubled. And morning was already waiting.

CHAPTER
FIFTEEN

September 12. Morning.

The next morning, Harper was back at his desk before seven. The techie had the phone data waiting for him. Harper sat alone in the office, a cooling cup of coffee by his elbow. A drive was tethered to the laptop, with the data from Calderón's phone.

The chaos from the apartment still clung to him. Malia's photos, the hog-tied doll, the smell of synthetic flesh and old obsession. But this part of the job required distance and precision. His shirt collar was open, the polo wrinkled. He hadn't really slept; he'd just closed his eyes long enough to forget the smell of Calderón's apartment. To dream of the doll's plastic skin and wake with the stink of synthetic flesh still in his nose.

He briefly glanced at the photo of Alyssa and Addie he kept on his desk. It was from their house back in Stonehaven, Addie riding on Alyssa's shoulders. Both smiling at the camera. He ran a thumb over the edge of his wedding ring, grounding himself.

He clicked through the data stream pulled from the phone.

Text logs. Social media screenshots. Browser history. And photos. Hundreds of photos, many clearly voyeuristic, cropped and zoomed from apart. None of that surprised him.

It was the GPS logs that mattered now.

He opened the timeline view and filtered for September 9, the day the Rainiers' boat had been at the Shilshole Point Marina.

This was it. The piece that would put Calderón on the boat, tie him to the Rainiers. Harper braced himself, waiting for the hit. At first, his pulse quickened: Calderón's phone pinged at the marina that morning, right where the yacht had been moored. But an hour later it was already south on I-5, then locked all day at the Pierce County courthouse in Tacoma. By late afternoon, it hit a cafe downtown, then an address Harper confirmed was his mother's house in South Tacoma, where it stayed.

Harper sagged back in his chair. While the Rainiers' yacht slipped out of the marina, Calderón had been nearly fifty miles away.

The device stayed there for the next two days. September 10: another cafe, another courthouse entry, then back to his mother's house. Not until the morning of September 11 did the GPS show him returning to Seattle, right before Harper and Maguire went to interview him.

Fuck. Harper slammed his fist onto the desk. The one thread he thought would unravel the case had just snapped in his hands.

Harper picked up the phone and called the Pierce County Sheriff's Office.

"Pierce County, Deputy Stevenson," a female voice answered.

"Good morning, Deputy. This is Special Agent Harper, CGIS. I'm investigating a homicide suspect. His GPS showed him at the Pierce County Courthouse all day on September 9 and 10. I just needed to verify he was there. Are you able to confirm that?"

"What was his name?"

"Rafael Calderón."

"Just a moment."

The line went to hold music. After a few minutes, a different voice picked up. Male and gruff.

"Detective Harrison. Special Agent Harper?"

"Yes, sir."

"I understand you were wanting to discuss Rafael Calderón's testimony yesterday?"

"Testimony?" Harper asked.

"Yes," Harrison said. "He testified in a cold case we reopened last year. Homicide down in Commencement Bay Marina, July of 2021. Victims were David and Renee Barringer. Husband was shot in the head, contact wound, small-caliber suppressed weapon. Wife was bound at the wrists, ankles, and neck. Hogtied, basically. Brutally raped. Then strangled to death. The body positioning was—" he paused, then said, "deliberate."

Harper's grip on the phone tightened. For a split second, the doll from Calderón's apartment flickered in his mind, hogtied in the bed. A cold flush crawled his neck. "He testified to what, exactly?"

"Back then, Calderón was working marina maintenance. He claimed he saw one of his coworkers follow the Barringers out the night they were killed. We tracked that guy down, a local meth head who'd been fired a few weeks earlier. Sketchy dude. He denied it, of course, but Calderón's grand jury statement gave us enough to spin the case up again."

"Was there anything else? In the testimony?"

"He said the guy had a thing for the wife," Harrison said. "Claimed he saw him watching her. Told us he was just trying to do the right thing. Handed us a journal he said the tweaker had left in the office before he was fired. Had detailed plans to do the couple in."

Harper was quiet for a moment. "Calderón's dead. Last night, he opened fire on me and a Seattle PD detective during a search warrant service. We'd identified him as a possible suspect in the disappearance of a Coast Guard officer and his wife. It looks like he took his own life before we could get inside."

"Jesus," Harrison swore. "Fuck man. I knew the guy was odd, but..." He paused again. "You think he was your guy?"

"He was planning something. Had a replica doll of the missing woman in his apartment, bound in the same way you just described in your case. Photos, fantasies, the whole shrine. But based on his phone's GPS, he was in Tacoma with his mother, and testifying in front of your grand jury, the entire day of the disappearance. So now, it's looking like he wasn't our guy. But he's no innocent."

Harrison's voice grew hard. "Shit. I always thought his statement felt too scripted. Now I'm wondering if he wasn't just a witness."

"Did you ever get DNA from the Barringer case?"

"Mixed profile," Harrison said. "Male. Never matched anyone in CODIS. The rapist used a condom, but he made mistakes: hair, touch DNA. You think we'd get something from your scene?"

"I'm guessing so. CSU's still working it. But I'll tell you this, Detective: the bindings, the staging, he'd thought it through. We even found a journal detailing plans to kill our victims in the same way yours were. He wasn't just fantasizing."

Harrison exhaled. "Send me whatever you've got. And if you pull prints or DNA, loop me in. I'll do the same."

"Will do. One more thing. Calderón's phone might have logs, notes, searches. You want access?"

"Absolutely."

"I'll package it up," Harper said. "Might have just cracked your case open by accident."

"Sir, you might've just *closed* our case," Harrison said. "But let's not call it luck. Let's call it what it is. A predator finally slipping up."

Harper hung up a minute later, already turning back to the GPS logs. Calderón hadn't killed the Rainiers. He'd been in Tacoma when the Rainiers went back out to sea. He couldn't have made them disappear. *But someone had.*

Harper sat still for a long moment, the hum of the office dim against the rising drumbeat in his chest. Calderón wasn't the one who killed the Rainiers.

"Goddamn it," he swore under his breath, pinching the bridge of his nose. Every hour chasing Calderón had only given the real killer room to breathe. Time to vanish. He knew the statistics. The chances of solving a homicide are cut in half if a lead isn't found within the first forty-eight hours. And they were going on more than seventy-two hours at this point.

Calderón was broken. Obsessed. Dangerous. But he hadn't been there. The timeline was airtight. Every piece of evidence that had pointed toward guilt had unraveled into something worse, something messier. Calderón had wanted to kill Daniel Rainier. Harper was sure of it. But someone else had beaten him to it.

And whoever had done it hadn't left behind obsession or fantasy.

They'd left silence. Deliberate. Clinical. Clean.

He shut the laptop and leaned back, eyes burning. He ran a hand through his hair. The false lead had bought the real killer time. Time to disappear. Time to destroy evidence. Time to plan what came next. The case had just shifted from a pervert with delusions to a ghost with precision.

Harper glanced at the case file on the corner of his desk, the Rainiers' names written in red. Malia's photo. Daniel's commission certificate. A string of printed messages from their social media accounts. A post from the marina.

It all felt too perfect. Too contained.

He looked at the pictures from the yacht. The too-clean cabins. The wiped logs. The missing dinghy. The untouched crime scene floating silently in the Sound.

He leaned back in his chair, eyes on the ceiling tiles. Someone had waited for the Rainiers to return. Someone had known exactly what they were doing. And they'd done it without leaving a trace. This wasn't over.

This wasn't rage. This was planned.

Harper could feel it in his gut. This was something else.

Something worse.

Something *evil*.

His phone buzzed. Alyssa.

"Hey love," he answered.

"Hey, yourself. You sound tired," she said.

"I'm fine," Harper lied, eyes on the Rainiers' file.

"Don't burn yourself out, Jake."

"I'm just working the case," he said, softer.

"You sure?" Alyssa said. He could hear the worry in her voice. She knew him too well.

"I'll be alright."

"Jake, I miss you. Please be careful...I need you around. *We* need you around."

"I will. I promise. I'll be home tonight. I love you."

"I love you," Alyssa replied.

He ended the call, the weight in his chest growing.

Harper's gaze drifted to a yellow sticky note pinned above his desk. A name scrawled in black ink.

Kincaid.

The pastor's smirk surfaced in his mind, slippery and hollow. Harper felt his gut tighten.

Maybe it was time to take another look at the good shepherd.

Part Two: Beneath the Altar

"Beware of false prophets, who come to you in sheep's clothing but inwardly are ravenous wolves."
— *Matthew 7:15.*

CHAPTER
SIXTEEN

They had been chasing ghosts.

Harper sat alone at his desk in the CGIS office at Base Seattle, the morning light slanting through the blinds in sharp, geometric lines. Coffee cooling by his hand, he started a fresh timeline on a yellow pad.

The Rainiers had sailed north for their babymoon on August 26, sunlight and smiling in the San Juans. On September 8 they were last seen alive, and by the next morning AIS showed their yacht returning to Shilshole Point Marina, only to leave again hours later. It drifted back into Elliott Bay after dark, abandoned. No blood. No belongings. Just a wiped tablet and silence.

The same day, Pastor Asher Kincaid filed a stolen vessel report, claiming he had purchased *The Halcyon Way* days earlier in cash, through a broker named Trevor Oliver. But Harper and Kincaid had so far been unable to locate the broker or verify any transfer of funds. No funds. No broker. No trace.

At the marina, Rafael Calderón had been teetering on the edge, fixated on Malia Rainier and planning to kill her husband, but someone had beaten him to it. Now Calderón was dead, and the case was back to square one.

On Harper's pad, Calderón's name was written, then crossed off. Alibi. Deceased.

Below it, Harper wrote two more.

Asher Kincaid.
Trevor Oliver.

•••••

Maguire had said Kincaid was clean. And Trevor Oliver was a ghost. Harper began digging himself. He re-ran the background check. NCIC said the same thing: spotless. No criminal record in any state. A couple parking tickets from college. *Too clean*, Harper thought. Everyone had something.

Harper looked at the clock. 9:00 a.m. He picked up the phone.

"Northwest University, registrar, this is Judy. How can I help you?" The voice on the other end was warm and friendly.

"Good morning, this is Special Agent Harper, CGIS. I'm hoping to speak to someone in records about a former student?"

"Hold please!" she said in the same cheery voice.

The line clicked over to an instrumental rock cover of "Sweet Child O' Mine," muffled like it was playing underwater. Harper leaned back in his chair. *It always sounds like it's being played through a cardboard tube.*

After a few more mind-numbing minutes of the music, a new voice came on.

"Records, this is Jack Simons. How can I help you?"

"Good morning, Mr. Simons. I'm working a background related to an ongoing investigation. Just wondering what the process is for accessing an old student file, an Asher Kincaid?"

"Oh, sorry agent, FERPA doesn't allow us to share that without a court order."

"I can send a subpoena."

"Perfect. Fax it over and we'll get the ball rolling."

Are they always this cheerful there? Harper took down the fax number.

He typed up the request and brought it to Easton. Ten minutes later, the subpoena was signed, stamped, and faxed.

While he waited, Harper dug back into every public database he could access. Social media, court filings, license records, and voter rolls, all trying to find a Trevor Oliver who wasn't smoke and mirrors.

Nothing.

No one with the right age, location history, or any professional affiliations matching the supposed broker. No bar license. No record of any business operating under his name in Washington, Oregon, or Idaho. Just a handful of disconnected hits—an HVAC tech in Spokane, a guy with a DUI in Yakima, a high school basketball coach in Salem.

Whoever Kincaid's "broker" was, they didn't want to be found. And Harper was starting to think that was the point. He either wasn't real, or he wasn't using his real name.

Harper leaned back, resting his head on the seat back and stared at the ceiling tiles, hands folded in his lap. *So who would trust you enough to launder a murder?*

He turned back to the name at the top of the page. To Asher Kincaid.

He started typing again. Digging further.

Public records showed Kincaid moved to Washington in 2006, enrolling in Northwest University that fall. He graduated in 2010, bought a used Toyota that same year and registered it with a Bellevue address. Nothing special.

He leaned back in his chair and sighed, letting the frustration out through closed teeth.

Just then, an email popped into Harper's inbox. Northwest University.

He opened it.

The transcript confirmed what he already knew: enrolled 2006, graduated 2010. Then straight into the graduate program— Ministry Leadership and Theology—finishing in 2012.

But it was the application materials that caught his eye.

A diploma from an Idaho high school. *Coeur D'Alene High School.*

Harper sat forward. He ran a quick Idaho DMV records check and found a learner's permit issued in Kootenai County back in 2003. The address listed was in Hayden Lake, a tiny lake town just north of the city. No license renewal on file in Washington. And no public records at all between 2003 and 2006.

He picked up the phone again.

"Hayden Lake Records," came the flat voice on the other end. The woman sounded like she'd rather be anywhere else.

"Hi, this is Special Agent Jake Harper with the Coast Guard Investigative Service. I was hoping to speak with someone about an old juvenile record, or at least someone who might be familiar with local history."

The woman let out a breath, as if Harper's request was the most wearisome thing she's had to deal with in weeks. "What's the name?"

"Asher Kincaid. Born 1988. I believe he lived there in the early 2000s."

"One moment."

Another hold line. This one was static-laced piano jazz, something between a funeral dirge and elevator music. Harper drummed his fingers against the desk.

Then a male voice picked up, calm, clipped, and edged with curiosity.

"Chief Russ Jansen. You're looking into Asher Kincaid?"

Harper blinked. "You know the name?"

"Yeah, I used to be with Coeur D'Alene PD before I took this gig. Hayden Lake only has one officer—me. Everything else is contracted through the Sheriff's Office. I grew up here, and when I retired, they roped me back in." He paused. "But back then, I was the SRO over at Coeur d'Alene High. I remember Asher well. What's this about?"

Harper gave a brief rundown: a federal investigation, missing persons under suspicious circumstances, a questionable yacht sale with Kincaid's name on it.

"I'll be damned," Jansen muttered. "But I can't say I'm surprised."

That got Harper's full attention. "You're not?"

Jansen sighed. "Not really. It's not in any report you'll be able to pull, at least not without unsealing it. But yeah, I remember Asher. And his brother."

Harper sat up straighter. "He has a brother?"

"*Had* a brother. Twin. Name was Noah. Their mom was a true believer. Deep Old Testament stuff—signs, prophecy, all that. She used to say Noah was the chosen one. Asher was always the shadow. The other son."

"So what happened?"

There was a pause. "Listen, I've already said more than I should over the phone. The family still has influence around here. Land. Money. Church ties. You know what I mean?"

Harper did. All too well. "Chief, why don't I come to you?"

Jansen didn't answer right away.

"Chief," Harper said, voice low. "I get small towns. Before this, I was a deputy. I'm not full-time federal. This is a temp assignment. I know how to keep things quiet. No one needs to know it came from you, I just need a place to start looking."

Jansen exhaled. "You buying lunch?"

"Absolutely."

"Then yeah. Come on out."

Harper hung up, already texting Easton for a travel authorization.

The records might take weeks to unseal, if they even existed anymore.

But memories?

Memories didn't redact so easily.

•••••

"Hey love, what's up?" came Alyssa's voice on the phone. Harper had called her as he drove to the Seattle-Tacoma airport, the city sliding past in muted grays through the windshield.

"Hey yourself, love. I gotta run to Idaho for a day, maybe two," Harper said. "Got a lead on this thing."

"Idaho?" she repeated, surprised. "What's out there?"

"Kid stuff," he said, then paused. "That pastor we're looking at—Kincaid—turns out he grew up out there. On paper, he's squeaky clean. But I just found out he had a sealed juvenile record from back there."

148

Alyssa was quiet for a beat. "Whoa. Idaho. Didn't see that coming."

"Yeah. I'm going out to talk to the local police chief, says he knew the family. And see if I can get someone inside the juvenile detention center to open the records."

"Do you think it's connected? To the Rainiers?"

Harper exhaled through his nose. "I don't know. But if this guy's been hiding something like that, I want to know what else he's buried."

There was a pause on the line, soft static, and the muffled sound of their daughter giggling in the background.

"I wish you didn't have to go alone," Alyssa said gently. "You've been carrying so much of this."

"I know," he said. "I'll be careful. Promise."

"Addie's right here," she said. "Want to say hi?"

"Please."

There was a shuffle, then a little voice piped through the line, sweet and high, full of unfiltered joy.

"Hi Daddy!"

Harper smiled, his heart catching in his chest.

"Hey peanut. What're you up to?"

"I made a sun with crayons," she announced. "It has sparkles. And a rainbow!"

"I can't wait to see it."

There was a pause. Then, in a voice just shy of a whisper. "Daddy? I miss you."

The ache settled deep in his ribs.

"I miss you too, baby girl. I'll be home soon, okay?"

"I love you, Daddy."

"I love you more," Harper said, eyes stinging just slightly. "Be good for Mommy."

"Okay. Bye!" she sang.

Alyssa came back on the line, her voice soft. "Text me when you land?"

"I will."

"Be safe, Jake."

"Always."

He hung up as the exit for Sea-Tac came into view, the sun already beginning to slide lower in the sky. The shadows were getting longer.

So was the road ahead.

CHAPTER
SEVENTEEN

It was only a one-hour-and-ten-minute flight from Seattle to Coeur D'Alene. During the flight, Jake Harper's thoughts churned in a low, steady spin. Kincaid wasn't just suspicious, he was starting to feel like someone who'd spent his entire adult life outrunning something.

Harper had met plenty of men of God over the years. Some were the real deal—pastors who visited jails, bought groceries for struggling families, stayed up all night talking suicidal kids down from the ledge. The Stonehaven PD Chaplain was one such man, and he'd helped Harper plenty through some of the worst calls he'd been through.

He still remembered the first time he had to tell a parent their child wasn't coming home. Two young girls, killed by a driver who fell asleep at the wheel. Senseless. Harper had given the first notification without a hitch. But the second notification...the second notification was different. Before Harper could even speak, the father knew. He looked in Harper's eyes, and collapsed on the grass, a wail tearing loose as if the earth itself had given way beneath him. Harper had caught him, holding tight. Pastor Wayne was there in an instant, his arms closing around them both. Just three fathers mourning the harshness of the world together.

Harper could not have done it without Wayne's quiet strength.

What marked those men apart was not their sermons, but their presence. They didn't need a pulpit to prove themselves. They showed up in squad rooms at two in the morning, boots on the same stained carpet, hands steady when everyone else's were shaking. They held officers and detectives when they broke after seeing a dead child or a suicide. They didn't preach about service; they lived it. And that kind of faith had weight you could lean on.

But Harper had met the other kind, too. Men who wore the collar like a costume. Men who used pulpits to groom trust, manipulate the lonely, and silence the vulnerable. Kincaid's record might've been clean. But a clean slate could still cover a filthy past.

•••••

Then.

The sanctuary was warm with the late spring sunlight filtering through stained glass, casting streaks of color across the rows of pews in the shape of a cross. Seventeen-year-old Jake Harper sat with his family near the front of the sanctuary at *Trinitarian Baptist*. His father, Raymond, was on his left, with his mother, Abigail, next to him. On Jake's right, his younger sister Anna fidgeted with her church bulletin, and his kid brother Matthew traced shapes into the worn oak of the pew rail.

Jake wore slacks and a collared shirt, the sleeves rolled once. His earrings—small black studs—remained in, though he'd caught the glances from some of the older congregants. The looks didn't bother him anymore. But the tension in the air did.

Pastor Benjamin stood at the pulpit, a leather-bound Bible open in one hand, the other lifted in declaration. His voice carried strong through the rafters, practiced and sharp.

"This morning," the pastor said, "we come to the Word of God in *Romans*, chapter thirteen. 'Let every soul be subject to the governing authorities. For there is no authority except from God, and the authorities that exist are appointed by God.'"

Jake glanced at his father. Raymond sat still, arms folded. His face was unreadable, his brown eyes stoic, but Jake had heard the long phone calls, the whispers after service. He'd seen the concern in his mother's eyes.

"As believers," Pastor Benjamin went on, "we must submit. Not just to the law, but to spiritual authority. To the men God places over us to shepherd the flock. Rebellion is not a personality trait. It is sin. Rebellion is witchcraft—*witchcraft!*—and it opens the door to the enemy."

The cadence began to shift. Each sentence grew more emphatic, the pastor's voice tightening with intensity. His cheeks flushed. The pulpit became a battleground.

"*'Do not be deceived: neither the sexually immoral, nor idolaters, nor adulterers...'*" He paced, reading from Corinthians now. "*'...nor men who practice homosexuality, nor thieves, nor the greedy, nor drunkards, nor slanders, nor swindlers will inherit the kingdom of God.'*"

Jake stiffened. The pastor's eyes swept the congregation, then locked with his own. And stayed there.

"There are those among us," Pastor Benjamin said, "who wear the mask of righteousness. Who play at godliness but flirt with the flesh. They dance on the edge of sin, thinking their secret thoughts are hidden. Thinking God does not see. But he *does* see. He sees the lusts of youth, the pride of their fathers." The preacher was staring at Jake and his father now.

Jake's jaw tightened. His father leaned forward slightly, posture still calm, but alert now.

"Let me be clear," the pastor thundered. "The fire of hell is *not* a metaphor. It is real. It is torment. Unending. Reserved for the prideful, the lustful, and the disobedient. It is reserved for those that question God's appointed order."

The words scorched the room. Abigail reached over and gently touched Raymond's wrist. Her face had gone pale.

Pastor Benjamin's voice finally lowered, calm again but only in volume, not in tone. "He who has ears, let him hear what the Spirit says to the church."

Silence lingered. Then the piano began to play softly, and the congregation stirred to life.

After the benediction, Raymond was summoned by another Elder. He gave Jake a nod, *stay put,* and followed them through the side door. Abigail tried to keep the kids calm, but Jake's chest was tight. He knew something was wrong.

He hadn't noticed the Youth Pastor, Chad, approach until the man sat on the pew beside him. Chad was in his late twenties, buzz cut, with a pressed shirt tucked in just a little too tight. His smile didn't quite reach his eyes.

"Hey, Jake," Chad said. "Got a minute?"

Jake nodded slowly. "Sure."

Chad leaned in. His voice dropped to something softer, almost tender, but with a practiced edge.

"I've been praying for you."

Jake didn't respond.

"The Lord's been impressing something on my heart," Chad continued. "You've got a girlfriend—Mackenzie, right?"

Jake blinked. "Yeah?"

Chad gave a slow nod, as if confirming a suspicion. "She's a sweet girl. Comes from a good family. Cute too," he said with a wink. "We want the best for both of you." Chad exhaled through his nose, voice low. "I think you know where I'm going with this. There's...concern lately. About boundaries. About temptation."

Jake didn't answer, but he felt the tip of his ears burn.

"I want to ask you something, Jake. And I want you to really think about it." He paused, holding Jake's gaze. "Are you guarding her heart? And her body? Are you guarding your own?"

Jake felt his shoulders tense, but didn't answer.

"I know what it's like at your age," Chad went on, voice soft but laced with something more intrusive now. "The temptation. The pressure. The hormones. Especially when you're dating such a beautiful girl. But God calls us to something higher, something sacred."

He leaned in just an inch more, the fluorescent light glinting off his wedding band.

"Have you two been saving yourself for marriage? Really saving yourselves? Because it's not just about what you do, it's about what you allow. What you entertain. Where your hands go, where your *mouths* go. God sees it all. You know that right?"

Jake said nothing.

Chad held the silence for a beat longer, like he was trying to draw out a confession that never came. Then he shifted, smiling faintly, but it didn't reach his eyes.

"I've seen the earrings," Chad continued. "And the attitude lately. You show up late to youth group. You ask a lot of questions. And questions are fine, but too many? That's usually a sign of rebellion. And rebellion's not from God."

Jake's fist clenched beneath the pew rail.

"Look, I don't want to make this about your dad," Chad said, tone shifting as if to feign sympathy, "but his influence matters. The way a man leads his family—*spiritually*—it shapes everything."

He took a step closer, lowering his voice again like he was sharing something sacred.

"When a father steps out of alignment with godly authority, even just a little? It opens doors. It creates cracks. And sometimes those cracks pass down. Bitterness, pride, lust...confusion about your place. Confusion about Truth."

Jake stared at a scratch in the pew rail, jaw tight.

"I've seen it before," Chad said, as if diagnosing a disease. "Good kids from good homes who start slipping. And it always starts the same way. Questions, distractions, compromise. The enemy doesn't kick the door in, Jake. He finds a foothold. That's all he needs."

Jake's mouth was dry. He didn't trust himself to speak.

Chad smiled gently and stood, brushing invisible lint from his sleeves. "I'll be praying for clarity in your heart. Don't let the enemy get a foothold. Don't let him steal your future. And don't let him steal hers, either."

Jake watched him go, stomach churning.

Ten minutes later, Raymond returned, his face tight.

"Come on," he said to Abigail. "We're leaving."

The ride home was quiet, the car filled with the low hum of tires on pavement. Jake finally spoke.

"What happened?"

Raymond kept his eyes on the road. "I've been removed as an elder."

Jake's jaw dropped. "For what?"

"For asking the wrong questions," Raymond said softly. "About the church's finances. About Benjamin's use of funds. And for disagreeing with a few things in private meetings."

Abigail put a hand on his arm.

"They didn't say we were unwelcome. But they said it might be... spiritually healthier if we found another congregation. One more in alignment with our priorities."

Jake sat back, seething. "That's bullshit."

"Watch your language," Raymond said, then sighed. "But yes."

"They can't just kick you out for disagreeing."

"They didn't," Raymond said. "They just made it clear we weren't wanted."

Jake looked out the window, throat tight. "Why didn't you stand up to him?"

Raymond was quiet a long moment. Then he said, "I did, son. And that's why he feels threatened. Not every man behind a pulpit knows the heart of God."

Jake didn't answer. But something shifted in him as they drove. Not anger. Not just sadness. A subtle fracture in something he'd once taken for granted.

A seed, quietly planted.

•••••

Now.

The rattle of the drink cart against his elbow pulled Harper out of the memory. He waved off the juice, taking the coffee instead. The bitter heat grounded him, but his mind stayed tangled in the old ghosts—men who wore the cloth but twisted it to serve themselves. Authority as cover. Scripture as leverage. Always taking, never giving.

Just like Kincaid.

Harper couldn't yet see the shape of it, but the feeling was there, heavy, and certain: whatever mask Kincaid was wearing, underneath it all, he was cut from the same cloth as those men.

CHAPTER
EIGHTEEN

Noon.

After landing, Harper picked up a rental car. He had chosen a non-descript mid-size sedan, and the staff had given him a white Toyota Corolla. The drive took only ten minutes, but it felt longer, the town unfolding in postcards. Hayden Lake looked like a painting hung over a wound. White fences. Lakefront cabins with decks pointed like pews toward the water.

It was picturesque. But Harper noticed the sideways looks when he slowed at the cafe on Main. Outsiders weren't unwelcome here, but they weren't embraced either. Hayden Lake wanted to be seen as a refuge, the kind of place where nothing bad ever happened. As long as you didn't look too closely.

The police station was a single-story brick building tucked between the post office and an insurance agency. Neat and unassuming. The kind of place you could blink and miss.

Chief Russ Jansen was already waiting out front.

"Special Agent Harper?" the man called, extending a thick, calloused hand.

Jansen was stocky, maybe six foot, with a high-and-tight cut gone silver and a clean-shaven face behind a pair of small metal-frame glasses. The handshake was firm. Measured.

"Thanks for making the time, Chief," Harper said.

"Sure thing," Jansen replied. "C'mon back."

They walked through a modest front lobby and into a compact office. The walls were lined with framed photos: Hayden Lake in winter, a vintage fire engine, a plaque commemorating Idaho peace officers lost in the line of duty. Jansen settled behind a heavy wooden desk while Harper took the guest chair, a worn leather seat that creaked under his weight.

Jansen gave him a once-over. "Not often I meet a Puddle Pirate out here in North Idaho."

Harper raised his eyebrow at the nickname, used mostly by other branches to razz Coast Guardsmen.

"USMC," Jansen said, catching the look. "Ninety-four to ninety-eight. Too late for Desert Storm, too early for Iraq."

Harper thought he could detect a hint of defensiveness of his military record. He nodded. "I hear that. I never did get sent to the sandbox, either. Did a tour with MSRT myself, mostly counter-piracy stuff and drug interdiction."

"Well, nothing but respect for you boat guys. The Corps never forgot Douglas Munro."

Jansen took a drink from a chipped Hayden Lake PD coffee mug, then leaned back. "But enough ancient history. You're here about Asher Kincaid."

Harper nodded. "You mentioned a brother?"

"Right, yes. So first, just to be clear, Hayden Lake's department is me. One officer—the chief. Everything else is handled by the county. I've only had this gig a couple years, but I grew up here. Everyone knows everyone, or thinks they do. That's how this place works. The City wants this place to be a quiet refuge, and you'll keep it that way if you want to keep your job."

Harper said nothing. Just let the man continue.

"Hell, guy before me got shit-canned for questioning the mayor when he decreed that anyone going seven miles an hour over the limit got an automatic cite. Former chief refused, said it wasn't legal. Sued, and won, but he's still out of a job."

He set the mug down.

"I knew the Kincaids. They were well-connected. Asher's mom, Elizabeth, was the daughter of Judge Rolf, retired now. Her husband, Micah, was a traveling preacher. Hellfire and brimstone, snake-handling type. Took his show on the road."

Harper leaned in slightly.

"Rumor was it he got tagged by one of his own snakes. Didn't bleed it right. Usually they milk the venom before their revival stunts, make it look like divine protection. But that time? No miracle. Died on the spot."

Another man of the cloth out for his own gain, Harper thought, before turning his mind back to the mother. "So she came back here."

"Yeah. Brought the boys. Twins, Noah and Asher. Her daddy gave her a parcel of land near the north end of the lake. She homeschooled them at first, then put 'em in public school when they were maybe twelve or thirteen. Told them they had a mission, spread the 'gospel' at school. Especially Noah."

Jansen paused, setting down his mug with a quiet clink.

"She really fawned over Noah. Told anyone who'd listen he was chosen. A prophet." Jansen's mouth pulled into a grimace. "Asher was just the other one. The spare. It was weird, but the judge kept a lid on it. People just let it slide. Just another harmless religious nut in northern Idaho."

161

"You were the SRO at the high school?" Harper prompted.

"Yeah. Coeur d'Alene High. I was assigned there for six years. That's where I really got to know the Kincaid boys. Those two, Asher and Noah, they were inseparable as kids, but it got darker once they got to high school. Pressure, expectations, weird family discipline. It did something to them. Noah was student body president, ran the Evangelical Club, always quoting scripture. Asher...not so much. Got into drinking. Started slipping behind. Then the boating accident..."

"Accident?"

He paused.

"Yeah. Summer after sophomore year. They were out on the lake in their grandfather's boat. Asher was piloting. He was drunk. Crashed it into a rock face near the inlet. Noah went over. Prop tore him up. He bled out before the rescue boat even got halfway there."

"Jesus."

"Yeah. Asher took a plea. BUI, assault, dropped the manslaughter. Two years in juvie. He got out before senior year, finished school quietly, then disappeared. The family tried to get the record expunged, but Idaho law didn't allow it. They settled for sealed."

"Did you ever hear from him again?"

"Not a word, until you called. Honestly, I wasn't sure if he was even still around the Northwest."

Harper's mind was spinning, fragments clicking into place. Clean-cut youth pastor, now a rising church leader. Trusted by families. But that past? That wasn't clean. That was soaked in blood and silence.

He stood. "Thanks, Chief. I owe you one."

Jansen held up a hand. "You owe me lunch, remember?"

Harper managed a thin smile. "You got a place?"

"Coldest beer in the county. Meet you there."

Harper stepped out into the crisp Idaho air, the chill biting deeper than he expected. As he walked to his car, his thoughts circled back to the fanaticism Asher had been raised in. It wasn't so different from the world he'd known himself. The strict sermons, scripture wielded like a hammer.

But where Raymond had taught him that faith meant service, humility, and integrity, Asher's parents had twisted it into control and prophecy.

There but for the grace of God go I.

•••••

The place was called the Patriot's Draft, a low-roofed taphouse off Government Way in Hayden proper, sandwiched between an insurance agency and a vape store. The windows were tinted and the inside was dim, lit by overhead Edison bulbs and a row of wall-mounted flags—American, POW/MIA, the Gadsden. The back wall was all taps, thirty of them, gleaming behind the bar.

Jansen had changed into jeans and a t-shirt with a local fire department logo on the chest. His badge was gone, replaced with a pint of amber in one hand and a coaster under the other. He was already halfway through when Harper arrived.

"Figured you'd find it," Jansen said, gesturing to the open seat with his pint.

Harper slid into the booth across from him, taking in the room. Mostly men, older, flannel-clad, a few in baseball with

Vietnam or OIF/OEF patches. A dog lay curled beneath a stool by the jukebox.

Jansen lifted his glass. "House red. You want one?"

Harper shook his head. "Still working."

"Your loss," Jansen said. "Food's solid though. Burger'll soak up your sins."

Harper cracked a smile. "You ordering for both of us?"

"Damn right. You're still paying though."

Jansen waved over the bartender, placed two orders, and leaned back in the booth.

The burgers arrived. They were big and greasy, with steak fries and a side of slaw. Jansen dove in like a man who skipped breakfast. Harper picked at the fries.

He looked at Jansen. "You mentioned earlier that Asher kept his head down after juvie?"

"Yeah," Jansen said, scratching the edge of his pint glass. "It was like he came back...hollowed out. Not just remorse. Something deeper. Like he'd figured out the only way to survive was to disappear."

He took a sip, then set the glass down.

"Didn't hang out with his old friends. Didn't date. Didn't cause trouble either, not visibly. You'd hardly know he was even there. But his mother—"

He whistled low.

"She went off the rails. You'd hear stories about that family. Elizabeth showing up at PTA meetings with a Bible under her arm, demanding Halloween be banned. Asher sneaking six-packs behind the Sinclair station. Noah preaching over the school loudspeaker before football games. Half the town proud, the other half embarrassed as hell."

Harper knew exactly the type.

He shook his head. "After the accident, it got worse. Elizabeth was broken, but twisted it. Said God spared the wrong son for a reason. All that religious fanaticism she used to heap onto Noah? She redirected it. Made Asher her new project. Her mission."

Harper frowned. "So he was living with someone who blamed him, then tried to redeem him?"

Jansen nodded. "Exactly. Said his punishment had been diving preparation. That he had a higher calling now. I think she honestly believed he could become some kind of prophet himself. I think he started believing it too. And folks let her. Out of pity for the judge, out of fear of crossing her. In Hayden Lake, silence is survival."

"Where's his mom now?"

"Oh, she died a few years back. Overdose. Guess she started taking pills to cope after Noah died."

Harper pursed his lips and nodded. He had seen this happen before. Outwardly religious to compensate for a secret addiction.

"You said Asher did his time in JDC," Harper said after a moment. "Any idea who he ran with in there? Who he was close to?"

"Not really," Jansen said, mouth half-full. "Juvie was a black box back then. They didn't loop in school staff unless a kid came back with issues. But I know someone who might."

"Who's that?"

"Ray Spencer. He was a shift supervisor over at Kootenai County Juvenile One when Asher was locked up. Retired now, but still does part-time work there. Doing backgrounds for new hires, mostly. I'm pretty sure he still has access. He's one of those guys they never really let go."

"Think he'd talk to me?"

"Absolutely. Especially if I call ahead and tell him you're square." Jansen wiped his mouth with a napkin, then pulled out his phone. "You'll need a subpoena, but guessing that won't be a problem for a Fed. Since the records weren't expunged, just sealed, they still exist. You get one of those, Spencer'll get you what you need."

"Not a problem. I'll have it in my inbox before I get there." Harper felt the buzz of forward momentum again. A real lead.

"Appreciate it," he said. "What's Spencer like?"

"Bit of a bulldog. Knows the system inside and out. Still calls the kids 'residents' instead of inmates. Takes it seriously. He'll help you."

Jansen finished his beer and looked at Harper more closely.

"I'll tell you this, though. If you dig up what I think you're about to dig up, don't expect it to make sense."

"What do you mean?"

Jansen rubbed the back of his neck, eyes drifting toward the window.

"Asher wasn't born broken. He was made that way."

CHAPTER
NINETEEN

It was a bit after four in the afternoon when Harper pulled up to the low-slung brick building at 210 E. Dalton Ave. *District 1 Juvenile Detention Center* was spelled out in large, institutional block letters across the facade. The letters were sun-faded and chipped at the edges, as if the place wanted to be forgotten.

Behind the office, a tall wrought-iron fence ran the perimeter, topped with razor wire that shimmered in the heat. Beyond it stood a squat, windowless gray building: the housing unit. Stark and silent, it was meant to hold children, but stripped of anything resembling childhood.

Harper stepped out of his rental and closed the door with a solid thunk. The heat hit immediately, drier than Seattle, but searing, the kind that clung to your clothes and rose in waves off the blacktop. He'd already shed his jacket before lunch with Chief Jansen. Now he wore a black polo bearing the CGIS badge on his left breast.

Inside, the sterile atmosphere was instant—cooler, but no more welcoming. Pale linoleum, flickering overhead lights, and the faint scent of ammonia greeted him as he crossed to the reception window.

Behind the bulletproof glass sat a man in his fifties, thick around the middle with a full head of gray hair and the distracted look of someone halfway through a long shift. His nametag read Garrett Brown.

"Can I help you?" the man asked without looking up.

Harper slid his credentials into the slot at the base of the window. "Special Agent Harper, CGIS. I'm here to see Ray Spencer."

Brown squinted at the ID wallet, scribbled something into a logbook, and passed it back without ceremony.

"Have a seat," he said. "I'll let him know you're here."

Harper turned and lowered himself into one of the molded plastic chairs along the wall, the kind that seemed designed to make sure no one stayed long. He pulled out his notepad and began scribbling down what he could remember from the Jansen conversation while it was still fresh—names, dates, and impressions. A cracked clock on the wall ticked somewhere overhead.

A few minutes later, a heavy metal door at the end of the hall buzzed open with a mechanical clunk.

A man stepped through, smiling warmly. He had a full head of white hair, reading glasses hanging from a black cord around his neck, and a soft mid-section beneath a gray polo stenciled *JDC*. His ID badge swung from a lanyard as he walked.

"Special Agent Harper?" he asked.

Harper put his notepad away, rose and extended his hand. "Jake is fine."

"Ray Spencer. Ray's good too," the older man shook his hand with a firm, practiced grip.

Spencer led him through the secured door and down a short hallway that smelled faintly of disinfectant and something older, concrete and the weight of time. The walls were painted a dull institutional beige, the kind that hadn't changed since the Clinton era.

168

"We've had some renovations over the years," Spencer said, as if reading Harper's thoughts. "But not to this wing. Records and admin are still stuck in 1998."

Harper gave a half-smile. "Feels familiar."

Spencer gestured toward a small office with a drop ceiling and a battered wooden desk. The filing cabinet behind it was heavy steel, the kind with drawers that slammed shut like a bank vault.

"Have a seat," Spencer said. "Your supervisor's subpoena came through while you were driving. I've already pulled the file."

He opened the cabinet, flipped through a tight row of folders, and pulled out one marked **KINCAID, ASHER M.** in blocky, faded handwriting.

He set it down on the desk and gave Harper a look.

"I don't think this is the worst file I've ever read," Spencer said. "But it's definitely one of the loneliest."

Harper opened the folder. Inside were intake forms, incident reports, group therapy notes, disciplinary records A photo was clipped to the inside cover, a mug shot of a fifteen-year-old boy. Pale. Sullen. Dark hair cropped short. Bruising was visible under one eye, causing Harper to cringe inwardly.

"Was he assaulted?" Harper asked, tapping the photo.

Spencer nodded. "First week. Two-on-one in the rec yard. Didn't talk about it. Wouldn't give names. The psychologist noted 'hyper-vigilant affect.' You know, withdrawal, numbness, learned helplessness."

Harper turned the page. Notes from a counselor stood out:

"Inconsistent eye contact. Avoids peer interaction. Compliant with staff, but exhibits signs of guilt-induced emotional suppression. Mother visits weekly. No father involvement noted."

"He didn't fight?" Harper asked.

"Never. Not once in two years," Spencer said. "We had kids with real records. Gang initiations, assaults, attempted murder. Asher just...folded in on himself."

"Did he bond with anyone here?"

Spencer sat back, scratching his chin. "One. We had a kid in around the same time. In for armed robbery. They shared a dorm wing for a while. Used to play cards during free time."

That caught Harper's attention. He looked up. "Name?"

Spencer stood, walked over to a thin blue logbook on a side table, and flipped it open.

"Yeah. Here it is. Oliver T. Hugo. In for robbing a drugstore with a machete. No injuries, but it scared the hell out of the clerk. Got two and a half years for it."

An electric thrill ran through Harper's stomach, but he kept his face still. His pen was already moving. "What was Hugo's middle name?"

Spencer walked back to the cabinet and thumbed through the folders. "Looks like...Trevor."

Harper's eyes widened as he stared at the name he just wrote down. *Oliver Trevor Hugo.*

Oliver Trevor.

Trevor Oliver.

The broker.

The electric thrill increased, making the hair on Harper's arms stand on end. He looked up at Spencer. "Was Hugo local?"

"Originally? No. Came down from Sandpoint, I think. Ward of the state. Bounced between placements until juvie. Not a bad kid, just...wrong wiring. Didn't really stand a chance."

"Do you know where he went after release?"

Spencer shook his head. "That'd be in probation files, not ours. But if he kept his nose clean, he aged out at eighteen and walked free."

Harper flipped another page, seeing the same name pop up again. Oliver Hugo, "positive peer influence" in a staff group note.

"So they were close?"

"About as close as two inmates could be in a place like this," Spencer said. "Didn't talk much, but they sat near each other. Ate together. One of the counselors noted they prayed together sometimes. Strange pair. Hugo was volatile. He flipped a chair once when a counselor pushed too hard."

That gave Harper pause. "Prayed?"

Spencer nodded. "I remember it. One of those nights where the whole place went tense. Word was, someone brought a weapon back from rec. Staff did a full lockdown. While the rest of the dorms were acting out, those two just sat in the corner, heads down, praying. Kincaid had...gravity. Hugo orbited it, and seemed to turn it around after that."

Harper closed the file slowly.

Two broken boys, bound by guilt, silence, and shared belief. And now, one had reinvented himself as a man of God. The other...Harper would have to find.

"Ray, this has been extremely helpful."

Spencer smiled faintly. "Hope it helps your case. This place doesn't usually touch the real world anymore."

Harper rose and shook his hand. "It just did."

•••••

By the time he stepped back outside, the late-afternoon sun had begun its slow drop toward the pines. Heat shimmered off the asphalt as Harper slid behind the wheel of the rental, the folder heavy on the passenger seat. He sat there a moment, staring at it, letting the silence press in. Feeling the pieces of the case drop into place.

He called Maguire once he was back on the road, the rental humming beneath him as pine trees blurred past outside the window. He had one hand on the wheel while the other thumbed the speaker button as the line rang. The phone rang twice before the familiar gravelly voice answered.

"Jake, tell me you're not calling from some dirt road with a dead body in the trunk."

Harper smiled into the phone. "Not this time."

There was a pause, then a softer, more grounded question. "How you holding up?"

"I was about to ask you the same thing," Harper said. "How's leave treating you?"

"Ah, the OPA goons finally let up," Maguire, his voice lighter. "You wouldn't happen to know anything about that, would you?"

Harper smirked. "Maybe..."

"You son of a bitch," Maguire said, but there was gratitude beneath the grumble. "They convened a grand jury earlier today. Ruled the shooting justified. No bill. Internal's still got their box-checking to do, but I should be back in a day or two. Not bad, all things considered."

"Glad to hear it," Harper said. "You were solid. Everyone knows it."

"Still doesn't make it fun. Now, what the hell have you been up to?"

Harper settled deeper into his seat and gave a small exhale.

"Followed some leads. You're gonna want to hear this."

"Hit me," Maguire said.

"Calderón, for starters. You were right about him, the guy was nuts. I checked his phone's GPS and he was in Tacoma the day the Rainiers disappeared, and was there for several days. Testifying at a Grand Jury."

"For what?"

"Cold case down there from 2022. Another couple. Husband was shot in the head with a .22. The wife was raped and hogtied."

Maguire's sharp intake of breath was audible through the phone. "Same as the doll. So he *was* a killer."

"Yeah, but not *our* killer. He left for Tacoma hours before the Rainiers' boat did."

"Well shit. Wait, what was he testifying to?"

"He was tying the whole damn thing to a coworker. A meth addict who'd been fired at the marina they both worked at back then."

"Christ on a bike," Maguire said.

"Yeah. I filled the Detectives there with what we found on him, and they'll probably be able to close their case now."

173

"So that shrine we found... was just the prelude to something that never happened."

"That hadn't happened *yet*," Harper corrected. "He definitely wanted to kill Daniel, and was going to take Malia and do what we saw on the doll. Then would've killed her like he did to the woman in Tacoma. But someone else got there first."

"Well that's deeply comforting." Maguire's sarcasm was obvious through the car speakers. "So what now? Where are you?"

"Idaho."

"What? What the hell are you doing in Idaho?"

"That's the fun part. I dug back into Kincaid," Harper said.

"Thought he was choirboy clean?"

"I went back to the drawing board after Calderón dropped off the list. Dug deeper. Tate...his clean record's an illusion."

"Go on."

"Found out he grew up in Hayden Lake. Turns out he had a twin brother, Noah. Family was full-on religious extremist. His father died when he was young, but was a snake-charming traveling evangelist. His mother believed Noah was some kind of prophet."

Maguire whistled. "And?"

"And Asher killed him. When they were teenagers, he took the boat out drunk and crashed it. Noah went overboard and got torn up by the prop."

"Jesus," Maguire said.

"Yeah. He pled it down, did two years in juvie. Family got the record sealed. Local PD confirmed it, and I paid a visit to JDC while I was out here."

Maguire let out a low breath. "That changes the picture."

"It does," Harper said. "Kid gets blamed for killing the 'chosen one' and gets branded by his mother. Apparently, after he got out of lockup, mother was pushing him to be the new 'prophet.'

They get his record sealed, then he disappears from Idaho, and reemerges in Washington like none of it ever happened."

"And the church welcomes him with open arms."

"Exactly."

"So we've got a trauma-saturated religious nutcase with a martyr complex running a church and laundering stolen boats. That tracks."

"Wait, there's more."

"Oh goody." Maguire was quiet for a moment, then said, "You found anything else?"

Harper nodded, even though Maguire couldn't see him. "Yeah. While he was locked up, Kincaid got close to another inmate, in for robbing a pharmacy with a machete. Staff said they were inseparable. Ate together. Prayed together. Counselor even flagged them as a 'positive influence' on each other. Oliver Trevor Hugo."

"Oliver Trevor Hugo..." Maguire repeated. "Trevor Oliver. Our fake brother."

"It's gotta be," Harper said. "I think Hugo's still helping him. Might've been the one who moved the yacht. Maybe more."

"Jesus," Maguire said again. "We've got a religious golden boy with a sealed manslaughter record, a violent friend from juvie using a fake name, and a dead stalker who *would've* killed the Rainiers—if someone hadn't beaten him to it."

"That about sums it up."

Maguire exhaled. "Hell of a week."

"I'm gonna start digging into Hugo here, see where he landed after juvie. Trace his movements a bit. If he resurfaced in

Seattle around the same time Kincaid did, we'll have more than coincidence."

"Keep me posted," Maguire said. "And hey...nice work."

Harper shrugged to himself. "Wasn't much else to do in Hayden."

"Well, color me impressed. You sure you don't want to come back to the city and work on a nice quiet stolen catalytic converter case?"

"Tempting. But I think we're getting close. Don't get used to the peace and quiet."

"I already hate it. Thomas has me working on house projects non-stop."

"Hurry back, Tate. We've got some rot to dig up."

"Talk soon," Maguire said.

He hung up and merged onto the exit for the airport. The clouds ahead were darkening. But the storm inside Harper was already raging.

CHAPTER
TWENTY

September 12. Early Evening.

Harper had checked in to the Best Western in Coeur d'Alene and used his Government Travel Card to pay for one night. It was one of the chains he knew had a standing government rate. He chose a room on the second floor, with his window having a clear view of his rental car. The air conditioner worked surprisingly well, but his head still buzzed from heat from everything he'd uncovered.

Once in his room, he dialed Easton at the Seattle CGIS Field Office and filled him in, detailing his conversations with Jansen and Spencer, Kincaid's sealed juvenile record, and the new lead on Oliver Trevor Hugo.

Easton listened, giving affirmative grunts at the right places. When Harper finished, Easton said, "Good work. Dig deeper on Hugo. See what shakes loose."

"Yes, sir," Harper said.

Next, he called Alyssa and checked in, letting her know he'd be staying the night there. He said goodnight to Addie on the phone, and told her he'd see her soon.

He pulled out his laptop and notebook and set them on the room's desk. He settled in and pulled up his system logins. The screen blinked to life with the standard agency tools. NCIC, DMV,

LexisNexis, PACER, as well as a few others he had access to as a Special Agent. He took a long sip of lukewarm coffee and typed the name and date of birth slowly, deliberately.

OLIVER TREVOR HUGO.

Then:

Alias: TREVOR OLIVER.

He hit enter.

The screen loaded slowly. Harper knew it was the hotel's Wi-Fi connection, but it felt as if even the system hesitated to spill what it knew.

First hit: a juvenile arrest record, partially redacted. Just the bones: age fifteen, an armed robbery in Kootenai County. Victim injured, but survived. Case disposition: confined to Juvenile Detention Center for a two-year term. Facility: Kootenai County Juvenile One.

Next: adult criminal record. The hits stacked like brittle bones.

2011 - Possession of methamphetamine. Guilty. Thirty days jail, suspended sentence, drug court.

2012 - Petty theft. Dismissed.

2013 - Possession with intent. Six months, served three.

2015 - Resisting arrest. Plea deal.

2016 - Possession of heroin. Three years at Idaho State Correctional Center. Released after two.

Then…nothing.

Harper leaned forward. No records. No arrests. No registered address. No employer. No parole violations. Hugo just vanished.

Harper frowned and picked up the phone.

"Idaho State Correction Center," a voice answered on the third ring.

Harper introduced himself and asked to speak with the warden. After a short hold, a woman's voice came on the line.

"This is Warden Corbin. How can I help you, Special Agent Harper?"

"Thanks for taking my call, ma'am. I'm investigating a potential homicide out of Seattle. One of the names that has come up in my investigation is Oliver Hugo. He was an inmate there from 2016 to 2018. I was hoping to review his visitor logs?"

"Not a problem. However, I'm afraid those records aren't digitized yet," she said. "You'll have to come look at them in person."

"Any chance I could do that tonight?"

She gave a patient sigh. "It's nearly seven, Agent Harper. You caught me at home, they forwarded the line. All my records staff are at home for the day. But if you come by in the morning, I'll have them start pulling the files."

"What time?"

"Nine is the earliest they'll be in. They should have the logs ready by ten."

"Appreciate it. Thank you, ma'am."

He ended the call and made a few notes, then began typing everything into the case file. All the facts, timelines, and future investigative queries. He filed the update just before nine p.m., closed the laptop, and stepped into the shower.

The hot water hit like relief and weariness all at once, steam rising around him as he scrubbed away the heat of the long day. By the time he crawled into bed, the room had cooled, but his mind still buzzed with the weight of it all.

He turned out the light and was asleep before his head hit the pillow.

•••••

The phone alarm buzzed at 2:00 a.m. Harper dragged himself from bed, splashed cold water on his face, and got dressed quickly. He threw on jeans and a gray short sleeve button up, then laced up the new pair of Chucks he had picked up. Clipping his belt and badge to his belt, he walked outside and loaded the rental with his overnight bag. He dropped the room key in the slot outside the lobby and hit the road in silence.

The drive south stretched like a ribbon through darkness. Gas stations few, cell service spotty, just the hum of tires and the occasional freight truck eating up miles of highway. By sunrise, the desert plains gave way to farmland, then the city skylines of Nampa and Boise, before eventually the squat gray perimeter walls of Idaho State Correctional Center came into view near the town of Kuna.

He pulled into the visitor lot, parked the car where he could see it, and sat with the engine off for a moment, drinking the last of a gas station coffee that had turned bitter in the cupholder.

At precisely 9:55 a.m., he stepped into the admin building.

The front desk officer gave him a clipboard to sign in and called back to records. Five minutes later, a woman in her early 50s with a square jaw, dark-framed glasses, and a no-nonsense energy emerged.

"Agent Harper?" she said, offering a firm handshake. "Warden Elise Corbin. We've got Hugo's file ready for you."

She led him down a corridor to a narrow records room with a long folding table. A manila folder was waiting.

"Take your time," she said. "You've got the room."

Harper thanked her and sat. The file was thick with intake documents, discipline reports, and program entries.

But what he wanted, what he needed, was near the back.

The visitor logs.

He flipped through page by page, scanning each dated entry. Public defenders mostly. A few other recurring names, probably a girlfriend. Then he saw it.

Kincaid, Asher.

Three visits.

Clergy status.

Each entry was signed in clean cursive. The first visit was about six months into Hugo's sentence. The next two were spaced out over the following months. The final visit was exactly two weeks before Hugo's release.

Harper stared at the page, the name sitting like a smudge across the timeline of Hugo's life. This didn't read like spiritual guidance. It didn't read as mercy or visiting an old friend from juvie.

It read like grooming. *Recruitment,* Harper thought.

He checked the release documents and saw Hugo was released on parole. His parole officer was listed as J. Chishelm, located out of the Boise office. He jotted down the name, phone number, and address.

He snapped photos with his phone of the rest, one page at a time, then closed the folder. He had what he needed.

•••••

Harper drove the twenty-five minutes to the Probation and Parole Office in Boise. The tan building sat tucked into a quiet business park, its block-letter signage declaring simply: PROBATION & PAROLE. Across the lot, some kind of manufacturing plant rumbled quietly.

Inside, the front desk officer directed him to wait. *Waiting, and more waiting.* That was the hardest part of an investigation. All the damn waiting.

A few minutes later, a blond woman stepped into the lobby, her gaze immediately assessing him. She was in her late thirties, maybe. Tight blouse, jeans that didn't quite pass dress code. Her eyes swept him the way cops measured people, first for threat, then for story.

"Can I help you?" she asked, eyebrows raised.

"Special Agent Harper, CGIS." He offered his hand. "I'm looking into a former client of yours."

She shook it. "Jennifer Chishelm." Her grip was firm, but her tone shifted. It was warmer now, maybe curious. She gave him a second look, slower this time. A hunger, maybe. Harper noticed the faint tan line on her ring finger.

Recently divorced. He filed it away, not for judgement, just the read.

She led him back to a cramped office with a laminated desk and a faded poster about accountability on the wall. He took the seat opposite her as she sat and crossed one leg over the other.

"So," she said, voice softening, "how can I help you, Agent Harper?"

Harper opened his notebook with his left hand, letting the wedding ring catch the light as he flipped to the right page. He didn't say anything about it. Just let it sit.

"I'm working a missing persons case out of Seattle" he began. "One of the names that keeps coming up is Oliver Hugo. I saw you were his supervising officer when he was released in 2018."

She nodded slowly, her eyes lingering on his wedding finger. "Oliver. Yeah, I remember him. Quiet type. Didn't give me much trouble, actually."

"What was your impression of him overall?"

She shrugged. "Bit of a ghost, honestly. He made his check-ins, passed his tests. Didn't have a job on paper, but said he was doing maintenance for a church. Something with a reentry program."

Harper leaned forward slightly. "Did he ever mention a name? A church or contact?"

"Yeah..." she said, furrowing her brow. "That pastor guy. Kincaid. I remember thinking he was some kind of polished for working with ex-cons. Real smiley. Hugo talked about him like he hung the damn moon."

Harper pursed his lips just slightly. "So you actually met Kincaid?"

"Once," she said. "He came with Hugo to a meeting, just to vouch for him. Said he'd taken Oliver in. Gave him a place to stay, some kind of spiritual mentorship. Honestly, it was one of the easiest cases I had that year. Hugo vanished off my radar after his parole ended, but at the time?" She shook her head. "He looked clean. Like someone who really turned it around."

Harper scribbled a note, then met her eyes. "Did he ever say where he was living? The actual address?"

"Yeah, it was a place in Meridian. Hold on, I can pull it up."

She walked over to a filing cabinet and bent to open the bottom drawer. She moved deliberately slow, her posture angled so her rear was directly facing him. She glanced back to see if he was watching.

Harper kept his eyes on the page, pen tapping lightly against his notebook. He knew what she was doing, but wanted no part in it.

After a moment, she straightened and returned with a manila folder. She dropped it on the desk and slid a sheet free.

"Here it is...The Way Forward Foundation. Looks like the building was a converted house." She read off the address and handed it over, her fingers brushing his just a little too long. "Said the church covered it. Figured it was off the books. Usually is."

Harper closed his notebook. "Appreciate the time, Officer Chishelm."

She smiled. "Any time, Agent Harper. Before you go..."

He paused, saying nothing.

"You have lunch plans?" she asked, hopeful, letting the silence hang.

He gave a polite smile. "I've got to run this down before the trail cools."

"Another time, then," she said, leaning back in her chair.

Harper gave her a nod and turned for the door. He could feel her eyes on him all the way out.

CHAPTER
TWENTY-ONE

September 13. Early afternoon.

The house in Meridian sat on a quiet residential street lined with maple trees and minivans. It looked ordinary now, with fresh paint, a swing set in the yard, wind chimes whispering from the porch. A little boy darted out the front door chasing a ball, his mother calling after him.

Harper watched from the rental car, parked across the street with the engine idling low. He didn't get out. Didn't need to. The place had moved on. He opened the laptop on the passenger side and connected to his hotspot. A quick property search confirmed the place was sold in 2020, just months after Oliver Hugo's parole ended. Current owners listed as a married couple. He found no connection to Kincaid or Hugo.

Harper leaned back and exhaled, fingers drumming lightly against the keyboard. Just a ghost of a lead now.

He dug into the Way Forward Foundation next. A nonprofit registered in the greater Seattle area. Status: active. The listed mission was vague: "Faith-based reentry support, transitional housing, and spiritual mentorship for justice-involved individuals." The kind of boilerplate language that sounded noble until you scratched the surface.

Executive Director: Asher Kincaid.

No other staff was listed. No board of directors, no published annual reports. Just a mailing address, one tied to a PO Box near Bellevue.

Harper stared at the screen for a long beat, then closed the laptop. He'd squeezed what he could out of Idaho. The rest of the trail pointed northwest, back to Seattle. He shifted into drive and pulled away from the curb, leaving the house and the laughter of the child behind him.

Time to go home.

•••••

During the hour and a half plane ride back to Seattle, Harper had time to reflect on what he had learned. Kincaid hadn't just crossed paths with Hugo, he'd sought him out. Found him at his lowest. Offered redemption wrapped in obedience. A place to stay, a role to play. Not as a favor, but as a claim.

It wasn't mentorship. It was recruitment.

Hugo had taken the deal. Maybe not at first. Maybe not fully. But enough to disappear.

Harper stared out the window at the quilted clouds below, arms folded, the dull drone of the engines filling the cabin. The tactic was familiar. Use faith like currency, and trade absolution for control. He'd seen it before. Lived through it.

His thoughts drifted back. Not to Kincaid, but to another voice, another pulpit. Back to the heat of a late summer Sunday and the sharp creak of wooden pews.

•••••

Then.

It had taken Jake's family six months to find another church after what had happened at *Trinitarian Baptist*. After Pastor Benjamin had run the family out. Their new church, Grace Baptist, had become their new refuge by necessity, if not by choice. His father, Rich, chose not to pursue being an elder again. Always a helper, he threw himself into parking duty and setting up the coffee stations every Sunday morning without complaint.

Eighteen-year-old Jake was another matter. While he admired his father's stoic tenacity and humility in serving others, he struggled to feel anything but hollow during the hymns, wary during the sermons. His trust in the church—in men behind pulpits—had been burned to ash. He sat through most services with his arms crossed, tuning out after the announcements.

Until the day Pastor Devan Adams spoke.

He wasn't like the others. No fire and brimstone. No theatrics. Just a quiet voice, worn at the edges like an old coat. He spoke that morning about service. Not in abstract, but in motion. Washing feet. Feeding the hungry. Sitting with the outcast. He quoted James: *"Religion that God our Father accepts as pure and faultless is this: to look after orphans and widows in their distress..."*

Jake remembered sitting straighter in the pew. For the first time in a long time, he felt something stir. Not fire. Not shame. Purpose.

He watched as Pastor Adams knelt afterward to pray with an elderly woman in a wheelchair. The way he held her hand. The way he listened.

He remembered sitting in that pew, letting himself believe again. Believe that service could be pure, that faith could be about lifting others instead of binding them.

Maybe this, Jake had thought. *Maybe I could do this.*

Maybe being a pastor didn't mean control. Maybe it meant *serving*.

Jake jumped at the chance to intern for the summer with Pastor Adams. They went to homeless shelters and soup kitchens, brought food to migrant camps, and visited the elderly in assisted living. He loved it, and found a passion he had long felt missing.

They spent long afternoons chatting while Jake filed paperwork and helped Pastor Adams with his newsletters. Adams convinced Jake to apply to a Christian university and set his major as Christian Ministries, with a plan to attend seminary afterward.

Sometimes Jake would bring up Mackenzie, his girlfriend of a year. The small arguments, the long hours apart, the confusing intensity of young love. Unlike Pastor Benjamin at *Trinitarian Baptist*, Adams never made him feel ashamed for caring about a girl. He never demanded details, never circled the conversation back to sin or sex. Instead, he listened, offering simple encouragement: *"Real love grows when you learn to put her first. That's the kind of discipline God asks of us."*

Adams always reminded Jake to strive for restraint, but he left it at that. No prying questions. No suspicion. No shame. For the first time, Jake felt like a pastor saw him as more than a bundle of hormones and temptation. Adams made him feel called, not condemned. In those months, Jake began to believe that serving people—the overlooked, the hurting—might be the shape of his life's work.

Then came the arrest.

It was a Sunday like any other. Jake had just finished stacking chairs in the fellowship hall when he heard the radios, that clipped cadence of police communication. Two men in plainclothes walked in through the side entrance, badges clipped to their belts. They scanned the room like they already knew who they were looking for.

Jake watched as they made their way toward the front of the sanctuary, where Pastor Adams stood shaking hands, offering soft smiles to congregants.

"Devan Adams?" one of the detectives asked.

Adams had turned, his expression curious. "Yes?"

"You're under arrest," the detective said. "Suspicion of elder abuse and criminally negligent homicide."

The sanctuary went silent. A woman gasped. A bulletin fell to the floor like a whisper.

Jake stood frozen as the pastor's hands were guided behind his back and cuffs clicked into place. He felt the blood drain from his face as Adams didn't argue. Didn't even flinch. He just looked over at Jake. Not with fear, but with something like shame.

They walked him out the side door in silence.

Jake didn't move. He couldn't.

Later that night, he followed the news coverage. The details came in slowly. Pastor Adams had been caring for his elderly father, a man with advanced dementia. But neighbors reported a foul smell. And by the time anyone had checked, the man had been dead for three days—alone in a locked, sweltering bedroom while Adams had gone on preaching and praying and building newsletters about compassion.

The autopsy confirmed dehydration and heat stroke. Advanced neglect. The kind that doesn't happen by accident.

Jake sat at the kitchen table with the family's laptop open, the glow of the screen casting long shadows across his moleskin notebook. The one where he'd written sermon ideas. Verses about mercy. Notes for seminary applications.

He closed it gently.

He'd never open it again.

Later that night, he sat on the porch with his knees pulled up and his arms draped across them, the old boards warm from the day's sun. The air was thick and still, but finally cooling. Somewhere down the street, frogs croaked. The screen door creaked open behind him.

His father stepped out, two glass bottles in hand—root beers. He offered one without a word and sat beside Jake with a quiet grunt.

They didn't speak at first. Just sat, letting the crickets and porch fan fill the space between them.

"You were quiet at dinner," his dad said eventually.

Jake didn't answer right away. He took a drink and stared out into the night.

"He fooled me," he said. "I thought he was...different."

His father nodded slowly. "Pastor Adams."

"Yeah," Jake's voice cracked. "I wanted to believe it. That it could be real. That service meant something. That maybe I could..." He trailed off, rubbing a hand over his face.

His father shifted slightly but didn't move closer. "You still can, Jake."

Jake scoffed. "By doing what? Playing pretend? Wearing a suit and saying the right words until someone else gets caught in a lie?"

190

"No." His dad looked out at the dark street. "By not losing yourself in the failures of other men."

Jake didn't respond.

His father continued, voice low. "You were called to serve long before you ever heard a sermon. You were the kid that shoveled the neighbor's sidewalk before they woke up. Who helped load groceries without being asked. That's not something a pastor gave you. That's something God planted in you."

Jake looked over, eyes searching. "So, what do I do now? Just...pretend this didn't wreck me?"

"No," his dad said, firm. "You let it wreck the lies. But not the truth. You don't let someone else's hypocrisy steal your purpose. You don't necessarily need a pulpit to serve. You don't need a title. Just a willing heart, and a spine that doesn't bend when it counts."

Jake looked away, blinking tears out of his eyes.

"You figure out who you are, not who they told you to be," his dad added. "And when you do? You go where you're needed."

They sat in silence for a long time after that, watching the porch light flicker against the gathering night.

The next morning, Jake made a call to the Coast Guard recruiter.

He dropped out of college before the semester even started.

CHAPTER
TWENTY-TWO

Now.
September 13. Early evening.

After landing, Harper drove straight to the Coast Guard Investigative Service Office at Pier 36. The CGIS Seattle Field Office smelled like burnt coffee and old carpet, a strange comfort after the sterile chill of Idaho motels and correctional facilities. Harper stepped inside, the familiar weight of his holstered gun settling into place on his hip as he passed the front desk.

SSA Easton's door was already cracked open. Harper knocked once and stepped in.

Easton looked up from a thick case file and leaned back in his chair. "You look like hell."

"Appreciate it, boss," Harper said. "Didn't sleep much."

"Sit," Easton said, gesturing. "Let's hear it."

Harper recapped the Idaho trip in a clipped, steady voice—the juvenile records, the visitor logs, the parole officer, the house in Meridian. He handed over printouts and notes as he went. When he got to the part about Kincaid being listed as Hugo's spiritual mentor, Easton sat forward.

"The pastor," Easton said. "The one with the bill of sale. You think he's the thread tying this whole thing up?"

Harper nodded. "He visited Hugo three times in prison. Last one was two weeks before release. Took him in through The Way Forward Foundation, some re-entry nonprofit he runs. No board of directors, no oversight. Just a PO Box and vague promises about rehabilitation and redemption."

Easton flipped through the notes. "And Hugo's record?"

"Petty stuff until the heroin charge in 2016. Three years in prison, served two. Released in 2018, parole until 2020. Then he disappears."

Easton exhaled slowly, tapping a pen against the folder. "All right. So we've got a charismatic pastor, a reentry foundation with no transparency, and a missing couple who just happened to sign over their million-dollar yacht. What are you thinking next?"

Harper leaned forward. "The boat."

Easton raised an eyebrow.

"We did a preliminary search, but it was mostly surface-level. Techs checked the living areas forensically, but we found no trace of anyone. I want to go back. When I was a boarding officer, we would find things in the other locations. Chain lockers. Bilges, engine spaces. I want to look for any trace evidence we might have missed to explain why someone wanted that boat. Something about it has been bugging me."

Easton gave a slow nod. "You think they were killed on board?"

"I don't know," Harper said. "But I'm really starting to think they never left it alive. And I think whoever left it out there wanted us to believe otherwise."

Easton drummed his fingers once, then nodded. "All right. Draft a new search warrant. Be specific, forensics and mechanical inspection. Anything related to anchoring systems, ropes, lockers, fixtures."

"Already started on it on the plane. I'll get it finished and over to a judge."

Easton handed him the folder back. "Good work. Keep pulling the thread."

Harper stood, folder in hand. "Yes, sir."

He stepped out of the office and headed for his desk. The yacht was waiting.

•••••

The warrant and affidavit were finished just before four p.m. Harper emailed the packet off to Judge Keller, then leaned back in his chair, lacing his fingers behind his head as he stared up at the stained ceiling tiles. His eyelids fluttered, just for a second.

He hadn't realized they'd shut until Easton's voice snapped him back.

"Sorry to bug you, Harper. I know you've gotta be exhausted. You get that warrant off?"

Harper jerked upright and blinked. "Yeah. Just sent. Keller's in trial though, clerk said it might be six or seven before we get the signed return."

"Figures," Easton said with a grunt. "Well, while you wait, I've got something else. Lawson needs a second on a case."

Harper perked up slightly. "Kiera?"

Easton nodded. "Yeah. She's working a pretty solid sex abuse case. She wants to try and talk to the suspect, and needs a second agent in the room. Thought of you."

Special Agent Kiera Lawson was the one who'd made the call that pulled Harper into CGIS last year. She worked major cases, primarily sex crimes, and had a reputation for balancing empathy with tenacity. She and Harper had become friends, that kind grounded in mutual respect.

And, if he was being honest, he was happy for the break, even a short one, from the case.

"You bet," Harper said, already reaching for his phone. "I'll give her a call."

Easton nodded and ducked back into his office.

Harper stood and stretched, arms crossed over his chest, then leaned back until his spine popped in a staccato of relief. His neck followed with a slow, deliberate roll. He thumbed through his contacts and hit dial.

"Hey Jake," Lawson answered, her tone clipped but warm.

"Hey Kiera. Easton said you've got a suspect on a line. What's the ask?"

"I'm over at the Station. Suspect's out on one of the small boats. Meet me here and I'll fill you in."

Harper grabbed his windbreaker and headed out.

Coast Guard Base Seattle sat like a self-contained city on the waterfront. The administrative building housed high level commissioned officers, legal staff, and CGIS. Next was a series of buildings housing inspectors, MSST— the tactical Maritime Safety and Security Team—and the base galley where enlisted and officers alike gathered to eat. Near the base exchange store was Station Seattle, the rescue hub.

He crossed the asphalt lot toward the two-story concrete structure. Downstairs, Harper knew, were the overnight crew quarters, locker rooms, and command offices. The upper level held classrooms, a defensive tactics mat room, and the law enforcement section where the Maritime Enforcement Specialists worked.

Across from the station building, the docks stretched down a gangway, where the unit's small boats bobbed in formation. At the top of the ramp stood a metal sign Harper had read a hundred times:

"Down this ladder goes a crew on a mission, up this ladder comes lifesavers who have answered their call."

Lawson was waiting near the entrance, arms folded, gaze scanning the water. She turned as he approached.

At five-foot-five, she wasn't imposing, but few people commanded space the way she did. Her vibrant red hair was tied back in a crisp braid, and the wind teased loose strands against her cheek. She wore plain tactical pants and a fitted softshell CGIS jacket, the cut accentuating a compact, curvy frame built more for grit than show.

Harper took in the scene like a cop did—detail, posture, and readiness.

"Afternoon," he said.

"Glad you could make it," she replied, already shifting into briefing mode. "You up for a ride?"

"Always," Harper said. "What are we looking at?"

She nodded toward the pier. "Suspect's name is Cody Neilan. Twenty-four. Boatswain's Mate Second Class—just advanced last month. His girlfriend called in the day before yesterday. Her twelve-year-old daughter is making disclosures, ongoing sexual abuse. Says it's been happening for the last two years."

Harper's face darkened. "Christ."

"I got the kid into a forensic interview yesterday while Neila was on overnight duty. She gave us enough detail to corroborate timelines. Physical evidence lines up. Digital evidence too. We've got him. I just want to see if he gives it up without realizing how tight the case is."

Harper gave a short nod. "You want me playing the quiet type, or you want a two-pronged approach?"

"Dealer's choice," she said with a grin. "I just don't want to go in alone."

"You got it. What's his status?"

"He's out on a training mission right now, but I had the watch office recall the boat. He's the coxswain, but they got a waiver to run without a boarding team."

Harper raised an eyebrow. "So he shouldn't be armed."

"Correct," she confirmed. "He's just breaking in some new non-rates. Probably thinks he's coming back to refuel and hit the gym."

Harper followed her gaze toward the docks. "We staying out of sight?"

"Boatswain's Hole," Lawson said, nodding toward the floating gear shed at the dock's edge.

They made their way inside the small floating office, a converted equipment locker filled with coiled lines, navigation tools, and workbenches stained with years of oil and salt. The smell of sea rope and machine grease hung in the air. Located at the rear of the docks where the crew would tie off before heading up the ramp to the station, it was the perfect place to stay out of sight to avoid spooking the crew.

Special Agent Kiera Lawson leaned against the workbench and handed Harper a case file. Harper flipped it open and scanned the details.

Sara Weyland, twenty-nine, waitress. Met Neilan online, moved in with him two years ago. On Neilan's off-duty days, he played attentive stepdad. When Sara worked night shifts, Neilan watched Charity, her daughter.

Charity had recently become withdrawn. Refused to be alone with him. Finally opened up two days ago. Said Neilan would come to her room at night. Said he called it "bonding time." Always gave her something afterward. Stuffed animals when she was younger, and now, more expensive gifts. Most recently, he got her a cell phone. Neilan told Sara it was for safety.

"Motherfucker," Harper said, letting out a slow breath.

"Yep," Lawson said. "Pretty bad, but unoriginal."

"They rarely are. They're all working with the same playbook. Grooming. Isolation. Gifts. Bet he targeted Sara because she was a single mom."

"Oh, that's my guess too," Lawson said. "The whole thing was never about Sara. It was always to gain access to the child."

"Fuck this guy," Harper said.

"Oh yeah. I'm gonna bury him."

Harper stared down at the file. "You planning to arrest him today?"

"If he lawyers up or clams up? Yes. But if he talks?" She shrugged. "I'll let him hang himself first."

After about fifteen minutes, they saw the small boat motoring in, its hull carving clean through the chop. At twenty-nine feet, the Coast Guard response boat small—RBS—was made with six seats, five inside the covered pilothouse, and one on the large back deck. The twin engines sputtered as the boat moved slowly backwards, almost like parallel parking, along the dock. As it neared the dock, they could hear the crew calling distances.

"Five feet! Four feet! Three! Two...contact!"

The boat eased against the fenders, and lines were tossed and secured with smooth coordination. The twin outboards sputtered into silence.

They waited until the crew began disembarking. Voices carried through the boat house.

"Good work today, Freisen," one of the crew said.

As they got closer, Harper caught the name tape: NEILAN.

He and Lawson stepped from the Boatswain's Hole at the exact moment the crew neared the ramp, positioning themselves with subtle authority, blocking the path.

Harper met Neilan's eyes. "BM2 Neilan?"

The smile on Neilan's face faltered. His eyes flicked between them, then toward the water.

Lawson stepped forward, flashing her badge. "Special Agent Lawson, CGIS. We need to speak with you."

Neilan's face turned white and he froze for half a second, just long enough for Harper to register the shift. Then he bolted. He dropped his canvas gear bag and shoved past a stunned crewmember, knocking her into the water with a shriek and a splash, then kept sprinting back toward the small boat.

"Stop!" Harper barked, already in motion. He and Lawson gave chase, pushing past the remaining crew members, feet pounding across the dock.

Neilan vaulted onto the stern deck of the response boat, flipping on the breakers as he moved. He yanked open the glass

200

cabin door, slammed it shut behind him, and twisted the lock just as Harper reached the handle.

"Neilan!" Harper shouted, yanking at the door. "Open this door right now!"

Lawson moved to the side, gun drawn and pointing inside through closed glass windows. "Cody, don't do this! Open up—NOW!"

Inside the cabin, Neilan fumbled through the controls with shaking hands. Harper saw him throw the ignition switches and reach for the throttles.

"Goddammit," Harper shouted. "He's trying to run."

The engines coughed, then roared to life.

Harper shouted again. "Cody! You're not going anywhere. Shut it down!"

Neilan's eyes locked with Lawson's through the glass. Her gun never wavered.

Then he jammed the throttles forward.

The boat lurched violently. Harper barely caught the rail, slammed hard into the glass door as the mooring lines snapped taut with a deep metallic groan. The tension flung him back, his face smacking the doorframe. White-hot pain flashed across his brow.

"You good, Harper?!" Lawson shouted over the roar, still covering Neilan from the dock.

"Yeah—hold on!"

The boat strained against the lines, engine screaming in protest. Harper knew they wouldn't hold forever. He spotted the back storage lockers just in front of the straining engines, dropped to his stomach and low-crawled to the hatch. Once there, he yanked it open, and found what he needed: the battery master switches. With one motion, he cut the power. The engines choked and died. The boat settled into the water like a spooked animal finally muzzled.

Harper stood, blood trickling down his temple, pistol drawn and steady in his left hand.

"It's over, Neilan," he said coldly. "Step out. Hands up. NOW." He growled the last bit, his tone leaving no room for negotiation.

Inside the cabin, Neilan sagged like a deflated balloon. He slowly lifted his hands and opened the door.

"Keep 'em where I can see 'em!" Lawson ordered, voice sharp and controlled.

Neilan stepped out onto the stern, trembling.

Lawson cuffed him as Harper covered. "You're under arrest for assault on a Federal agent."

Neilan didn't resist. Just swallowed hard, his face pale as paper.

•••••

In the interview room, Lawson sat across from Neilan, her tone even. "Cody, I need you to walk me through June 14. Sara worked late that night. Charity said you came into her room."

Neilan's jaw clenched so hard he could have chipped a tooth. "That's not—she's making things up. Kids lie."

"She knew what the sheets looked like," Lawson said softly. "She knew what you said to her after."

Beads of sweat formed on his temple. Harper finally leaned forward, voice low and steady. "We've got your texts. Every gift. Every time you set her up to stay home alone with you. You're not walking out of here."

Neilan swallowed hard, eyes darting between them. His leg started to bounce under the table. "I–I didn't...it wasn't like that–"

"No. That's the thing," Harper interrupted, his gaze hard. "It's exactly like that. She remembers the *birthmark*, Cody. She knew the exact number of moles on your dick. You're done."

•••••

The interview room door clicked shut behind them.

Lawson let out a low whistle, then laughed as they stepped into the hallway. "You see him trying to tough it out? Whole 'I'm not scared of you feds' act? Then I laid out the receipts and the phone records–"

Harper smirked, wiping a drying smear of blood from his temple. "Guy turned sheet white like a sea-sick recruit."

"—and then puked right into the trash can," Lawson added, shaking her head. "Classy exit. Right after that confession, too. Might be the only perp I've had literally choke on his own bullshit."

Easton looked up as they stepped into his office. "How'd it go?"

"Like clockwork," Lawson said. "Folded like a lawn chair. Confessed to everything. Every damn detail. Tried to justify it as first, said he loved her, said she needed him. Then puked into a trash can for good measure."

Easton arched an eyebrow. "Hell of a detail."

Harper shrugged. "Guilt's a bitch."

After they finished briefing Easton, they were back in the hall.

Harper leaned against the wall, arms crossed. "Need help with the transport?"

"Nah. It's already en route. Charges are gonna be stacked. Full weight of the system coming down. Plus the assault charges on you. He's fucked."

Harper nodded. "Good."

Lawson looked over at him. "Thanks for backing me up today."

"Anytime," Harper said. "Always happy to ruin a predator's day."

CHAPTER
TWENTY-THREE

B ack at his desk, Harper refreshed his email. Still nothing.
9:00 p.m.

Guess Judge Keller's reviewing it tomorrow.

He leaned back, rubbed his eyes, and took stock. There were too many threads to chase tonight. But one detail gnawed at him. Something felt off, something he'd missed. He decided to call an audible.

He pulled out his phone and dialed.

"Harper?" came the familiar voice, groggy but alerting quickly. "What's up?"

"Sorry to bug you so late, Logan. I need a consult."

"Same case?" Cross' voice was fully alert now.

"Yep. I need a boat guy."

A pause, then a low chuckle. "So you wake up a Boatswain's Mate on the East Coast?"

"You're a Chief now. Comes with the territory."

"Fair enough. Lay it on me."

Harper paced the floor as he updated Cross on everything that had happened the last few days, including Calderón's misdirect, Pastor Kincaid and his too-smooth charm, and Trevor Oliver—now unmasked as Oliver Hugo.

"Damn," Cross said when he finished. "You cannot stay out of trouble, can you?"

"Learned from the best," Harper replied.

"So, what are you thinking here?"

"I'm thinking someone killed them and cleaned it up damn well. The yacht was spotless. No prints, no blood, no personal effects. I need to know what else I should be looking for. Something they might've missed."

Cross didn't answer right away.

"If they were selling the boat," he said finally, "there should be a manifest. Inventory for the buyer. Gear lists, maintenance logs, that kind of thing."

"That makes sense. I'll check for one."

"And if there was a murder on board..."

"Yeah?"

"Check for missing anchors."

Harper stopped pacing.

"Say that again?"

"If you were out on the water, no body, no mess, and needed to weigh someone down...hell, Jake, those bow anchors are built for that. Big ones are fluke or plow style. Tie someone to one and toss it over? That's the kind of quiet people never come back from."

It hit Harper like a lightning strike through bone. He saw *The Halcyon's* bow again in his mind. Clean, gleaming chrome, the chain tucked just so.

There hadn't been an anchor.

Not on the bow.

"Logan," he said slowly, "you ever think about changing careers?"

Cross laughed. "Nah. Melanie's already mad at how often I've been shot at. She'd leave me for sure if I added a badge."

Harper smiled. "Well, thanks for the insight. I owe you one."

"Nah, we're even now," Cross said. "But let's do dinner the next time I'm in your neck of the woods."

"Deal."

They hung up.

Harper sat down again, mind already working. He opened Malia's social media on his laptop and began scrolling, searching for one photo. One timestamp. One piece of proof.

It wasn't long before he found it.

A selfie, posted on September 8. The day before they vanished.

Malia sat on the bow, legs dangling over the edge. Daniel stood behind her, his arms loosely wrapped around her shoulders. Both were beaming, sun-kissed and carefree.

But Harper's eyes went lower, beneath Malia's legs.

The anchor. It was mounted on the bow, clearly visible. Gleaming steel and a coiled chain.

He opened the photo set from his walkthrough of *The Halcyon Way*, the initial sweep. Flipped through until he found the same angle. Same bow rail, the same curve of the hull.

No anchor. Just an empty mount.

He pulled the two images side by side on his monitor.

On September 8, *The Halcyon Way* had an anchor mounted to the bow.

On September 10, it did not.

His stomach dropped.

They hadn't just vanished. They'd been sunk.

.K. WOLFE

This was no longer a missing persons case. It was officially a homicide investigation.

Despite the exhaustion clinging to his limbs, he felt the familiar jolt of adrenaline that always seemed to accompany a major break in an investigation. He pulled up his notes and digital evidence, retracing the full picture.

On September 9 at 15:43 *The Halcyon Way* departed Shilshole Point Marina, heading west into Elliott Bay, then north into Puget Sound. It looped in a wide arc just beyond Elliott Bay before pushing farther north toward Whidbey Island.

Around 18:30, the yacht came to a dead stop in the middle of the shipping channel. It remained there for nearly an hour. Then, just after 19:20, it turned around and raced south, clocking 30 knots. Faster than a pleasure cruise.

At 23:19, the vessel stopped again, this time just north of Elliott Bay. Then it drifted, idle, until morning, when Seattle Harbor Patrol found it adrift and empty.

He now had a timeline. And a likely dump site.

Harper plugged in the GPS coordinates from the 18:30 stop. His heart sank.

Dead center of the Whidbey Basin, one of Puget Sound's three deepest sections. The chart showed a mean depth of 203 feet.

Too deep.

Too vast.

Even a dive team wouldn't stand a chance.

If he was right, Daniel and Malia Rainier were gone, claimed by the deep.

Still, he had to try.

He picked up his phone and dialed the Coast Guard watch office.

"This is Special Agent Harper, CGIS. I need to request immediate search assets—helo and small boat team. I've got coordinates on a possible body disposal site. Two presumed victims."

He gave the location, his cell number, and asked to be called directly with any findings.

•••••

September 14. 2:53 a.m.

Harper stepped quietly through the front door of the Seattle rental, the silence of home settling around him like a different kind of weight.

The SAR office had called it.

Five hours on the water. Nothing found. No sign of the Rainiers.

Harper was deflated. He had known it was a long shot, but hope springs eternal. He had let himself hope they would have been found, and now, all he had left were the ghosts of the Rainiers and his own guilt at not bringing them home.

He set his overnight bag down and dropped his dirty clothes into the hamper. On the way to the bedroom, he paused to check Addie's room. She was asleep, her arms sprawled over a tangle of blankets, breathing soft and steady.

He leaned down and kissed her head.

In the bedroom, the dark was warm and still. He heard Alyssa stir.

"Mmm...hey, babe," she said sleepily.

"Sorry," he whispered. "Didn't mean to wake you."

"It's okay," she said. "Just glad you're home. Come to bed."

He showered quickly, washing off the salt, sweat and failure. When he slid beneath the sheets, Alyssa was already asleep again. He pulled her close, her warmth anchoring him.

This time, he didn't dream.

CHAPTER
TWENTY-FOUR

September 14.

The alarm blared shrill and insistent, despite the soft acoustic track Harper had set the night before. His head throbbed. Sleep had been shallow and restless. Eight a.m. came too soon, and the sleep debt of the week was catching up to him.

He rolled out of bed with a groan, moving like a man twice his age. He threw on a fresh pair of slacks, polo and Chucks, then put his gun and badge back on his belt.

In the living room, the day had already begun.

Addie sat curled beneath Alyssa's arm on the couch, her curls a wild halo as she giggled at Elmo. Alyssa sipped from a mug, tired eyes still soft with love. The morning light caught her belly in profile beneath the throw blanket, a quiet reminder of everything Harper carried into the job with him.

He kissed Addie on the top of her head, then leaned down to press his lips to Alyssa's.

"Be safe," she said, her hand brushing his wrist.

He nodded, grabbing his to-go coffee mug from the kitchen counter. He shrugged into a light jacket then walked outside.

Back into the fray.

He pulled onto SR-99, Seattle waking up around him. Steam rose from gutters, cyclists braved the morning chill, and ferries cut across gray water like slow moving ghosts. His eyes were gritty. His heart was heavier.

Visions of Malia Rainier haunted him. On the bow, alone. The water swallowing her scream as she went down into the cold deep, pregnant and terrified. The weight of another life wrapped inside of her. A mother. A daughter. A wife. Gone.

And Daniel. Though Harper had never met him, he could feel the shape of the man as he pushed the investigation. Steady. Protective. The kind of man who would've fought until his last breath to save her.

Harper ran a hand over the stubble dotting his face. He hadn't had time to shave the last couple of days.

He glanced at the travel mug he had grabbed. "World's Greatest Dad." It had been a Father's Day gift from his daughter— picked out with Alyssa's help, of course. It was his favorite, with the chipped ceramic lid he refused to throw out. That tiny domestic detail struck him hard. He could still kiss his wife. Hold her hand across the center console. Malia and Daniel would never have that again.

If Harper was right, the Rainiers had lost everything in the space of an evening. A future stolen, a family erased. And he couldn't shake the thought that some part of him was racing that same tide, fighting to hold onto the fragile good in his own life before it slipped under the waves, too. Every moment he spent chasing shadows felt like stealing time from his own family. Time he couldn't afford to lose.

He signaled left, merging into traffic. The city swallowed him whole.

Time to work.

•••••

He parked in a visitor spot in the SPD parking garage just past nine, the morning traffic having chewed up most of the commute. The structure echoed with the hum of engines and the occasional squeal of tires rounding corners too fast. Harper slotted into a visitor space near the elevators and hung the laminated placard from his mirror: **CGIS - OFFICIAL BUSINESS**. The plastic swayed slightly as he shut the door.

His footsteps rang out across the cold concrete, the air tinged with exhaust and rain dampening off tires. Somewhere a car alarm chirped lazily, ignored. Stepping into the elevator, he hit the button for the detectives' floor and watched the steel doors groan shut with a tired sigh. The elevator lurched upward with the mechanical grind that seemed to define every public building he had ever been in. It seemed no matter where he went, government efficiency—or the lack thereof—was standard.

The homicide bureau sat behind glass doors etched with the SPD crest. Harper stepped through into the hum of printers, low conversation, and the scratch of pen on paper. It smelled of burnt coffee and old air conditioning, home to any cop who'd spent years in the grind.

To Harper's relief, Maguire was already at his desk.

The tall detective cut a distinct silhouette, even seated. Broad-shouldered, silver-haired, with clean lines in a dark button-down rolled at the sleeves. His full gray beard was neatly trimmed, catching the light from the windows. Wire-frame glasses slid slightly down his nose as he reviewed the files before him. The tattoo sleeve on his left forearm peeked out beneath the fabric, showing the Celtic knots and mythic symbols inked in black and green. The quiet markers of the Irish Pagan soul.

Harper paused a beat, watching him work. Maguire read with quiet intensity, pen tapping lightly against his lower lip. An old habit, Harper had come to realize, when he was already connecting dots faster than the evidence could keep up.

Then Maguire looked up and met his eyes.

"Morning, sunshine," he said dryly. "You look like hell."

"Didn't sleep much," Harper replied.

Maguire gave a one-sided smirk. "You're a father and a cop. That's the default setting. Speaking of, how's the little crotch-goblin?"

Harper blinked, then laughed. "Crotch-goblin?"

"What? Thomas and I never wanted kids. We're much happier being the fun uncles to everyone else's rug-rats. We get to spoil 'em when they're cute and charming, then hand them off when they start throwing juice boxes."

They shared a laugh, Harper's quieter, but real.

"Haven't seen the family too much lately," he admitted. "Between flights and interviews..."

"I can see that," Maguire said, gesturing at the files spread out before him. "But it looks like you've been putting the time to good use. Thanks for sending over the updates last night. You made serious headway with Kincaid and Hugo."

"I got more than that," Harper said. He filled him in on the missing anchor, the AIS track, and the likely dump site near Whidbey Island.

Maguire sat back, jaw tight. "So we're officially looking at a homicide investigation now."

"Yeah," Harper said. "One with no bodies."

"Harder, but not impossible to prove," Maguire replied, his voice thoughtful. "Juries don't always need corpses. They need a story that sticks."

Harper nodded. "Speaking of anchors, I got another warrant. Judge Keller signed late last night." He tapped his phone. "We're clear to go back aboard. I want another look at the bow. Double check the missing anchor. If we're gonna call it a murder, we'd better be damn sure."

Maguire reached for a fresh folder and flipped it open. "Before we do that, I found something you need to see, Jake."

He pulled out a copy of the bill of sale and slid it over. Harper leaned over the desk as Maguire placed his finger on the signature of Daniel Rainier.

"Look at Daniel's signature. Looks clean, consistent. We'll have to match it against a verified sample, but at first glance, it holds."

Harper nodded. "Okay..."

"But Malia's?" Maguire tapped her signature. "Look at the 'R' at the end of *Rainier*. It's...wrong. Like a different hand finished it."

Harper squinted. Sure enough, "Malia" was written in smooth cursive, same with most of "Rainier." But the final *R*? It was a bit blockier. Hesitant. Disconnected, just slightly, from the rest of the name.

"Looks deliberate," Harper said. "Like someone forged it."

"Or," Maguire said, "she did it on purpose. As a signal. A way to tell us something was off."

"Like she signed under duress," Harper said, connecting the dots.

"Exactly." Maguire ran his thumb along the bottom edge. "And here, look. It's notarized."

Harper leaned closer, reading aloud. "Cindy Glorevich. Seattle-based?"

Maguire pointed to his notepad. "Already ran her. Local address. Runs her shop out of her house."

Harper nodded. "If this notary watched them sign it, we need to find out what she saw."

Maguire stood up, finishing his coffee in one long sip. "Yeah, after the warrant, let's go find Cindy Glorevich."

CHAPTER
TWENTY-FIVE

They met back at Pier 36 on Coast Guard Base Seattle. *The Halcyon Way* sat under rotating guard, with Coasties and Harbor Patrol taking shifts to keep gawkers and any opportunities from slipping past the faded yellow crime scene tape strung across the gunwales.

Harper stood for a moment at the edge of the pier, wind tugging at his hair, the salt-stung breeze hinting at the weight beneath the surface. He took a slow breath, then walked along the dock until he reached the bow.

There it was. The absence.

The anchor cleat was empty.

"It's gone," he said, lifting his phone. On-screen, Malia smiled into the camera, legs dangling off the bow, the polished stainless steel anchor just visible below her feet. He lifted the phone to eye level, holding it next to the real thing, now conspicuously empty.

"That's not all that's missing," Maguire said from behind. He leaned in, pointing over Harper's shoulder. "There. Behind them."

Harper stared at the photo. Just behind Daniel, nestled against the bow railing, was a small Zodiac. The yacht tender.

"Well, now we know how they got off the boat afterward," Maguire said grimly.

"Yeah," Harper replied, "AIS had them cutting the engine just north of Elliott Bay. I'd bet they launched the dinghy there and let her drift."

"Wonder where the tender ended up?" Maguire mused aloud.

"I'll notify the CG watch and Harbor Patrol," Harper said. "Have them search the shoreline west of the last AIS ping. Maybe it washed up."

He looked back toward the yacht. "In the meantime, let's find a manifest. If they were selling, they'd have an inventory—everything the buyer was getting with the boat."

They pulled on blue nitrile gloves and stepped aboard. For the next two hours, they searched through every compartment, locker, and storage nook. They checked under cushions, lifted floor panels, and scanned for hidden cubbies. No anchor. And no sign of the manifest.

Maguire huffed from the starboard cabin. "Maybe they torched it."

Harper crouched by the head, his brows furrowing. "Not necessarily." He ducked into the small compartment and examined the plumbing beneath the sink. "If they panicked...or didn't want to leave trash on board...they might've flushed it."

"Flushed it?" Maguire echoed, incredulous.

Harper opened the access panel under the marine toilet and followed the sanitation piping to the Y-valve, a diverter that, by law, had to be wired shut in domestic waters to route waste into the holding tank rather than overboard. He gave the wire a tug. Still intact.

"Y-valve's sealed. Which means if they flushed anything, it went into the tank."

He stood, stripped off his gloves, and headed back to the car. A few minutes later, he returned with a respirator, safety goggles, and a cordless Sawzall.

Maguire raised a brow. "Jesus. Do you just keep that in your trunk?"

Harper shrugged and set the gear down. "Old habits."

He pulled on fresh gloves and crawled into the engine bay. The holding tank was tucked beneath the generator. Sixty-eight gallons of potential evidence. With a whispered prayer to the gods of homicide, he strapped on the respirator, braced himself, and began cutting a small access hole in the aluminum metal. The metal screeched as the blade bit through.

Once the section was loose, he peeled it back, flicked on his flashlight, and leaned in.

There wasn't much sludge inside. The tank had been recently emptied, either manually or via pump-out. But there, floating atop the last inch of liquid waste, bobbed something white and rectangular.

Harper reached in with two fingers and pulled out a laminated sheet, streaked with filth and tinged slightly yellow. He held it up in the beam of his flashlight.

"Bingo," he said into the respirator.

From the hatch above, Maguire peered down. "Please tell me that's not what I think it is."

Harper climbed out, holding the laminated paper with one hand while he peeled off the respirator with the other. "Manifest."

He carried it to the galley and laid it out on the counter, blotting it dry with paper towels from the kitchenette. The list was standard: life jackets, marine radio, stereo system. At the bottom: *Bow-mounted 100 lb. stainless steel anchor with 2,000 lb. capacity chain. Eleven-foot Zodiac tender.*

Maguire stared at it, then shook his head. "How the hell did you even think to look there?"

"Had a gut feeling," Harper replied.

Maguire grunted. "That's one hell of a gut instinct."

Harper tapped the laminated page with his finger. "Anchor, tender...everything that's missing. And it wasn't floating in there by accident. Someone flushed it. They were in a hurry, maybe thinking it'd be gone forever."

Maguire leaned on the counter, staring at the smeared list. "So either they didn't know the Y-valve routes to the holding tank, or they panicked."

"My money's on panic. It fits," Harper said. "You kill a couple on a boat, suddenly you're staring at a crime scene. You scrub the decks, dump the bags, wipe the electronics. But then you're holding this laminated list that ties you straight back to what you took. You're out of time, so you shove it down the head and hope it disappears."

Maguire gave a slow shake of his head. "Only it didn't. It sat there, waiting for us."

Harper nodded. "Bodies sink. Anchors too. But paper floats."

Maguire pulled out his phone and dialed the office. "We need Forensics back out here. Tell them to bring the scope kits and swabs. I want every inch of that sanitation line tested."

•••••

The forensics team was still working when Harper and Maguire stepped off *The Halcyon Way*. One tech was swabbing the sink drain with a long cotton applicator. Another was feeding a flexible scope into the holding tank, muttering about the smell through a doubled-up mask.

"They're going to be a while," Maguire said, scrubbing his palms with a wipe. "Let's grab coffee before I start hallucinating burnt toast."

"Exchange is just down the pier," Harper nodded. "Let's go."

They walked side by side, their shoes echoing against the planks of the pier. The sky had shifted to overcast, the marine layer creeping in. It felt heavier than usual, like the Sound itself was mourning.

Inside the Coast Guard exchange, the coffee corner was wedged between racks of boat shoes and sunscreen displays. Maguire grabbed a large dark roast and dumped in two sugars. Harper went for black. No frills, he was too tired for anything else.

"Remind me to never climb into a holding tank again," Harper muttered as he pulled a lid from the dispenser.

"You did it for the drama," Maguire smirked. "Theatrics and trauma. Cop fuel."

They walked back to the pier, steaming cups in hand. Harper took a long pull from his mug and leaned against the piling. Maguire perched one foot on a cleat, eyes on the forensic team still buzzing around the yacht.

"This ever get easier for you?" Harper asked quietly.

Maguire took a moment before answering. "No. You just get better at carrying it."

Harper didn't reply. He stared out at the gray water, the wind teasing at the surface, trying to unearth secrets buried in the deep.

Twenty minutes passed before one of the forensics techs approached. It was the same woman from the first sweep, with the short, dark ponytail tucked through her ball cap and a laminated ID badge clipped to her vest. Her gloves were off now, and her expression had shifted.

She was walking with purpose.

Harper straightened. Maguire tossed his empty cup into the nearby bin.

"You got something?" Harper asked.

She nodded, pulling out a small folder and flipping it open.

"We ran the trace kits on the sink drain and the plumbing inside the head. Swabbed the pipe junction at the Y-valve and scoped the holding tank. We picked up multiple positive hits for blood trace. Partial hemoglobin readings. Weak, but consistent."

Maguire's brow rose. "You sure it's human?"

"We did a presumptive test on site. It's not conclusive, but the proteins match human blood, not fish or other marine contamination. The concentrations were highest in the pipe just below the sink. Lower in the tank itself."

"So," Harper said slowly, "someone washed their hands."

"Most likely," she nodded. "And probably pretty soon after the incident. The samples weren't contaminated by raw sewage, which suggests the tank hadn't been used much since."

Harper glanced at Maguire. "They wiped the boat down top to bottom. But they didn't think about the plumbing."

Maguire gave a grim smile. "The devil's in the drainage."

The tech handed over a printed summary. "We'll send this to the lab for full confirmation, but if you're building a homicide case, this helps."

"It helps," Harper said. "A lot."

"Let us know if you need the tank removed or held for court. It'll take some wrangling, but we can coordinate with your evidence technician."

"We'll be in touch," Harper replied.

The tech nodded and turned back towards the forensics van.

Harper exhaled slowly, feeling the wind brush over his shoulders again.

Maguire nudged his arm. "Well, partner...looks like we've got blood in the pipes and a manifest in the muck. You don't get much clearer than that."

Harper didn't answer at first. His gaze was fixed on the yacht bobbing gently against the pier, as if nothing had ever happened on board. "They thought they'd cleaned it. Thought they'd erased the story. But the boat remembers."

Maguire glanced at him, then back to the forensic folder in his hand. "Looks like we just moved from missing persons to homicide."

Harper's reply was quiet, but steady. "Yeah. It's definitely now a murder case."

CHAPTER
TWENTY-SIX

September 14. Two p.m.

They took Maguire's car, an unmarked city-issued sedan that still smelled faintly of old coffee and department-grade upholstery cleaner. Harper rode shotgun, manila envelope on his lap, the notary's name circled at the top of the bill of sale. After forensics finished with *The Halcyon Way*, they had decided to go pay her a visit.

"Cindy Glorevich," Maguire said, turning off the main road. "Google says she works out of her house, runs a mobile notary business. Retired legal secretary, looks like."

"Think she knew what she was signing off on?" Harper asked.

Maguire shrugged. "If she didn't, maybe she's a pawn. If she did? We'll find out."

The car slowed as they approached a worn-down craftsman that looked like it used to be nice, back when someone had time to care. Peeling paint flakes from the eaves. A gutter hung low on one corner, heavy with leaves. The lawn was patchy and dry, gone more golden brown than green, with weeds sprouting near the cracked walkway. A sun-bleached plastic scooter, with one wheel bent, lay on its side near the leaning white picket fence, the paint chipped and gray at the edges. A child's pink Croc rested halfway off the porch step, like someone had kicked it off mid-tantrum and no one had bothered to pick it up.

In the front window, a tarnished brass placard read:

Cindy Glorevich, Notary Public - By Appointment Only

Maguire parked at the curb, cut the engine.

"Ready to see if Cindy Glorevich has a conscience?"

Harper nodded once, hand already reaching for the file. "Let's find out who she saw on that boat."

They walked up the front path. Harper clocked the crooked blinds in the living room window, the plastic play kitchen barely visible behind them, and the faint smell of stale diapers riding the breeze.

As they reached the two concrete steps leading up to the door, Maguire tilted his head towards the dusty doorbell camera mounted beside the frame. He knocked instead. Three sharp raps that made their purpose clear.

The door swung open a few seconds later with surprising speed.

"Closed today," the woman barked, her tone sharp and weary.

She was short and plump, maybe mid-thirties, with soft features that might have once read as cheerful but now just looked tired. Her chin-length hair had once been trendy, cut asymmetrically, one side longer than the other, but the roots were grown out in streaks of brown and gray. A few errant strands stuck to her forehead with sweat. Her oversized T-shirt was streaked with what Harper instinctively recognized as toddler-level chaos: peanut butter smears, juice stains, maybe dried formula. Her jeans were sagging the knees, the hem frayed.

Dark circles framed her eyes. Her nails were chipped. Her face was flushed, not from embarrassment, but effort.

Harper's instincts kicked in. She wasn't just annoyed. She was drowning.

"Ms. Glorevich?" he asked gently, holding up his ID. "I'm Special Agent Harper. This is Detective Maguire. We just have a few questions about a notarized bill of sale. Won't take long."

Her eyes widened, just a flicker, and her shoulders drooped. Not in relief, more like she was bracing herself.

"Of course you do," she said under her breath, stepping back to let them in.

Harper stepped inside, noting the smell of reheated takeout, the noise of a cartoon playing in another room, and the stack of unopened mail leaning precariously on a hallway table. Cindy shuffled to the kitchen table and swept an arm across the cluttered table, shoving crayon drawings and dried glue sticks to one side, making just enough space for them to sit.

"Please," she said, weariness in every syllable, "have a seat."

"Ms. Glorevich," Harper began as he settled into the worn wooden chair. "We're investigating the disappearance of a couple. We were hoping you could help us."

"Call me Cindy," she said quickly, rubbing her palms against the sides of her jeans. "I'm not sure how much help I'll be, but I'll try."

Maguire took over smoothly. "They were last seen aboard their yacht, *The Halcyon Way*. Found yesterday morning drifting near Elliott Bay. No one on board."

227

Harper added, his voice gentler now, "They'd been sailing the San Juans. A babymoon. She was pregnant, their first child." He let the words linger, his eyes drifting to a child's drawing on the table. A stick figure family, smiling under a crooked sun.

Cindy followed his eyes. Her pupils tightened. Harper clocked the flicker of tension — not the confusion of someone blindsided, but the bracing of someone who'd already rehearsed a version of the story.

"Okay..." she said slowly. "So how can I help?"

Harper reached into his file folder and withdrew the bill of sale. He slid it across the table. "Is this your signature and stamp?"

She glanced at it, then nodded. "It is."

"Do you remember the notarization?"

Cindy shrugged faintly. "I do a lot of these. They blur together sometimes."

"Do they?" Harper asked quietly, glancing again around the cluttered kitchen behind her. Takeout containers, coupon mailers, and a half-drunk cup of cold coffee sat on the counter.

She looked back down at the paper. Her voice was tighter now. "I do remember it better now. The Rainiers, right? They came in that morning. Told me they were selling the yacht. Something about preparing for the baby. Downsizing. They seemed in a good mood."

"Did you see their IDs?" Maguire asked.

"I did. I always do. That's the law."

Harper pressed. "Do you remember what they looked like?"

"Yeah. I think so." She spoke too fast, then slowed, as if correcting course. "The husband was tall, Black, clean-shaven. He looked military. The wife was shorter, pregnant, with long dark hair, maybe Hawaiian or something. They looked so happy. It's... awful they're missing."

Harper's gaze sharpened. He felt Maguire glance his way.

"You're sure about the hair?" Harper asked. "Long and dark?"

Cindy hesitated, then nodded. "Yes. It was past her shoulders, definitely. Dark. Black or really dark brown."

Maguire said nothing, but his jaw shifted slightly.

Harper didn't press, not yet. "Do you mind if we see your notary log book?"

"Sure," Cindy said, rising. She left the room and returned a moment later with a thick brown ledger. She flipped through its pages with practiced fingers, then set it on the table and turned it toward them.

"There. That's them," she said, pointing to an entry dated last week.

Harper leaned in. Two signatures — *Daniel and Malia Rainier* — written in flowing cursive, neat and consistent. He compared it to the bill of sale. The version of Malia's signature on the sale form had the awkward, altered "R" at the end. Different. Like someone had tried to fake it and lost confidence mid-stroke.

He took out his phone and snapped a photo.

Cindy's brow furrowed. "Hey, um, actually, you're not really supposed to take pictures of the logbook. It's private information."

"Cops, remember?" Maguire interrupted with a smile that didn't reach his eyes.

Harper tapped the corner of the bill. "Did you notice this when they signed?"

"Notice what?"

"The 'R' at the end of Malia's name. It's not like the rest. Looks like someone changed style mid-signature. A little sharp, blocky. Out of place."

Cindy's fingers twitched on the edge of the table. "Oh. Um, yeah, that's....how she signed it. That morning."

"You're sure?" Maguire asked, calm but watchful.

"Pretty sure," she said quickly. "Maybe she was just nervous. Or maybe... I don't know, the pregnancy. Hormones. Pregnant women can get shaky sometimes."

She laughed faintly at her own excuse. No one joined her. Her smile was tight, her tone overly casual. Harper saw the wheels turning behind her eyes.

"What time did they come in?" he asked.

"Around ten."

"One thing I noticed," Harper said, "this form here, the bill of sale. Did you notarize this *at the same time* as the log entry?"

Cindy hesitated. "No... not exactly. Same day, but not the same time."

"When did the buyer come in?" Maguire asked, flipping the bill of sale back over.

"Oh, same day, but later. Early afternoon. He and his guy came by, uh, Pastor Kincaid and some other man. Trevor, I think. He had all the paperwork. I remember because they were in a hurry and I almost told them to come back later."

"And did they sign in front of you?"

"Yes. Both of them. Kincaid and the broker. They signed right here," she said, tapping the spot on the bill.

"You didn't find it odd that the seller and buyer weren't here at the same time?" Harper asked.

Cindy shrugged. "Happens more than you'd think. People are busy. Some sellers want privacy. As long as the paperwork's in order, everything's fine."

"If you remember anything else, anything at all," Harper said, putting his business card on top of the logbook, "don't hesitate to call."

"Please do," Maguire said, firmer this time. "We're trying to find a pregnant woman and her husband. Every detail matters."

Cindy forced a smile that never touched her eyes. "Of course."

They saw themselves out. As the door shut behind them, Harper didn't say a word, just tucked the bill of sale back in the folder and started down the steps. As they got in the car, he exhaled slowly.

Maguire broke the silence. "She lied."

Harper nodded. "About more than one thing."

"She got the hair wrong."

"Yeah," Harper said, not looking up. "She never saw the Rainiers in person. I'd bet my badge on it."

"She described Malia like she'd seen that ultrasound photo. Or a DMV license photo. Not real life."

Harper nodded slowly. "And the signature in her notary log? Clean. Normal. Nothing like that weird "R" on the bill of sale."

"She flinched when we asked about it," Maguire added. "Said Malia was excited. That it made sense. But she was thinking on her feet."

"Panicking," Harper said. "And we gave her just enough rope to hang herself later."

Maguire glanced over. "So what's the play? Bring her in?"

"Not yet," Harper said. "She's scared. We lean too hard now, she lawyers up and we lose any shot at flipping her. Let her sweat a little. We'll circle back."

"She's protecting someone," Maguire said. "Or got paid to look the other way."

Harper nodded once. "Agreed. Let's find out which it was."

Part Three: The Cup of Wrath

"But God remembered Babylon the Great, and gave her the cup filled with the wine of the fury of his wrath."
— Revelation 16:19

CHAPTER
TWENTY-SEVEN

September 14. Late afternoon.

The Industrial District always smelled like old iron and hot asphalt, like the ghosts of factories that hadn't worked in decades. Trucks rolled by in slow succession, rattling the cracked streets. The Way Forward Foundation's address sat at the edge of it all, registered out of a squat warehouse with fading paint, its front door framed by dust and neglect.

Harper parked at the curb, staring through the windshield. "Hell of a place to redeem souls."

Maguire snorted. "Looks like more where you come to hide 'em."

They climbed out, shoes crunching over broken glass scattered near the sidewalk. The building's front door had a flimsy keypad lock, the kind anyone with a screwdriver and half a minute could bypass. A paper sign— "THE WAY FORWARD FOUNDATION"— was taped crookedly on the inside of the glass, sun-faded until the words looked more like a shadow than an identity.

Harper tried the handle. Unlocked.

Inside, the air smelled of dust and stale carpet glue. The place was a skeleton of an office: mismatched desks, filing cabinets against the wall, a couple of chairs still in shrink wrap. On the reception counter sat a stack of unopened mail, envelopes curling at the edges.

Maguire picked one up, turning it over in his hand. "All post-marked months ago." He let it drop back onto the pile. "Guess the Foundation's not big on correspondence."

Harper ran a finger across a desk and lifted a line of dust. "Or staff."

The whole room felt staged.

Through glass doors, the executive office looked just as abandoned. Stacks of unopened mail sat on a wooden desk beside a desktop computer that hadn't been powered on in years.

"We're gonna need a warrant," Harper said.

"Way ahead of you." Maguire held up a sheet of paper, SEARCH WARRANT written across the top.

Harper cocked an eyebrow.

"You sent over your updates. I figured we'd get here, so I had it drafted and signed this morning. Just didn't get a chance to tell you."

"Sure you weren't waiting for the perfect dramatic reveal?"

Maguire smirked. "Maybe. Worked, didn't it?"

Harper shook his head, smiling despite himself. He pulled on nitrile gloves and tried the knob to the executive office. Locked.

"Good thing you've got that warrant," he said.

"Want the honors?" Maguire asked.

"Nah. You've got the leverage, tall man."

Maguire didn't need a second invitation. One hard kick splintered the frame, sending the door swinging inward.

They stepped inside and got to work. Harper took the desk while Maguire pulled binders from a bookshelf. The mail on the surface of the desk was routine—bank statements, utility bills, form letters from missionaries looking for support. Harper opened the top drawer, finding more of the same unopened mail. Same story.

The second drawer was different. These letters had been opened. He thumbed through them. Each one was handwritten, thank-yous in looping penmanship, too polished and eager.

One caught his eye.

Asher,

Thank you for the support you've given. Without the generosity of The Way Forward, we would have lost our house. My children eat tonight because of you. If I can ever do anything to repay you, please, let me know.

—Suzanne

Harper let the page hang between his fingers, unease prickling the back of his neck.

He found more of these letters, with similar messages of gratitude. As he continued to leaf through, he found another stack of letters, rubber-banded together. He pulled one from the stack and read it:

Asher,

I do not know how to truly thank you. Not only for your generosity, but for your wisdom. God truly has given you the gift of Sight. The things you spoke over me, no one else could have known. When you told me my struggles were a test, I felt a burden lift, as if the Lord Himself had spoken through you. I believe now more than ever that you were sent to guide us, that you are the prophet you claimed to be.

I have done as you asked. The papers are in order. The life insurance will go to The Way Forward, with your name as the beneficiary. My will has been updated to transfer the house to you upon my passing. It is a comfort to me, knowing that what I leave behind will serve your purpose and further the Kingdom you are building.

I will continue to do all I can in this life to support your vision. And when you call, I will answer, as I always have. Whether in prayer, counsel, or in your arms, you have shown me what it means to be chosen. I am yours, Asher, body and soul.

> *Entwined,*
> *Annette*

The sweat on the back of Harper's neck turned cold as his mind began to wrap around the scope of Kincaid's scheme. He worked through the stack, letter after letter, every one from a woman. Each called Asher a prophet. Each pledged something. Insurance policies. Homes. Savings. Many pledged more. Their bodies. Their obedience. Their silence.

Asher had himself a goddamned cult.

"You've got to see this," Maguire said, breaking the silence of the room, and the tension in Harper's head.

Harper lowered the letter he was reading and looked over at Maguire. Maguire put one of the binders down on the desk, flipping to the middle.

"Check this out," he said. "Here. It shows assets coming in. Unexplained cash. Sometimes large amounts. Property transferred. Donations labeled as 'gifts of faith.'"

Harper leaned in. The handwriting was careful, almost reverent. Columns of names filled the pages, with amounts beside them. Some of the amounts were in the hundreds. Some, the tens of thousands.

He felt his stomach turn. The names weren't strangers. He'd just read them in the letters rubber-banded in the desk drawer.

Eight women in particular showed up again and again, their contributions ballooning over time. One of them: Cindy Glorevich.

Maguire cleared his throat. "Looks like our notary's got more than one signature on her soul."

Harper grunted and kept flipping. Interspersed among the women's names were others, men with criminal records. Known associates in the system. Maguire pointed at one name: Ezra Silas.

Harper looked up at him. "Name mean something to you?"

"Yeah," Maguire said slowly. "Street-level dealer I used to deal with back when I worked narcotics. Got popped for distribution. Skated on a technicality with a high-priced lawyer he shouldn't have been able to afford. Been in and out on petty stuff since."

"Guess we know how he afforded that fancy attorney," Harper said, piecing it together.

The entries next to Silas' name weren't gifts of faith. They were numbers. Cash in, cash out. Large numbers, spaced over months. Classic laundering patterns.

"He's using the Foundation to wash dirty money," Harper said, his lips turning up in disgust.

"Looks that way," Maguire said. "Drug cash in, clean donations out. Women cover the front, Silas moves the product, and Kincaid sits in the middle."

Harper turned to the back of the ledger. A page marked with a sticky note read: *Acquisitions*. It was a handwritten list with bullet points, each one a prize.

Lakefront house - acquired
BMW X7 - acquired.

Private retreat property - sale pending.
Luxury yacht -
The word wasn't crossed out like the "acquired" entries were.

Harper stared at it, bile rising in his throat. The last entry, scrawled in almost ornamental script, read: *2003 Sea Ray 560.*

That was the exact model of *The Halcyon Way.*

Maguire leaned in, voice low. "Well. We might have just found our motive."

Harper closed the binder with a sharp snap. His pulse was steady, but underneath, he felt the burn of fury. Kincaid hadn't just wanted the Rainiers gone. He'd wanted their lives, their boat, and stolen their future. Coveted it enough to kill for it.

Maguire blew out a slow breath and leaned against the desk. "So the bastard wanted a yacht, and the Rainiers had the bad luck of owning the exact one on his wish list."

Harper nodded, tapping the binder once with his finger. "Motive's there. Pattern's there. But we've still got a gap."

"Proof," Maguire said.

"Exactly. Right now it's circumstantial. A ledger, some letters, and a list with a boat name scribbled on it isn't enough to hang a murder indictment—"

"Especially a 'no-body' murder case—"

" —and we need someone inside his circle to say it out loud. To tie Kincaid to the Rainiers' death. To the whole damn scheme."

Maguire lifted his head, already guessing. "Cindy."

"She's in deep," Harper said, setting his jaw. "She notarized the sale, signed letters pledging herself to him, donated money. She's in the cult, no question. But she's also a weak link. You don't leave a baby at home if you're ready to go down for a false prophet."

"You think she'll flip?"

Harper stared at the stack of letters again, the words blurring for a moment. "I think she's scared. Question is, is she more scared of us or of him?"

Maguire picked up the binder and tucked it under his arm. "Then I guess our next move is to find out."

Harper stripped off his gloves and tossed them into the bin by the door. He felt the weight of the case pressing heavier than ever, like the Sound itself had settled onto his shoulders. They finally had motive, a trail of money, and names that tied it together. Now they just needed a voice, one person willing to stand up and say the truth out loud.

He looked at Maguire. "We put Cindy in a room, give her the chance to save herself. If she's smart, she takes it."

"And if she's not?" Maguire asked.

Harper opened the office door, stepping back into the dust and stale air of the empty foundation. "Then we find out just how far this cult really goes."

CHAPTER
TWENTY-EIGHT

D arrin Fulton's suit was as impeccable as his reputation: sharp, pressed, and not a wrinkle in sight even at six in the evening. He carried himself with the same discipline. His thin build, full head of brown hair combed with precision and a clean-shaven face made him pass for early forties even though he was pushing fifty-three.

Harper had read his name enough times on case law summaries to recognize it instantly. Fulton had been with the King County Prosecuting Attorney's Office for over two decades, hired right out of law school. He'd made his bones in the misdemeanor rotation, then cut through the domestic violence unit with a conviction rate that turned heads. But it was his time in the child sex abuse team that made him a name, the kind of prosecutor defense attorneys whispered about in courthouse hallways. Ninety-five percent conviction rate. Average sentences running thirty years or more.

That reputation had carried him to the Violent Crimes Unit, then to the elite Most Dangerous Offenders Project, a select group of senior deputy prosecutors who responded to every homicide in the county. The responding deputies embedded with detectives from the first day of an investigation, shaping a case for trial from the ground up.

Now Fulton stood at the head of the conference table at Pier 36, a fresh legal pad in front of him and a pen balanced neatly across the top. Beside him, Assistant U.S. Attorney Kari Summers crossed her arms. Both wore the same scowl, aimed squarely at the investigators. Harper and Maguire were seated, with SSA Easton next to them. The case files were stacked in front of them, with photographs of *The Halcyon Way* and the Rainiers spread out next to the folders.

"We should have been consulted from the start," Fulton said, voice clipped.

"We did reach out—" Maguire began.

"To say you had a *missing persons* case, not a homicide," Fulton snapped. "My team is supposed to be looped on *every* homicide from the jump. Not after you've already trampled the scene."

Harper leaned forward. "We made it clear there was potential for homicide from day one. Your office reviewed multiple warrant affidavits that said exactly that. We didn't cut you out. Someone on your end chose not to call you in." He turned to the AUSA Summers. "And I've looped in the US Attorney's Office from the beginning. SSA Easton was sending multiple updates a day."

Summers gave a diplomatic nod. "That's true, my office was kept apprised. We just assumed Violent Crimes or MDOP was on board, too." She pronounced the acronym as "Em-Dop."

"Well, we weren't. *I* wasn't," Fulton shot back. "And that is unacceptable. Now I get to clean up the mess. I expect this from a rookie Fed, but not from you, Maguire. You should have known better."

Maguire's face turned red, the muscles at his temple flexing with his jaw. Harper saw the storm coming and cut in before it broke.

"With respect, Mr. Fulton, neither of us are rookies. Detective Maguire's a twenty-year veteran. I've worked homicides and trafficking cases before you even knew about this. If your office sat on the information, that's on your politics, not our investigation."

Summers tried to ease the tension. "Darrin, Special Agent Harper's technically a reserve—"

Fulton barked a bitter laugh. "You put a *weekend warrior* on a fucking homicide case? Jesus Christ, Kari—"

"As I was saying," Summers pressed, "he's one of our most experienced agents—"

" —I'll be calling your boss, the Attorney General, and Seattle PD command—"

" —our office has full faith in CGIS handling this—"

The room erupted into crosstalk until Easton slammed both palms on the table. The crack silenced everyone.

"ENOUGH!" he roared. The air in the room seemed to contract.

Easton's eyes locked on Fulton. "You want credentials? Harper's a detective out of Stonehaven PD. You might've read about him—the trafficking ring and multiple homicides he tore apart in Oregon? Or the work he just did back east with organized crime? He and Maguire have been shot at, bled for this case, and they're the ones who proved it was homicide while your office sat on its hands.

Now, if you're done measuring dicks, can we please get back to work?"

The room went quiet. Even Fulton shut his mouth. Harper caught the corner of Maguire's smirk. He couldn't help his own crooked smile.

Fulton cleared this throat and straightened the edge of his legal pad, the only sound in the room for a long moment. When he finally spoke, his tone was cooler, but the bite hadn't disappeared.

"Fine," he said. "You've proven it's a homicide. You've earned my attention. But if this case is going to stand in court, every step from here on out runs through me. We do this by the book."

Summers added quickly, "Which is why we're here now, for coordination, not conflict." She looked between the investigators, Easton, and Fulton. "The evidence you've uncovered so far—the manifest, the blood traces, the Foundation paperwork—that's enough to shift this firmly into homicide territory. But it's circumstantial, at best, until you can put someone on that boat at the time the victims went over."

"And preferably, someone who can confirm they even *went* over," Fulton jumped in.

Harper leaned forward, tapping the file in front of him. "That's where Cindy Glorevich comes in. We believe she forged the signature on that bill of sale, or at least lied about seeing them in person. Either way, she lied to us. And the records we found in the Foundation office put her as one of the subjects in Kincaid's little cult. She's close enough to him to at least know some of how this was done, and to tie him to this."

"Or close enough to take the fall," Fulton said flatly.

Maguire shot him a look, but Harper kept steady. "Either way, she's our crack in the wall. We get her talking, we get inside Kincaid's operation."

Summers nodded. "Then the question becomes how. Do we go at her hard? Threaten charges and see if she flips? Or do we dangle protection, immunity, something that gets her talking without a fight?"

Fulton leaned back, pen tapping against the legal pad. "My instinct? Pressure. Show her the letters, the bank records, and the forged bill of sale. Put the fear of prison in her. If she's got half a brain, she'll fold."

"That's one way," Maguire said. "But she's been in Kincaid's orbit a long time, from the records we found. Loyalty runs deep in cults. Fear alone might just drive her further into him."

Harper glanced between them, then said quietly, "Sometimes it's not about fear. It's about showing someone they've already been abandoned. If we can prove Kincaid used her, cut her out of the money, left her holding the bag on this, she might realize he's not the prophet she thinks he is."

Easton rumbled his agreement. "I think we try it Harper's way. Gentle push. Scoop her up, first thing in the morning. If she won't bend, then Fulton, bring the hammer."

Fulton gave a thin smile, finally scribbling a note on his pad. "Fair enough. But you'd better bring me something solid when she cracks. Because once she's in play, the whole case hangs on her."

Summers closed her folder with a quiet snap. "Then it's settled. Cindy's the next move. If she flips, we've got leverage. If she doesn't, well..."

"Then we'll know how deep this goes," Harper finished.

"And we'll have to find another way in," Maguire added.

The room exhaled as one. Harper leaned back, his crooked smile gone, replaced by the familiar weight pressing down on his chest.

They had a homicide. They had a motive.

They just needed someone to talk.

•••••

Harper pulled into the driveway just as the last glow of sunset bled out behind the trees. The house lights were on, warm rectangles against the deepening blue. Inside, he could already hear Adelyn's voice, lilting and animated, telling some story only a four-year-old could string together. As he got out of his car, he rolled his shoulders to shake off the lingering tension from the meeting with the prosecutors.

Alyssa met him at the door, her hair tied back, hands on her swollen belly. "You're just in time," she said softly, kissing his cheek. "Dinner's almost ready."

He kissed her deeply, then pulled her into an embrace, whispering in her ear. "I missed you."

She smiled at him, and mouthed, *I love you.*

The smell hit him then—garlic, tomatoes, and bread warming in the oven. His stomach rumbled as he realized he hadn't eaten all day. It was so normal it felt absurd, the way everything else in his life was not.

Adelyn barreled into him and wrapped herself around his leg. "Daddy! Guess what? Mommy let me stir the noodles all by myself!"

He bent and scooped her up, pressing a kiss into her hair. "That so? You didn't burn the kitchen down?"

She giggled, shaking her blond hair. "Noooo. I'm a good stirrer! I'm helper number one!"

"You sure are!" Alyssa called out.

At the table, Harper tried to anchor himself in the rhythm of dinner: the clink of forks, the chatter of his daughter, Alyssa's steady presence across from him. But every time his mind drifted, it went back to Cindy. To Kincaid. To the Rainiers. The weight of it pressed harder with every bite.

"You're a million miles away," Alyssa said gently, catching his eyes.

He exhaled. "Sorry. It's...it's been a lot with this one. Everything about it—everything reminds me of what we have here." He gestured at the table, to their daughter. "They lost everything. And it looks like all for one man's greed."

"What's greed, Daddy?" Adelyn asked.

Harper turned to her and smiled. "Well, Addie...greed is when someone wants more than they need. And sometimes they take stuff that isn't theirs."

"Like when Natalie takes my toy?" she asked, thinking of a daycare incident.

"Yes, sweetie. Just like that. And daddy's job is to help stop people like that," Alyssa finished.

"Like the bandits on my show!" Adelyn exclaimed, launching into a full retelling of the latest cartoon episode.

Later, after putting her to bed, Harper and Alyssa resumed their conversation on the couch.

"I can see this is wearing on you, Jake. Are you okay?"

"Not really, love. But I will be, I think. Once we close this."

"Are you close?"

"I think so. Closer than we've been. But tomorrow...tomorrow might be the hinge."

She reached across the couch, her hand resting on his. "Then don't let tonight slip by. Be here, just for now."

Harper looked at her. She was beautiful. The lamplight from the side table caught the red highlights in her auburn hair, framing her face. He nodded, forcing himself to let the case slide to the edges of his mind. For one night, he'd keep the ghosts at the door.

He reached over and put his hand on her belly. "Has he been kicking today?" he asked.

"Like you wouldn't believe," Alyssa laughed. "He's either gonna be a soccer player or an MMA fighter!"

As if on cue, Harper felt the fluttering kicks under his palm, answering their laughter.

"I can't wait to meet him," Harper whispered, mesmerized.

"Me either," Alyssa said, love in her eyes. "Our perfect little growing family."

They stayed like that for a while, feeling the movement, the life inside her. Feeling hope. Feeling the shape of their future.

And yet, as Harper held his hand on Alyssa's belly, a shadow pressed at the back of his mind. He thought of Malia Rainier, of the child she'd never bring into the world. Of the promises cut short by another man's greed. He kissed Alyssa's temple, breathing her in, forcing the thoughts away.

CHAPTER
TWENTY-NINE

September 15. Nine a.m.

Cindy Glorevich's craftsman house looked the same as yesterday—run-down, weary—but now, knowing it was likely bought with Kincaid's money, it seemed to sag under something darker. The sun-bleached plastic scooter still lay on its side in the yard. A breeze stirred the notary sign hanging on the porch, its chain creaking and breaking the silence of the morning.

Harper knocked three times, hard, against the wooden door. It opened to reveal a woman in her sixties, short and plump, her features a softened mirror of Cindy's.

"Yes?" she asked.

Harper and Maguire showed their badges. "Good morning, ma'am. Special Agent Harper, CGIS. Is Cindy Glorevich here?"

The woman tilted her head, suspicion flashing across her face. "I'm her mother. Can I ask what this is about?"

"I'm sorry, I can't get into the details, ma'am," Maguire said smoothly. It's important we speak with her."

After a long moment, the woman turned and shouted over her shoulder. "Cindy! There are cops at the door!"

Footsteps. Then Cindy appeared in the hallway behind her mother. For a split second, her eyes widened—fear, recognition, guilt—but she smoothed it over. "It's ok, mom. I've got this. Go back to the kids."

Her mother scowled at them before retreating inside. Cindy shut the door firmly behind her.

"What's this about?" she asked, but her voice carried a thread of dread she couldn't hide.

"Some things have come up in our investigation since yesterday," Harper said evenly.

"What things?" she asked, her eyes flicked rapidly between them.

"I think it's better we discuss it down at the precinct," Maguire replied. "Keep things private."

"Do I have to?" she asked, her hand twitching toward her sleeve.

Harper stepped closer. "It's in your best interest to come voluntarily, Ms. Glorevich. Is your mother here to watch the kids?"

"Yes. I guess I can spare a few hours." She glanced toward the door. "I'll grab my car keys—"

"We'll drive," Maguire cut in.

"O-kay," she said slowly, her tone sliding into resignation. She cracked the door just enough to call inside, "Mom! I'll be back in a bit!" before shutting it again, cutting them off from the world inside.

Harper and Maguire led her to the sedan. She climbed into the back seat, the door shutting with a click that sounded much like a lock.

The ride to the precinct was quiet. Cindy sat in the back, her arms folded tight across her chest, staring out the windows as if the passing streets might offer her an escape. Harper caught her reflection in the glass once. Her jaw was tight, muscles flexing, lips pressed flat. She had the look of someone rehearing excuses she already knew wouldn't hold.

When they arrived, Maguire swiped them in through the side entrance. The hallways were still buzzing with morning traffic: Detectives clutching coffee, uniforms hustling paperwork. Harper kept his pace steady, not looking back until they reached the interview room.

Inside, the space was bare—just a table, three chairs, and the faint hum of the ceiling vent. Harper pulled out a chair for Cindy. She hesitated a beat fore sitting, her eyes flicking toward the mirrored wall and the camera mounted above it.

"This isn't an arrest," Harper said evenly as he set a bottle of water in front of her. "You came voluntarily, remember. We just need to clear a few things up."

Cindy gave a quick, brittle laugh. "You drag me down here and stick me in a box with a mirror, and you want me to believe this is casual?"

Maguire dropped into the seat across from her, folding his arms on the table. "We want to hear your side before assumptions get made. That's why you're here."

Cindy's gaze darted between them. She twisted the water bottle cap until it squeaked, her knuckles whitening. "I already told you what I know yesterday. Nothing's changed since then."

Harper leaned forward, resting his forearms on the table. "That's the thing, Cindy. A lot has changed since yesterday. And if you're smart, which I think you are, you'll want to be the first one to get in front of it. But as you pointed out, this isn't really a casual interview." He recited her Miranda rights, his tone steady, professional, then slid the waiver across. She signed fast, too fast, the pen scratching like she just wanted it out of the way.

"Alright," Maguire said, his voice flat. "Tell us again how you met the Rainiers."

Cindy took a breath, then repeated the script from the day before, but sweat had already started to pearl along her brow. Harper slid the bill of sale across the table. "Daniel signed here?"

She nodded.

"And Malia signed here?" He tapped the mismatched *R*. Another nod.

"In front of you?" Harper pressed.

"Of course."

He pulled out the photo of the notary log book he had taken and set it down next to the bill of sale. He pointed to the Rainiers' signatures. "Here too?"

"Yes," Cindy said. The sweat at her brow had increased to a full sheen.

"Do you see a problem with the signatures?" Harper asked.

Cindy's eyes flicked back and forth between the copies. "No...they don't have to be exact..."

Harper nodded at Maguire. "Tell us again what they looked like?"

Cindy looked at both of them. "Like I told you yesterday. He was tall, black, military. She was Hawaiian. Long, dark hair."

"You sure?" Maguire asked.

"Yes!" she said, exasperation evident in her voice.

Harper dropped the photo of Malia, short red hair blazing in the sunlight. "This was taken the day before she supposedly was in your home, signing that—" he stabbed his finger down on the bill of sale.

"I—she was wearing a hat," Cindy blurted. She folded her arms and tucked her hands into her armpits to hide them, but not before Harper noticed the tremor in her right hand.

"No." Harper cut in sharply, raising his palm to stop her. "She wasn't. Don't lie to me. Lying to a federal agent is a crime, Cindy."

Maguire leaned forward, his voice like gravel. "And so is murder."

Cindy's eyes flared. "I didn't—"

Harper again interrupted her. "No, Cindy. She wasn't wearing a hat. You didn't *see* her. We know that. What we don't know is *why*. This is a big deal, Cindy. But we need your help."

Cindy's eyes looked directly into Harper's. He had her.

"We need to know why you helped Asher Kincaid."

At the mention of Kincaid's name, Cindy's mouth closed and her face hardened. Her lips pressed into a thin, defiant line. She stared at him, unblinking. Harper felt the temperature in the room change. Whatever tether they'd had on her was gone.

"Let's take a quick break," Maguire suggested, picking up the same sense Harper had. "Do you want anything, Cindy? Water? Soda?"

"A diet coke would be great," she replied, her tone terse.

They stepped out of the room and walked over to the vending machine.

"I think we lost her," Harper said. "Something shifted as soon as I said Kincaid's name."

"She's brainwashed by that charlatan," Maguire responded, feeding a dollar bill into the machine.

255

"Yeah, agreed. I feel like we missed something." Harper took the soda from Maguire. "I think we need to bring in Fulton. I'll get this to her and wait for you guys in there. I want to ask her something else real quick."

Maguire raised his eyebrow. "Don't spook her," he said.

"I'll do my best."

Harper walked back in the room as Maguire pulled out his phone to call Fulton. He sat down across from Cindy again and slid the soda over to her. She glared at him as she pulled the tab open with a pop and took a long drink.

After she set the soda down, Harper began again, his tone softer this time. "Cindy, your kids. Where's their father?"

Cindy looked at him, but said nothing.

"Asher's their father, isn't he?"

A single tear rolled down Cindy's cheek. The beating at her temples was visible as she clenched her teeth together repeatedly. But still, she said nothing.

"I can't imagine how tough it must be, raising them on your own, with just your mother to help. Struggling to make ends meet with your notary job. And all the while, he offers to help you, but isn't *there* for them like he should be..."

"You have no idea what you're talking about," she finally said. Her tone was defiant, her lips pursed.

Just then, the door to the interview room opened, and Darrin Fulton walked in with Maguire behind him. He set a folder down neatly, pulled out a chair, and sat across from Cindy. His pen clicked once before he spoke.

"Ms. Glorevich, my name is Senior Deputy Prosecuting Attorney Darrin Fulton. I represent the King County Prosecutor's Office, and I'm assigned to this case." His tone was clipped, courtroom-polished. "I want to make something very clear at the outset. We are not here because of *you.* We are here because of Asher Kincaid."

Cindy's eyes flicked toward Harper, then back to Fulton, her lips still in a thin line.

"My role," Fulton continued, "is to evaluate evidence and determine whether prosecution is viable. At this moment, Ms. Glorevich, you occupy a gray zone. You have exposure to potential charges—forgery, conspiracy, accessory after the fact, possibly more—but my office is not interested in pursuing you if your cooperation leads us directly to Kincaid."

Cindy said nothing. She continued to stare forward, barely blinking. Fulton let the silence stretch.

He opened the folder, slid a single-page document toward her, and turned it so the signature line faced her. "This is a formal proffer agreement. In plain language, it grants you total immunity from prosecution for your involvement in this matter, contingent on your full cooperation and truthful testimony. Once signed, this binds my office. You would not be charged for anything you disclose. Not now, and not later."

Fulton laced his fingers together on the table. "This is, to be blunt, the only opportunity you will receive. If you decline, this offer expires the moment you leave this room. There will be no second changes. Do you understand?"

Cindy stared at the paper. Her shoulders raised and lowered several times as she inhaled through her nose. For a moment, Harper thought she might reach for the pen. Instead, she pushed it slowly back across the table, her hand steady.

"No."

Fulton blinked, as if he hadn't heard correctly. "Excuse me?"

"I said no." Her tone sharpened, carrying a sudden, almost zealous certainty. "I don't need your deal. I haven't done anything wrong. And Father Kincaid—" her voice hitched, " —is a good man." She leaned back in her chair and crossed her arms in front of her again.

The word *Father* hung in the air. Harper felt a cold weight settle in his stomach.

Harper began softly. "Cindy, I want you to think long and hard on this. Think of your children—"

"*Fuck* you," she spat. "Get me a lawyer."

The room fell silent.

"Yeah, that's right. I'm done talking to you pricks without an attorney."

Fulton exhaled slowly, the mask of professionalism cracking for just a second before he snapped the folder shut. "Very well. Then we're finished here." He slid his card over to her. "Have your attorney give me a call."

Cindy tore his card in half slowly, then flicked it back at him.

"Go fuck yourself." She stared at Fulton, venom in her eyes.

They all stood up as one and filed into the viewing room, the door closing with a soft click. Through the one-way glass, Cindy sat at the table, arms folded tight across her chest, eyes fixed forward as if she could bore a hole through the glass itself.

Fulton tossed his folder down on the counter with a snap. "Jesus fuck. You two weren't kidding. She's not just uncooperative, she's indoctrinated."

"She's in deep," Maguire said quietly.

"Deep?" Fulton shot back. "She tore my card in half. In twenty-two years, I've had gang members, murderers, and predators try to bluff me. But I've never seen someone spit on full immunity like that." He ran a hand through his neatly combed hair, messing it for the first time Harper had seen. "She doesn't think she *needs* us. That's not deep, that's delusional."

Harper leaned forward on the counter. "It's worse than that. He's the father of her kids. That's why she won't break. Not for a deal, not for anything. She thinks protecting him is protecting them."

Fulton froze mid-step, staring back at Harper. "You're serious?"

"As a heart attack," Harper said. "We missed it before, but it's obvious now."

"Shit." Maguire shook his head.

"Christ almighty," Fulton muttered. For a long beat he said nothing, just stared at Cindy through the glass. Finally, he shook his head. "Alright, cut her loose. We'll regroup. If she won't save herself, we'll have to bury Kincaid without her."

The room fell into silence. On the other side of the glass, Cindy picked up her empty soda can, set it down neatly, and resumed her cold, unwavering stare. A soldier for Kincaid, even here.

CHAPTER
THIRTY

Afternoon.

Maguire's desk looked like a paper bomb had gone off. Case files were stacked at odd angles, yellow sticky notes clinging like leaves after a storm, half-drained coffee mugs scattered. Harper sat across from him, elbows on his knees, staring at the floor.

Cindy's face was still fresh in his mind. The way she'd looked at them, unafraid, unbroken, and *defiant.* Like she'd already picked her side, and it wasn't theirs.

Maguire tossed a folder onto the pile in front of them. "Well. That was a waste of shoe leather."

"Not a total waste," Harper said, finally looking up. "She showed us something important. We're not cracking her. Not now, maybe not ever. She's too far gone. Which means we need another angle."

Maguire leaned back in his chair, fingers laced behind his head. "Lucky for us, I've got just the guy." He tapped the folder with one finger. "Ezra Silas. You remember the name?"

Harper nodded. "From the Foundation records. Money in, money out. Big numbers."

"Bigger than any of those women could've covered," Maguire said. He flipped the folder open and pulled out a photocopied rap sheet, spreading it across the desk. "Armed robbery. Assault. Narcotics distribution. Multiple priors, all violent. Did six years, got out in '19. Should've gone right back in after he damn near beat a guy to death in a bar fight, but guess who bailed him out and hooked him up with a lawyer."

Harper signed. "Kincaid."

"Bingo," Maguire said. "And now Silas is our in. He's not loyal like Cindy. He's a business partner. Business partners crack when the money stops flowing."

Harper studied the file, the mugshot staring back at him. Silas had a square jaw, a crooked nose, and tattoos creeping his neck. He looked like the kind of guy who thrived on fear and used it like currency.

"He's gotta still be dealing to be producing the kind of numbers we saw in the books," Harper said.

Maguire smirked. "Oh yeah. Narcotics has him flagged. I gave them a call. They're going to set up a buy. We'll have him in cuffs before he even realizes the game's changed."

Harper sat back, the tension in his shoulders easing just a fraction. For the first time since Cindy walked out of the interview room, he felt the shift, the weight sliding off dead ends and onto something they could grab.

"Alright," he said. "Let's squeeze him."

The call to Narcotics went fast. Within an hour, a task force sergeant and two detectives were crammed into Maguire's cubicle, the air thick with burnt coffee and the stink of old carpet. They pored over Silas' sheet, cross-referencing recent tips, known hangouts, and phone pings that put him in South Seattle twice a week.

"Guy's sloppy," Sergeant Mark Carver said, flipping through a log of surveillance notes. He looked more like a washed-up biker than a cop: short, thick around the middle with a protruding gut, a long graying ponytail trailing down his back, and a goatee that ran halfway down his chest. A silver badge gleamed at his hip, but it looked almost out of place next to the biker cuff strapped to his wrist.

"He deals out of his car. Same silver Tahoe, plates registered to his sister. Works late. Starts circling around nine or ten, meets his regulars. If you want him, we can have an informant make the call tonight. Classic controlled buy with a wired up informant."

Maguire leaned back in his chair, eyeing the sergeant's beard with a smirk. "Jesus, Carver, you moonlighting with ZZ Top or what?"

Carver didn't look up from the file. "I get that a lot," he said flatly, thumbing another page.

Harper hid a smile.

"Do it. While you're getting your buy ready, we've got other angles to chase. When you're set, give us a call. After Silas bites, we'll help box him in. But instead of a narcotics interrogation, we'll take first crack."

Carver nodded once, already pulling out his phone. "You'll have your buy tonight. Just be ready when we call. Silas doesn't run on schedule, he runs on impulse. That makes him dangerous."

He started dialing, lining up the informant and buy money, his low voice carrying over the low hum of the cubicle computers.

Harper stepped away from the table, leaning against the wall near the window. Outside, the September sun had gone flat behind a gray marine layer, the city wrapped in a dull haze. His hand rested on the Glock holstered at his hip. Familiar. Steady.

Maguire joined him, slipping a toothpick into the corner of his mouth. "You look like you're about to storm Normandy."

Harper gave a dry half-smile. "Just don't like sloppy operators with nothing to lose. Guys like Silas, they go for broke."

"That's why we're not giving him the chance." Maguire clapped him on the shoulder. "Relax. It's a buy-bust, not a gunfight."

Harper didn't answer. He just watched the city through the window, the streets already buzzing with evening traffic. Somewhere out there, Ezra Silas was tuning up for a night's work. Work that helped finance Kincaid's cult.

Maguire finally broke the silence. "We've got a few hours until narcotics is ready. Know what that means?"

Harper glanced at him. "Homework."

"Bingo. House church meet tonight. Kincaid's flock, women included. If Cindy won't talk, maybe one of her sisters-in-devotion will without knowing it. Let's get eyes on who's coming and going."

Harper nodded. "Alright. Let's see what God's chosen family does when they think no one's watching."

He walked to the vending machine, fed in a crumpled dollar, and studied the buttons. For a moment he hovered over the diet soda, then changed his mind and hit the root beer instead. The can dropped with a metallic clatter. He cracked it open, the hiss and sweetness hitting him at once. One sip and the taste pulled him back—back to warm summer nights on the porch, a tired old truck cooling in the driveway, and his father's voice carrying over the hum of crickets.

•••••

Then.

Eighteen-year old Jake felt tears sting his eyes as he stuffed clothes into his bag. His chest hitched in uneven spasms as he fought to keep control.

She doesn't love me anymore.

He had gone to Mackenzie's house that afternoon, the promise ring burning a hole in his pocket. He was going to ask her to wait for him while he was at Basic. Too young to marry—barely—but he had a plan.

He would go to boot camp. They would write letters during the eight weeks while he transformed into a Coast Guardsman. Then she would fly out for graduation, and he'd propose for real. He had even researched ring stores in Cape May, planning to use his recruit pay for a modest diamond. After graduation, he'd get his first duty station, and they would plan the wedding long-distance. A year later, when she finished high school, they'd marry before he shipped to A-School.

Jake loved Mackenzie. A year younger, athletic and headstrong, she had been his anchor through the storm of late adolescence. They had met after another boy broke her heart on a school field trip. Jake had sat with her on the ride home, holding her as she sobbed, never asking for anything in return. By the time the bus pulled into the parking lot, she had kissed him and asked him to call her.

From there, their romance had bloomed. She was his first dance. His first time. The first girl he ever said "I love you" to. The first person he imagined a future with.

Which was why, when he laid out his plan that afternoon, he hadn't expected her reaction.

Mackenzie listened quietly, her hands folded in her lap. When he finished, she gave a smile, small and strained, the kind that never reached her eyes. Jake felt it immediately, something in his gut tightening.

He tried to ignore it at first, pushing ahead, waiting for her excitement to catch up to his. But her silence lingered, heavy in the space between them.

"What do you think?" he asked finally.

"It sounds...nice," she said after a pause. Her voice was thin, unenthusiastic.

Jake's chest hollowed. He knew that tone. He'd felt it before when friends were trying to spare someone's feelings. The way her eyes slid away from his, the way her fingers twisted in her sweatshirt. All of it told him more than her words.

"Do you still love me?" he asked quietly.

She didn't answer. Not with words. Her silence was an answer of its own.

Jake swallowed hard. "You want to break up, don't you?"

Mackenzie finally looked up at him. Her eyes brimmed with tears, her lips trembling as she gave a single, pained nod.

"Jake, I'll always love you," she began. "But this is too much. I want to enjoy my senior year. I want to go to football games. To youth group. I want to go to prom again and not have to explain that my boyfriend is off in the military."

He nodded, his chest numb. They had hugged, promising to stay friends. He drove his beat-up pickup truck the two miles home, and went to his room where he wordlessly finished packing for Basic. When he finally had his bags zipped up, he fell to his knees and buried his head in his hands, and let the tears flow.

That night, after a final family dinner together, Raymond asked Jake to come sit on the porch with him. As was tradition, Raymond brought two bottled root beers as they sat side-by-side on the wooden steps. Raymond was quiet beside him, the porch light buzzing faintly overhead, the crickets loud in the summer dark. For a while, Jake didn't say anything. Just sat with his elbows on his knees, watching the gravel drive like it might hold the answers.

"I know that look," Raymond said finally, his voice low, steady. "Feels like the world just caved in on you."

Jake nodded, unable to trust his voice.

"I noticed Mackenzie's absence at dinner tonight. I'm guessing that has a bit to do with it."

Jake nodded again.

Raymond took a slow breath. "Son, there are two kinds of hurt in this life. The kind that breaks you, and the kind that makes you. You don't get to choose the pain. You only get to choose what you do with it."

Jake lifted his head, eyes wet. "I thought she was it, Dad. I thought I knew."

Raymond's gaze softened, but his tone carried weight. "That's the thing about love, it's not just feelings. It's choosing the best for the other person. Even if that's not you." He let the words hang a moment, then added, "You can't make her choose you, Jake."

Jake swallowed hard, the words cutting deeper than the heartbreak.

Raymond leaned back, eyes on the night sky. "You're at a crossroads right now. She's still in high school, and you're moving forward with your life. You are choosing a life of service, of integrity.

You've got a journey ahead of you." He took a long drink from the root beer. "The Coast Guard's gonna break you down and build you back up. Don't drag this heartbreak with you. Let it make you tougher, but not harder. Let it push you to be the man you were meant to be. One day you'll look back, and you'll thank God she left, because you'll have become more than she ever could've imagined."

Jake looked at his father, trying to breathe through the ache in his chest. Raymond's words didn't fix the pain, but they gave it shape. They gave it something to carry instead of to drown in.

Raymond reached over and gripped his son's shoulder. "So stand tall, tomorrow, Jake. Don't let this be the thing that defines you. Let it be the fire that tempers you. Integrity's not about how you feel. It's about what you do when it costs you."

CHAPTER
THIRTY-ONE

Evening.

They parked two blocks down from the address Maguire had flagged off the Foundation's files. Buried in a stack of "outreach reimbursements", the same property was listed over and over, always coded as a "Tuesday expense." They were dressed for surveillance in the cool Seattle air: Maguire in jeans and a gray-sweatshirt with "USNA" printed across the front, Harper in jeans and a green flannel rolled at the sleeves.

The older rambler itself sagged behind overgrown hedges and a chain-link fence gone to rust. The porch light was on, throwing a dull yellow glow across the patchy front yard. A row of mismatched cars lined the curb: dented sedans, a minivan with a cracked windshield, and a late model Lexus that didn't belong.

"Looks like Bible study night," Maguire muttered, lifting his binoculars.

From their vantage point, Harper watched the trickle of arrivals. Mostly women, some with kids in tow. A few men too, though they walked a half-step behind, eyes down. Everyone carried something. Casserole dishes. Bibles. Grocery bags that sagged with supplies.

"They're not dressed for Sunday," Harper noted. Jeans, sweatshirts, everyday clothes. Normal enough to vanish into any

Seattle street. But the way they moved, the hush as they entered, made it feel different. Coordinated. Almost rehearsed.

They sat in silence for a few minutes, the rumble of passing traffic filling the car. Finally, Harper said, "I want to get closer."

Maguire lowered the binoculars. "Closer how?"

"Inside."

Maguire gave him a sharp look. "You walk in there, you're tipping Kincaid that we're on to him."

Harper shook his head. "Cindy already tipped him. You know it, I know it. He's expecting us. So what's the harm in me listening to the show he puts on?"

Maguire leaned back, chewing the inside of his cheek. "It's a cult meeting, Jake. Not Sunday school. You sure you want to walk into that snake pit?"

"I grew up in places like that, Tate," Harper said. "Revival tents, potluck basements, Bible camp cabins. I know the rhythm, the language. They won't look twice at me."

"Kincaid will," Maguire said sharply.

Harper said nothing.

For a long moment, Maguire studied him, then sighed. "Alright. But you keep your phone on you. I'm going to text you every ten minutes. You stop responding, I'm coming in after you. No hero shit."

Harper gave a small nod. "I have a better idea." He dialed Maguire, then locked the phone while the call was open and slipped the phone in his pocket. "Poor man's wire. I'll keep the call open. You'll hear everything going on. If I'm in trouble, the safe word is 'lighthouse.' You hear that, you come get me."

Maguire laughed and shook his head. "Lighthouse. Of course."

270

Harper slipped out of the car and started up the block, the faint sound of music drifting from the house. An acoustic guitar and voices rising in practiced unison could be heard three houses down. As he approached, he pulled the bottom hem of his flannel up and over his badge and gun, making him look like any Seattle hipster.

He walked up the cracked path to the front porch, the faint hum of the guitar and voices spilling through the thin walls. The door was half-open, propped by a shoe. A sign read "All Welcome." He slipped inside.

The living room had been converted into a sanctuary of sorts. Couches were pushed to the walls. Folding chairs lined the carpet in neat rows, the air warm with the smell of crockpots and candle wax. A dozen women sat scattered through the room, heads bowed and voices low. A few children leaned against their mothers, coloring quietly or fidgeting with toys.

At the front of the room stood Asher Kincaid. No pulpit, just a mismatched wooden chair turned backward, his forearms resting on the back as he leaned toward the group. The posture was casual, intimate even. His voice carried across the room with practiced ease.

"Faith isn't just what you show on Sundays," Kincaid was saying. His voice was warm, conversational, almost gentle. "It's what you sacrifice when nobody's watching. When it costs you something. That's where the proof is."

Heads nodded. A soft "Amen" rippled.

"Take Suzanne here," Kincaid continued, turning toward a woman in her thirties near the front row. She lowered her gaze, but a faint smile tugged at her lips. "Suzanne has given herself fully to

God's commandments. She has borne children, just as Scripture commands in Genesis 1:28. 'Be fruitful and multiply, fill the earth and subdue it.'"

A murmur of approval passed through the room. Harper took a seat in the back row. Nobody challenged him. He knew house churches thrived on the image of open arms.

Kincaid leaned forward on the chairback, lowering his tone to a confidential hush. "But fruitfulness is more than children, brothers, and sisters. Paul wrote in First Corinthians that a husband and wife must not deprive one another, except for prayer. And in First Timothy, we are told that those who serve the prophet are worthy of double honor." His gaze swept the room, pausing when it found Harper. The faintest flicker of recognition crossed his face before he smiled again, easy and warm.

The room was silent now, breath held.

"So what does that mean?" he asked softly, letting the silence deepen before answering. "It means that obedience in marriage is obedience to God. That when the prophet calls, the faithful do not withhold. A husband honors God when he allows his wife to serve. A wife honors God when she gives herself, body and soul, to the prophet. In that obedience, blessing flows."

The air seemed to tighten. A few women nodded, murmuring assent. One man shifted in his chair, lips pursed, but he kept his head bowed.

"Sacrifice is never easy," Kincaid went on, his voice rising again. "It cuts. It hurts. As men, handing your wife to another may feel like betrayal. But jealousy comes from the enemy. As women, lying with the prophet may feel like rebellion. But the prophet's seed is not betrayal, it is blessing itself. To give joy and pleasure to your prophet, to bear his children, is to multiply God's will in this world."

His cadence lifted now, the practiced rhythm of a revival preacher. "That is true faith! When you give not just from your wallet, but from your body, your home, your very life! That is when heaven takes notice. And God multiplies what remains!"

The chorus of "Amen" that followed was uneven, shakier this time, but still obedient.

As if rooted in fear. Harper sat still in his seat at the back of the room, hands folded, but inside his pulse quickened. He knew this cadence. The rise and fall, the careful weaving of scripture into rhythm, the way a verse became a weapon when put in the wrong hands. He'd heard it in revival tents, at summer camps, and in churches where people shouted "Amen" because silence would have felt like dissent.

Only this time, the twist was sharper. Darker. He could hear the rot behind the words, like mildew hidden under fresh paint. Where his father had once spoken of service and humility, Kincaid preached ownership. Where Harper had once learned that love was patient, Kincaid dressed lust up as blessing.

Kincaid's voice dripped with charm as he told the husbands to give up their wives to him, and the wives to give up their bodies. Harper's face stayed unreadable, but bile rose in his throat. He glanced at the bowed heads around him. Women nodding in weary obedience, and men too cowed or complicit to speak.

For the first time since the Rainiers disappeared, Harper understood—viscerally—how Kincaid had convinced them all to play along.

And then, like a whisper from another lifetime, he heard his father on the porch: *"Integrity's not about how you feel. It's about what you do when it costs you."*

The memory settled, grounding him. Kincaid could wear the mask of righteousness all he wanted, but Harper knew the truth: masks cracked under pressure. Integrity held.

"And sometimes," Kincaid continued, never missing a beat, "God sends us strangers. Men on a journey. Men searching for something." His gaze locked on Harper's, the words floating between them like a dare.

Harper sat a little straighter in the folding chair, hands loose in his lap. He could feel the weight of the phone in his pocket, knowing Maguire was listening. He met Kincaid's eyes, steady as stone. He smiled and nodded once, then said loudly enough for Kincaid to hear:

"And some men don't search. They just take what was never theirs to claim."

The air snapped. A few women clutched their children closer. A man's chair scraped as he half-stood, fists clenched. Irritation flickered across Kincaid's face, a twitch at the corner of his left eye, before his smile reasserted itself like plaster over a crack.

"Tell me, Jacob Harper," Kincaid said, drawing out the name like a schoolmaster calling on a child. "Have you come seeking God? Or have you come to intimidate His servants?" His arms spread wide, the posture of a shepherd shielding his flock, though his eyes stayed fixed on Harper.

"I'm not the one twisting his words to lure women into my bed, Asher."

"You'll speak to the prophet with respect!" one of the men barked, springing to his feet.

Kincaid lifted a calming hand. "Peace, brothers and sisters, peace. We were all seekers once. We were all wanderers before the Way found us." His voice was velvet again, gentle enough to soothe the room back into submission. The man reluctantly sank into his chair.

But Harper didn't look away. He let the silence between them stretch like wire.

Kincaid's smile thinned. "Strangers who come to mock the Word—they do not leave unchanged." His tone was for the flock, but his eyes never left Harper's. "The fire of truth burns away pretenders. Either they are purified...or they are consumed."

Harper didn't flinch under Kincaid's gaze. His voice stayed level, but each word cut like glass.

"You preach sacrifice," Harper said, fire burning in his gut, "but you twist Paul's words until they serve your lust. First Corinthians wasn't written to give you women. It was written so husbands and wives could serve *each other* in love."

A stir rippled through the room. A few heads lifted, uncertain.

"And Genesis?" Harper pressed on. "You love quoting 'be fruitful,' but you leave out the part where Adam and Eve walked together, side by side. Not under the thumb of a self-proclaimed prophet."

For a split second, Kincaid's smile faltered. His jaw twitched, his fingers flexing against the chairback before he forced the mask back into place.

"Careful, Jacob," he said, voice tighter, the warmth thinning into steel. "Scripture cuts both ways. The prophets were mocked in their time, too. And those who mocked them—"

"—they were real prophets," Harper cut in. His tone sharpened. "Not thieves dressing lust up as a blessing. Not little boys anointed by their mommies because daddy couldn't handle a snake."

Gasps spread through the flock. A woman clutched her child tighter. A man shoved to his feet, fists clenched. Kincaid's eyes flared—raw, angry—for the first time. He didn't motion for calm.

Instead, two men near the door stepped forward, shoulders squared, blocking Harper's exit.

Harper held his stare. "Do they know Asher? About Noah? About what you did? How you killed your own brother?"

Kincaid leaned harder on the chair, the casual posture gone rigid, his knuckles pale against the wood. His voice was stripped bare to anger. "You've got a wife at home, don't you, Jacob? Carrying your child. A boy, if I remember right." His eyes gleamed with menace, the smile gone sharp and humorless. "Wouldn't it be a shame if temptation—or tragedy—visited your house before the harvest came due?"

The air in the room tightened, brittle as glass. Every face turned toward Harper. The men by the door edged closer, not rushing him, just closing the circle.

Harper stayed still, pulse pounding, refusing to look away. His left hand dropped down to his side, to where his holstered Glock was hidden by the flannel. His father's words rang in him again— *integrity's about what you do when it costs you.* He whispered one word. "Lighthouse."

"What was that?" Kincaid asked, as the men stepped even closer still.

And then a voice cut through the charged silence.

"Jake."

Harper turned his head just enough to see Maguire standing in the doorway, his large frame silhouetting the darkness outside, his badge glinting on his belt, his pistol visible at his hip. His tone was firm, measured, but his eyes were hard. "We need to go."

The room shifted, murmurs rolling as Kincaid sat back, smiling like a man who'd just tested the fence and found where it would bend.

Harper backed away from his chair slowly, meeting Kincaid's stare one last time. No words, just the steady weight of defiance. Then he moved toward Maguire, the two men at the door parting reluctantly as the investigators stepped out into the cool night air.

CHAPTER
THIRTY-TWO

Night.

The sedan was silent for three blocks before Maguire finally spoke. His hands were tight on the wheel, teeth grinding his molars down to dust.

"Did you lose your goddamn mind back there?" he said at last. "You don't poke a rattlesnake just to see if it bites."

Harper sat back in the passenger seat, arms folded, his eyes on the rows of streetlights flickering past. "I wasn't poking. I was testing."

"Testing?" Maguire shot him a look. "You walked straight into his den, called him out in front of his flock, brought up his mother and his dead brother, and let him get close enough to breathe a threat about your pregnant wife. That's not testing, that's suicide."

Harper didn't answer right away. He could still hear Kincaid's voice, honey dripping over poison, telling husbands to hand over their wives, telling women to serve their prophet. The bile was still there, bitter in the back of his throat.

"He showed us more in fifteen minutes than we've seen in days," Harper said finally. "His ego's too big to hide. He didn't shut me down, didn't throw me out. He wanted to spar, wanted to prove he could twist the Bible better than me. And he made it clear he's not running. He thinks he's untouchable."

Maguire snorted, shaking his head. "Yeah, well, I don't want to find out how untouchable he is while I'm zipping your wife into a widow's dress."

Harper turned, meeting his partner's glare. "I needed to see it. Needed to hear it for myself. Now I know. He's not just playing prophet. He believes this. Every word. And so do they. That's why they'll follow him straight off a cliff."

Maguire was quiet a beat, then blew a breath through his nose. "You scare the shit out of me sometimes, Coastie."

Harper looked back out the window, his reflection ghosted in the glass. "Good. Then we're both paying attention."

They drove in silence for another block before Maguire flicked on the turn signal, his tone shifting back to business. "Narcotics texted while you were playing Bible trivia with discount Moses. Silas is working tonight. They're setting up the buy right now."

Harper straightened, his pulse steadying. "Good. Let's put this one in cuffs and see how loyal he is to our prophet."

Maguire smirked around his toothpick. "Amen to that."

They pulled into a coffee shop parking lot and turned off the car.

Carver's mini-van was already there, parked nose-out by the dumpster. He leaned against the hood, wearing a faded PD raid vest, sipping something that looked too black to be coffee.

"Evening, gentlemen," Carver said, tossing the cup into a bin. "Here's the play. Our friendly is meeting Silas in about thirty at the Safeway lot over on Rainier Avenue. He'll make the buy, get back in his own ride, and roll. Silas will think it's business as usual. We let him pull out, get moving, then we box him on the street. Safer than jamming him in a crowded lot."

"Rainier Ave. Ironic," Harper said.

Maguire nodded, then turned to Carver. "What's our role?"

"You two vest up and ride tail-end with me," Carver said. "My guys will initiate the stop, I'll call the move. If Silas decides to rabbit or draw down, I want extra hands in the stack. We'll pull him out hard and clean, cuff him curbside. Then he's yours to work."

Harper popped the truck of Maguire's sedan. Ballistic vests sat folded inside, black plates dull under the dim lot lights. He strapped his on, the familiar weight settling over the tension in his gut. Maguire did the same, adjusting the front zipper snug over his chest.

"Your CI solid?" Harper asked.

Carver gave a dry chuckle. "He's not Ivy league, but he knows his part. He's facing some serious jail time, and detox is a bitch to do in jail."

Harper shut the trunk with a solid *thunk.* "Ready when you are, then."

Carver gestured them toward his Tahoe. "Convoy forms up in ten. Once the friendly checks in, it's game time. Don't blink, Silas is the kind who'll burn rubber first and think second."

Harper exchanged a quick look with Maguire, the kind of look only partners shared: a mix of readiness and the quiet acknowledgment that things could go sideways fast.

"Showtime," Maguire said, slipping into the driver's seat.

•••••

The Safeway lot was half full, sodium lights buzzing overhead, throwing long shadows across rows of shopping carts and sun-faded sedans. Shoppers shuffled in and out, bags swinging. Ordinary life, oblivious to the sting about to unfold in the far corner.

Harper and Maguire sat two rows back in their sedan, vests hidden under sweatshirts draped over their chests, ready to pull off at a moment's notice. Their eyes were on the silver Tahoe idling by the garden center entrance. Silas. Even at a distance, Harper could make out his restless posture behind the wheel—window cracked, cigarette ember glowing like a tiny beacon.

Carver's voice crackled low over the tac net. *"Friendly is mobile. Everybody sit tight."*

Across the lot, a battered Honda rolled in. The informant, greasy hair under a ballcap pulled low, drove casual, swinging into the space two slots down from Silas. He cut the engine, got out, and stretched like he was just another late-night shopper.

Silas flicked his cigarette out the window, then closed the window. The CI slid into the Tahoe's passenger seat, door shutting with a hollow thump.

"The deal is starting," one of the narcotics detectives said over comms, posted at the far edge of the lot.

Seconds ticked. Harper's eyes scanned the rows of parked cars, the entrances, the oblivious shoppers passing within twenty feet of a felony. His hand hovered near the radio clipped under his sweatshirt, ready.

"Friendly gave the signal," Carver's voice came, clipped. "Buy's complete."

The passenger door opened. The informant got out, gave a lazy wave like he'd just talked sports, and ambled back to his Honda. He started the car and pulled out of the row, headed toward the lot exit.

Silas stayed put, lighting another cigarette. He didn't even bother to check his mirror.

"Deal confirmed. Friendly handed over the dope. We've got PC," the narcotics detective from earlier said over comms, using the shorthand term for probable cause.

Bingo.

"Stand by," Carver said. "We let him go mobile. Box him on the street, not in front of soccer moms with shopping carts."

Maguire drummed his fingers once on the wheel, tension bleeding into motion. "Come on, Silas. Let's go."

As if on cue, brake lights flared. The Tahoe rolled forward, turn signal blinking lazily for a left onto Rainier Avenue.

"All units," Carver's voice snapped, sharper now, "move with him. Tail for position, wait for my mark for takedown."

Engines rumbled to life around the lot. Unmarked units peeled off from their corners, headlights snapping on in practiced sequence.

Harper pulled off the sweatshirt draped over his body, exposing the CGIS marked vest underneath. He gave Maguire a quick look. "This is it."

Maguire smirked. "Hope this traffic stop doesn't come with any fireworks. I don't need any more days off."

They eased in behind the convoy of ghost cars. The tac net filled with clipped updates:

"South on Rainier. Approaching South Andover."

"Left turn, South Oregon."

"Might be a burn run," Carver cut in. "Dominguez, switch up. Take Alaska and parallel."

"Copy," another voice answered.

Harper pointed at the green Tacoma surging ahead. "That's Dominguez. Stay on him."

"On it," Maguire responded, pushing the pedal down causing the sedan to drop a gear to match speed.

The radio crackled again. "Passing 39th."

"Turning south on 41st."

Harper thumbed his phone map. "Flip it. Go north on 38th, there's a park. Conover cuts right past it."

Maguire swung the sedan around, engine growling low.

"Turning right on Conover," the tail unit confirmed.

"Parking lot there," Harper pointed. A small community center sat on the corner, its rear lot spilling onto Conover like a funnel.

Maguire cut the lights and rolled in, tucking the sedan against the back edge.

Seconds later, headlights swept the upper lot. Silas's Tahoe nosed in, killed its lights, and went dark.

"He's onto the tail," Maguire said flatly.

"Yeah, he burned them." Harper keyed the radio. "We've got eyes from the community center lot. Holding here. Best box-in spot you'll get."

"Copy," Carver's voice came back. "Alright, converge on the community center. Harper, Maguire, you guys jump in the box as soon as you see us move in."

"Copy," Harper replied.

The sedan sat in tense silence. Silas' Tahoe remained dark, but Harper could hear the faint tick of cooling metal through the cracked window.

Then—headlights. Dominguez' green Tacoma swung into the lot, followed by a Subaru and Carver's minivan. The three vehicles fanned around Silas' Tahoe like wolves circling prey.

The Tahoe's headlights flared, engine coughing to life.

"He's gonna run!" Harper barked.

Maguire jammed the gearshift forward. Their sedan lunged, emergency lights and siren exploding to life in unison with the other units.

They closed fast, boxing in the Tahoe. The Tacoma on the driver's side, Subaru on the passenger, Maguire's sedan on the nose. For a heartbeat, it looked contained.

Then the driver's door flew wide. A mountain of a man spilled out, shoving past the gap and sprinting hard toward the playground.

"On foot!" Harper shouted, already out the door. His Converse slapped against asphalt as he took off after Ezra Silas.

Silas was bigger than Harper expected. His broad shoulders filled his short-sleeve shirt, muscled packed into a frame like a linebacker. Sweat glistened on his bald head under the orange glow of the lights. And he was fast.

But Harper was faster.

"Stop! Police!" Harper's voice cut through the night. Silas didn't break stride.

They tore through the playground, bark chips spraying beneath their feet, dodging swings and a low slide. Silas juked left, then hard right, cutting a zigzag toward the street. Harper ignored the feints, driving straight through, shaving off distance.

Five feet. Four.

Silas risked a glance over his shoulder, just a flicker of hesitation. It was enough. His foot caught a low divot in the grass. His leg buckled and he sprawled forward, face-first into the wet earth.

Harper was on him before he could rise. "Silas! You're under—"

WHAM. A rear elbow smashed into Harper's cheekbone. White light exploded in his vision, blood hot on his face. A wave of dizziness washed over him, but he pushed through the pain pounding in his temple. Gritting his teeth, Harper clamped onto Silas' left arm, wrenching it behind his back. Silas roared, surging up, raw power driving against Harper's leverage.

"Not today," Harper growled, and drove his own elbow into the back of Silas' skull.

The big man sagged back to the ground, groaning. In a practiced motion, Harper snapped the cuffs over his wrists just as Carver and the others arrived, shoes pounding on the grass.

"Damn, son. You've got wheels," Carver puffed, catching his breath.

Maguire's eyes locked onto Harper's bloodied cheek. "You good?"

Harper stood, chest heaving. "Had worse."

"You're gonna be wearing a shiner," Maguire said, squinting at the spreading bruise. "But it's not broken."

Silas groaned again as detectives yanked him upright, fury twisting his face.

"That wasn't smart, Silas," one of them said.

"Fuck you," he spat, lips curling.

"You first," the detective shot back, shoving him toward the waiting cars.

Harper rolled his shoulders, the ache in his cheekbone pulsing with every step as he turned away. His pulse was still jacked from the chase, but the night air cooled the sweat on his neck, sharp with the smell of cut grass and exhaust.

Carver clapped him once on the back as they passed. "Nice collar for a Fed. But don't make a habit of eating elbows for free."

Harper gave him a thin smile, wiped the blood at his eye with the back of his hand, and kept walking toward their sedan. Maguire fell in beside him, muttering around his toothpick.

"Hell of a sprint, partner. But you know that was the easy part, right?"

Harper grunted, eyes already sliding back to the Tahoe surrounded by flashing reds and blues. *The real work starts when Silas opens his mouth.*

CHAPTER
THIRTY-THREE

Midnight.

The same interview room they'd used for Cindy felt smaller tonight, the walls closing in under the low fluorescent hum. The table was bare except for a bottle of water, condensation pooling into a ring.

Ezra Silas sat cuffed to the steel ring bolted into the tabletop, shoulders slouched, legs spread wide like he owned the place. His lip was split from the chase, but the grin he wore was all teeth. He'd signed his Miranda waiver without hesitation, bragging that he "knew the game" and wasn't about to get tripped up by a couple of narcs.

"Man, you clowns really think you got me?" he said, voice carrying that mix of bravado and slur from a hit of adrenaline. "I'll be out before you finish your paperwork. Little possession beef, maybe intent to distribute if you're feeling spicy. Seen it before. Walked out before."

Harper sat down across from him, calm and quiet, sliding a legal pad onto the table. Maguire leaned against the wall, arms crossed, letting the silence hang.

Silas filled it fast. "What, you think cuffing me out in front of a playground's gonna make me sweat? I know the game, man. You pop me, I sit a day, maybe two, and I'm back on the street. All you did was waste gas money." He leaned forward aggressively, eyes gleaming with cocky energy. "Hell, maybe I'll file a complaint. Pretty sure that boy scout over here cracked my skull."

Harper didn't bite. He flipped a page in his notebook like he was checking a grocery list.

Maguire finally spoke, his voice low and dry. "Ezra, you're treating this like it's about dope. Like that's the biggest problem in your life right now."

Silas grinned wider, exposing the gold cap on his molar. "Isn't it? I mean, hey, we're in Seattle. It's a slap on the wrist here. Everyone knows that."

Harper looked up from his notes then, calm as stone. "No. Not even close."

Silas smirked, leaning back in his chair. "So, lay it on me, Detective." The last word dripped with sarcasm.

"It's *Special Agent*, actually," Harper corrected, flipping his badge open and laying it flat on the table. "Coast Guard Investigative Service."

Silas leaned forward to peer at it. "Special Agent—"

"Which means earlier? That elbow to my face? Assault on a federal officer." Harper's voice stayed even. "That alone can get you eight years in the pen. The *federal* pen."

"Wait, what—"

" —and that's before we even bring up the murder—"

" —what the fuck?!"

" —which falls under both State and Federal jurisdiction. Since it happened at sea, we're looking at Murder in the SMTJ—"

Silas blinked. "The SMT—what now?"

"The Special Maritime and Territorial Jurisdiction," Harper said, slow and deliberate. He put the folder down and looked directly into Silas' eyes. "Federal waters. Which means you'd be eligible for the death penalty."

The cocky grin disappeared completely from Silas' face. Sweat beaded at his hairline. "Death penalty? You're outta your goddamn mind. I don't know shit about—"

"I think a jury would disagree," Harper cut in smoothly. "Two missing people. Killed at sea. One a decorated military officer. His wife? Pregnant."

The blood drained from Silas' face. "Pregnant? What do you mean? I didn't know she was—"

He stopped cold, but it was too late.

Harper let the silence swell, the words hanging in the stale air like smoke. Then he spoke, voice flat as a blade: "Yeah, Ezra. That's right. She was pregnant. You're getting the needle."

Silas' mouth opened, then shut again. His head started to shake.

"You know how it works?" Harper said, almost conversational. "First drug relaxes you. The second paralyzes your muscles. The third stops your heart. Clinical. Like you never mattered at all."

Silas' eyes were locked on the table now, sweat dripping down his temple.

"But here's the thing," Harper leaned in. "That doesn't have to be your fate. There's one way out."

Silas' eyes finally lifted to meet his.

"You tell us what you know. All of it. You hold nothing back."

Silas swallowed hard. "And what do I get out of it?"

Harper stared directly into his eyes. "Life. You're going down for the murder either way, Ezra. But let's be real. No one in this room believes you were the mastermind. You're muscle. A trigger man. Somebody else called the shots." He paused, watching the shift in Silas' eyes. "We need his name. His involvement. Every detail. You give us that, Ezra, and you might just walk away with decades instead of a needle."

The silence stretched. Silas' jaw worked, and finally, he muttered a single word:

"Kincaid."

Harper gave the faintest nod, his voice calm, coaxing. "Good. Now give me more."

Silas' mouth twisted. He took a long, shaky breath, and shook his head once. "I want it in writing."

"Not a problem." Harper leaned back, turning his gaze toward the one-way glass. He gave a single, deliberate nod.

The door clicked open. Darrin Fulton stepped in, a folder under his arm, and slid into the seat beside Harper like he'd been waiting for his cue.

"Mr. Silas, my name is Senior Deputy Prosecuting Attorney Darrin Fulton." His tone was clipped, professional. His introduction mirrored what he'd told Cindy Glorevich the day before. Just like then, he pulled a single-page document from the folder and slid it across the table.

"This is a plea agreement, Mr. Silas. My office, along with the U.S. Attorney's Office, is prepared to offer you life without parole for the murders of Daniel and Malia Rainier. In exchange for a guilty plea, your full cooperation, and truthful testimony, as well as corroborating evidence, we will take the death penalty off of the table."

Fulton steepled his fingers, studying Silas. "Well? What do you say, Mr. Silas?"

For the first time all night, Silas' bravado cracked into something smaller. His gaze dropped to the page, lips moving silently as he read the bold print at the top. His cuffed hands fumbled with the paper, rattling the chain against the steel ring.

Finally, he looked up. His voice was low, gravelly, and tired. "...Pen."

Fulton slid him one. The room went dead silent as Silas hunched over and scrawled his name across the signature line.

Harper leaned forward, eyes locked on him. "Now, Ezra. It's time. Talk."

Ezra's eyes flicked from Harper to Fulton, then to Maguire, and back again. He wet his lips, shoulders sagging.

"I didn't know," he muttered. "I didn't know she was pregnant. I swear to God." His voice cracked. He shifted in his chair, chains clinking, before the next words forced their way out. "And I didn't know...I didn't know we were going to kill them."

Harper let the silence sit, heavy. "But you were there," he said finally. Not a question. Certainty.

Silas licked his cracked lip. "I was just supposed to...move some money. That's it. Just keep it clean."

Maguire leaned forward, voice hard. "Bullshit. You don't move fentanyl and stash cash through a church if you're just a bagman."

Silas flinched, but tried to laugh it off. It came out thin. "Man, you think I'm the big bad wolf here? Nah. I was just muscle. He...he had the plan. He always had the plan."

"Kincaid," Harper pressed, calm as stone.

Silas shook his head. "You don't get it. He's untouchable."

"No, he's not," Harper pushed. "Tell me more."

Silas swallowed, jaw twitching. "He–he said it was just about the boat. Paperwork. That's all. Next thing I know, the anchor's gone, they're gone, and I'm holding a bag of cash I didn't even want."

Maguire's voice jumped in, sharp. "Save the choir song. You were in it up to your neck."

Silas shook his head frantically. "I didn't lay hands on her! I didn't! They were just supposed to sign it over. But the husband, he wouldn't listen. So Kincaid—I just—I just did what he told me..."

Harper's voice cut low. "And he told you what?"

Silas sagged, eyes closing. His voice came out low, broken. "To clean it. Make sure the boat was spotless. That was me. But the rest? That was Kincaid...and his buddy. That Hugo guy. And her."

Harper's gaze sharpened. "Her?"

Silas' lips pressed tight, but his eyes flickered. Fear behind them. Guilt. He shook his head, once. "She followed him like the rest of us. Did what he asked. We all did."

Maguire leaned forward. "What do you mean, Ezra? Spell it out."

Silas rubbed his cuffed wrists against the steel ring. "Man, I don't even know where to start."

Harper's voice cut in, calm but firm. "Then start from the beginning. Tell us everything. Everything you saw. Everyone involved. No more games."

Silas licked his cracked lips again, a tremor in his jaw. When he finally spoke, the words seemed to drag him down with them.

"They brought us out on the water...thought it was just business. But Kincaid...he had other plans. He always did."

"Come with us, let us lie in wait for blood; let us ambush the innocent without reason."
— *Proverbs 1:11*

INTERLUDE

Then.
September 9.

The water was calm that night, the Sound stretched wide and black under a clouded sky. *The Halcyon Way* rocked only gently, its running lights dimmed, its anchor chain humming a low, metallic vibration with each shift of tide.

Ezra Silas remembered the way the air tasted. Salt and diesel, dinner scraps still clinging faintly to the galley sink. He hadn't wanted to be there. Not really. But when Asher said *come,* you went. When Asher said *wait,* you waited.

Daniel Rainier sat across the cabin table, trying to keep his voice level, his arm wrapped protectively around his wife. Malia had pulled her hood up against the chill and tugged a knit beanie low over her ears, hiding most of her newly cut hair. Only a few strands slipped loose, catching the flicker of the cabin lights with a copper-red sheen. Her other hand rested unconsciously over the swell of her stomach. She looked like she wanted to be anywhere else. Anywhere but there.

Asher Kincaid leaned in, wine glass in hand, his smile all charm and teeth. Beside him, Oliver Hugo loomed quiet, the muscle behind the words. Ezra stood back near the bulkhead, eyes darting between them, pulse pounding in his ears.

This wasn't what he'd signed up for. He thought it was about paperwork. About the boat. A quick hustle. Like they had done with the women in his "church." Get them to sign over the boat. Maybe get them to join. Maybe threaten them. But then

Asher's voice had shifted, slipping into that preacher's cadence, smooth and slow, as he laid the bill of sale out on the table.

"Sign," Kincaid had said, his voice velvet and steel. "Sign, and this all goes easy."

Ezra's eyes slid toward Hugo, who stood in the corner like a shadow waiting to be unleashed. Taller than both Rainier and Kincaid, he was lanky at first glance, but it was the kind of frame built from coiled muscle. Wiry, quick, all tension and no softness. Tattoos climbed both arms, crude black ink that spoke of time and violence. Spiderwebs at the elbows, jagged letters, half-faded skulls inked with a shaky hand. A short crew cut bristled against his scalp, a patchy mustache shading the hard line of his mouth.

Hugo had the look of a man who'd lived too many fights and lost too few. Knuckles swollen and scarred, eyes quick and mean. He didn't need to say anything. The message was clear: Hugo was the one who did the dirty work. And enjoyed it.

"You can't be serious. You're a pastor! We're not giving you the boat for free!" Daniel protested, his voice tight with disbelief.

Kincaid's eyes flicked to Silas, then back to Daniel. Calm as ever, he stepped forward and drove his fist into Daniel's gut. The sound was a sick, muffled thud. Daniel folded with a gasp, knees buckling, as Malia screamed.

"Shut the fuck up, bitch!" A woman's voice cut through, sharp and venomous. A crack followed—the sound of skin on skin—and Malia's head snapped sideways. Her lip split, warm copper filling her mouth.

She stared, wide-eyed, at the face before her.

"How could you?" Malia's voice broke. "We trusted you. You...you brought your child."

Cindy Glorevich smirked, the same lips that had once smiled over notary paperwork, now twisted with contempt.

296

"Exactly," she said. "You'd never have let us on otherwise." Her eyes flicked toward Kincaid with something like reverence. "Father said sacrifice is proof of faith. My boy will grow up blessed because I obeyed. And you? You'll serve a higher purpose than you ever imagined."

At those words, Daniel's heart sank. Panic flooded his veins. He tried to rise, but Hugo's boot slammed into his stomach, causing him to fold over again.

How had they fallen for this?

It had all started with the email. Hugo, speaking on Kincaid's behalf, had written that the pastor's congregation was praying for a vessel—a boat just like theirs—for "ministry and outreach." Kincaid himself followed up, congratulating them on their pregnancy. He'd said the church was willing to pay above market value, "a gift for your growing family."

Daniel and Malia had talked it over the whole way back from the San Juans. The idea had made sense. A bigger house, maybe even one with a yard. A real place to raise a child. Selling *The Halcyon Way*, their home on the water, hurt to imagine, but for the baby? Worth it. They reached back out to Hugo, and said they were interested. They set up a time to take Kincaid out for a test cruise before final purchase.

That morning, Hugo had suggested bringing along "the pastor's agent" to help finalize things, and Daniel hadn't thought twice. When the group showed up at Shilshole Point Marina, it was bigger than expected. Kincaid with Hugo, plus another man he introduced as a mechanic, "just to check the engines." And then Cindy, with her toddler on her hip, introduced as Kincaid's wife.

297

It was Cindy who disarmed them. The soft voice, the little boy shyly clinging to her leg, the promise that this was a family, just like theirs. What danger could there be?

Now Daniel could taste the bile in his throat, cursing his naïveté. He and Malia had poured the wine, set out cheese and bread, even laughed politely at Kincaid's smooth anecdotes while the boat slid into the calm waters of the Sound. Cindy had sat by Malia, even asked to rub her belly. When she asked to have her child take a nap so early in the dinner, they hadn't hesitated to offer the use of the master cabin.

But then the mask slipped.

Kincaid pulled out the bill of sale, laid it flat on the table, and smiled. "I'll take the boat," he said. "As a donation to God's work."

The words hadn't landed at first. A joke, maybe. A test. But the look in his eyes—cold, expectant—told Daniel otherwise.

And now, with Hugo's fist still poised and Cindy's smile twisting into something cruel, Daniel realized the truth: there had never been a deal. There had only been a trap.

Malia was sobbing, shoulders shaking as she clutched at her stomach. Daniel straightened slowly, ignoring the ache in his ribs, and put a steadying hand on her knee.

"Shh," he whispered, forcing calm into his voice. "It'll be alright, love." He lifted his eyes to Kincaid. "We'll sign. Just...just let us go afterward."

Kincaid's smile was wide and serene, the smile of a man convinced of his own righteousness. He leaned back, spreading his arms like a preacher at the pulpit.

"I knew you'd see reason, and God's will. Of course we'll let you go afterward. After all, the faithful are always rewarded."

He slid the bill of sale back across the table. Hugo yanked Daniel up by the collar, then shoved him back down hard in front of the paperwork, looming over the couple like a shadow ready to strike.

Daniel reached for the pen with shaking fingers. He signed quickly, his breath catching on every letter. "Don't we need to get this notarized?" he asked, his voice thin.

"Oh, don't worry about that," Cindy cut in smoothly, her smile never wavering. "I'm a notary."

Malia's head snapped toward her, eyes wide, betrayal cutting deeper than the slap had. "You..." she whispered.

"Ok, do you need us to sign the logbook?" Malia finally asked, her voice breaking.

"Oh, we can take care of all of that later," Kincaid said lightly, his eyes already on the envelope.

A chill ran through Malia's spine. She looked at Daniel, the fear mirrored in his eyes. Then she pressed the pen down, scratching out her name. When she reached the final "r" in *Rainier,* she stopped. She left it incomplete, a silent act of defiance.

Kincaid didn't notice. He snatched the bill of sale, slid it into a waiting manila envelope, and patted it as though it were scripture safely bound.

"Thank you for your service to the church," Kincaid said.

"And to the prophet," Cindy added, her tone sharp.

"For the prophet," Hugo echoed, his voice like gravel.

Kincaid's eyes moved from Silas to Hugo, then back again. He nodded once. "Tie them. Blindfolds too."

Malia screamed, raw and panicked. Daniel surged to his feet, fists clenched, but Hugo was faster. His punch cracked against Daniel's nose with a sickening snap, sending him sprawling.

Silas moved toward Malia, hands open, almost gentle. She spat a scream in his face and drove her forehead into his nose. He staggered back with a curse.

"Oh, for fuck's sake!" Cindy snapped. She grabbed Malia by the hood of her sweatshirt, yanked her upright, and slammed a fist into her stomach. Malia dropped instantly, gasping, both arms curling around her belly as sobs tore free.

Hugo was already pulling lines from the cleats. Cindy helped, working with a practiced efficiency. In minutes, Daniel and Malia were bound, wrists raw against the rough cord.

"The bow," Kincaid growled, his voice dropping its false warmth.

Hugo and Silas dragged the couple forward, shoes scuffing across the deck. They forced them down at the bow, tying them back-to-back, line clinched cruelly around their chests and arms. Malia wept softly, Daniel whispering broken reassurances through blood and swelling, trying to soothe her though his own breath came ragged. Cindy took strips of clothing and tied rough blindfolds over their eyes.

Hugo cracked his knuckles, then crouched by the anchor locker and unhooked the chain with a grinding snap of metal. The links spilled across the deck, clattering in the dark, a sound that carried finality.

Through the blindfolds, Daniel and Malia could only hear the heavy scrape of steel being dragged closer. Malia's body shook against his, sobs wracking her chest.

"What about our baby boy?" she cried, voice breaking.

Daniel reached back until his fingers found hers. Their hands locked, rope biting their skin, but their grip held tight. "Where we're going, he'll be with us," he whispered.

"I don't want to die," Malia sobbed.

"I know, love." His voice trembled but stayed steady enough for her. "It'll be okay. It'll be okay."

The first cold coil of chain pressed against them. Hugo looped it around their torsos, threading the steel through the lines already binding them. Each wrap tightened, sealing their fate.

Malia wept softly, but Daniel lifted his chin and began to speak, voice firm even through swollen lips.

"Our father, who art in heaven..."

Cindy laughed. A low, cruel sound that made the hair rise on the back of Silas' neck.

"Hallowed be Thy name. Thy kingdom come, thy will be done..."

Footsteps retreated across the deck.

"On earth as it is in heaven."

The anchor slid from the rail with a final shriek of metal. A splash followed, deep and heavy, and the chain screamed across the deck.

"Forgive us our trespasses, as we forgive those who trespass against us..."

The chain snapped taut. Daniel's voice rose over the roar.

"Lead us not into temptation—"

The line yanked them backwards.

" —but deliver us from evil."

Their bodies vanished over the rail, swallowed into the black water, prayer and breath torn away by the Sound.

CHAPTER
THIRTY-FOUR

Now.
September 16. Early morning.

In the interview room, Harper fought to force his face into stillness as Silas finished recounting the Rainiers' last night. They'd let him tell it all in one uninterrupted flow the first time, the words tumbling out like poison. The second time, Harper was ready, his pen scratching across the pad, every detail weighed, key phrases marked.

He glanced once at the camera in the corner, its red light steady. The record was rolling.

"So," Harper said evenly, "confirming it was Oliver Hugo who wrapped the chain around them? Hugo who beat Daniel Rainier and tied them back-to-back?"

Silas nodded, gaze fixed on the cuffs biting into his wrists.

"I need you to say it out loud, for the record."

Silas swallowed. "Yeah. That was Hugo."

"And Cindy Glorevich?" Harper flipped a page, eyes on his notes. "She struck Malia Rainier in the stomach...and laughed while the anchor dragged them into the water?"

Silas' voice was quieter now. "Yeah."

"Who unhooked the anchor?"

"Hugo. And...she helped him."

"Who? Glorevich?" Harper pressed.

Silas flexed his jaw. "Yeah."

"Tell me exactly what she did."

"She walked over, lifted it off the hooks with him. They dropped it together. That's when she laughed. As it went over."

The silence in the room stretched. Harper's hand hovered over the page, his pen steady. "And you didn't know that was the plan?"

"No, man." Silas finally looked up, eyes raw, desperate. "I thought we were just gonna shake 'em down. That was it. I swear."

"Why didn't you try to help them once you realized the plan?" Maguire jumped in now.

Silas turned toward him, no hesitation this time. His answer was flat, cold with survival. "Because then it would've been me in the water with them."

The coward's words hung like a foul stench.

Harper's pen froze above the page. For a split second, he pictured Alyssa's face, her swollen belly under his hand, Adelyn's laugh drifting down the hallway. Then the image shattered against Malia's sobs, Daniel's voice steadying her in the dark, both of them bound to an anchor—and to each other.

He pictured her slipping into the black water, mouth open in a final cry. She would not have been able to sob and hold her breath at the same time. The truth struck like a blade: her last breath had gone to terror and grief.

His hand trembled once before he forced it still, the only sign of the storm clawing inside.

Integrity's not about how you feel. It's about what you do, when it costs you.

His father's words whispered through the roar in his ears.

He tapped his pen once against the paper, steady again, and looked back at Silas with eyes flat as glass. "Noted," he said. His voice was calm, professional. But beneath it, Maguire caught the edge—the quiet promise of reckoning.

"So, Silas," Harper continued evenly. "How do you prove this?"

Silas shifted in his chair. "Phones," he said finally. "Burners. We each had one. Hugo bought 'em in cash, handed them out like candy. Said it kept things clean. I still got mine stashed. Numbers'll link to his. To Hugo's. To Cindy's. You'll see the calls that night."

Harper's eyes narrowed. "Where?"

"My place. Back of the freezer, under the tray. Dead battery, but it's there."

Maguire leaned in, voice sharp. "That's something. But not enough. What else?"

Silas licked his lips, sweat tracing the line of his jaw. He spoke rapidly, desperate. "The dinghy. From the Yacht. After they went over, we cruised back to Elliott Bay while I cleaned the boat up. When it was done, we let it drift. Kincaid made us launch the Zodiac. Said we couldn't come back in on the yacht right away, that it was too obvious."

"And then?" Harper asked, after Silas had gone silent a beat too long.

"Then we rode the dinghy in, tied it off by the pier near Harbor Island, and ditched it. He said someone would move it. Maybe it's still there. Maybe you find who took it. Either way, it proves what I'm saying."

Harper said nothing, just stared at Silas. He struggled to keep his face blank, to not show the disgust and rage he was feeling just under the surface.

Silas leaned back and exhaled through his nose, the fight completely gone out of him. "That's what you needed right? I get the deal?"

Fulton didn't answer immediately. He looked first at Harper, then Maguire, then back at Silas. "Here's how it works, Mr. Silas. You've taken the first step. But the deal holds only if my investigators corroborate every detail you've given us, and you testify once we've got the rest of them in custody. You try to play us, or you hold back, and the needle goes back on the table. Am I clear?"

Silas nodded faintly, the cuffs rattling as he shifted in his chair.

The three men stood and filed out, leaving the interview room heavy with silence. In the viewing room, Fulton stopped at the glass. He watched Silas slumped at the table, head down, and muttered, "Cowardly fuck." Disgust carried in every syllable.

Maguire gave a single nod. Harper, though, kept his expression flat, all steel. "I'll draft the warrant for his place. You'll have it for review within the hour."

"Good," Fulton said, already thumbing his phone. "I'll get it fast-tracked with a judge."

"I'll also prep federal subpoenas for the burner phones, including logs, GPS, the works."

Fulton's head bobbed once, sharp. "Good, good. Hey, Harper. Maguire."

They both looked at him.

"Let's nail these motherless fucks."

Harper gave a short nod and turned away, the weight of the case still pressing down like wet stone.

Maguire clapped Fulton lightly on the shoulder as he passed. "Don't worry, Counselor. We'll gift wrap 'em for you."

Then he fell in beside Harper, laying a steadying hand on his partner's shoulder.

"You alright, Jake?"

"Yeah," Harper said after a moment. "We've been here all night. Just need to check in at home."

"Do that. I'll give Thomas a call too."

They split off in the hallway, Harper ducking into a quiet conference room. He shut the door behind him, the hush settling around him. Then he pulled out his phone and checked the time. 6:45am. His thumb hovered for a moment before he dialed. It rang once, twice, then Alyssa's voice came through, warm and tired.

"Hey, love."

Just hearing her eased something tight in his chest. He sank into one of the conference chairs, rubbing the bridge of his nose. "Hey. How are you two holding up?"

"We're fine. About to make some breakfast. Addie's been begging for pancakes with chocolate sauce on them." He could hear their daughter's laughter in the background, muffled but bright, the sound hitting him like sunlight through storm clouds.

"Put me on speaker for a second?"

Alyssa must have done so, because a second later, Addie's voice came clear as a bell. "Daddy! Guess what? I drew you a picture! It's of you and Mommy and baby brother! But you're bigger, cuz you're a police *ossifer*!"

The mispronunciation cracked through the heaviness in his chest. Harper felt a smile tug at his mouth.

"That's perfect, sweetheart. I can't wait to see it when I get home."

"When are you coming home, Daddy?"

"Hopefully tonight, love," Harper said, glancing at the blank conference wall. He wanted it to be true. "I just have a little more work to finish first."

"To catch the bad guys?"

"Yes, sweetie. To catch the bad guys."

"Okay! Mommy says it's time to eat now. Love you, Daddy!"

"I love you too, Addie-bear."

There was a shuffle as Alyssa came back on.

"She's scarfing down the pancakes. I put whipped cream on them, too."

"Good," Harper said softly. "She deserves it. She's an amazing kid."

"Yeah she is," Alyssa said. Then her voice changed, gentle, like she could hear the weight through the line. "I can hear it in you, Jake. You're carrying it heavier than you normally do."

Harper leaned forward, put his hand on the wall, staring at the floor. "We're close, Lyss. Closer than we've been. But it's ugly. Worse than I imagined."

A pause. He heard her exhale. "Then don't let it take you with it. Remember who you are. Remember us."

He closed his eyes, picturing her in their kitchen, one hand on her belly, the other cradling the phone. "That's the only thing that keeps me steady," he admitted.

"See you tonight?" she asked.

"Yeah, hope so," Harper said, voice thick. "I'll be home when I can."

"I'll keep the light on," she whispered.

They said goodbye. When the line went dead, Harper stood a moment longer, phone resting heavy in his palm. Addie's laugh still echoed faintly in his ears—this time, not drowned by Malia's sobs, but standing apart, bright and alive. A reminder of why he couldn't stop.

He squared his shoulders and slipped the phone back into his pocket. The challenge coin was there too—Foster's coin, cool metal pressing against his palm.

Right is right, no matter the cost.

The words echoed both Foster's and his father's voices, two men whose lessons had shaped him in different ways but led to the same truth.

Harper took a breath, steadying himself.

Back to the case.

Back to the hunt.

CHAPTER
THIRTY-FIVE

Harper claimed a corner desk in the Homicide conference room, laptop open, a half-cold coffee sweating onto a stack of manila folders. Fluorescents hummed. Printers chattered. He tuned it all out and finished the last paragraph of the affidavit.

...the above facts give me probable cause to believe the cellular telephone used by Ezra SILAS is secreted under a tray inside the freezer at 5543 SW Dawson St, Seattle, WA, and that evidence of the crimes of RCW 10.95.020 Aggravated Murder in the First Degree and 18 USC § 1111 Murder within the Special Maritime and Territorial Jurisdiction of the United States will be found therein, including: location data, subscriber information, call logs, text messages, encrypted application content, image/video files, and metadata bearing date/time/geo coordinates...

He added the freezer detail as a separate particularity section—to obtain photos of the kitchen, packaging, latex gloves, tape, wipes, cleaning solvents—and a clause authorizing seizure of external storage and cloud backups linked to the device. Then he tightened the Attachment B list: phone, SIM/ESN/IMEI, charges, and "any notes indicating passcodes or unlock patterns."

Send.

He fired the packet to Fulton and AUSA Summers, cc'd SSA Easton, and immediately pivoted to the admin subpoenas Silas had just bought them: three burner numbers for Hugo, Cindy and Kincaid, one week window around the disappearance, tower dumps limited to three hours each side of the AIS data, plus subscriber/IMSI/IMEI for any number that touched the burners more than twice. He printed, signed his portion, and walked them down the hall to scan and send to Easton.

By the time he had refilled his coffee, Easton had countersigned and scanned. Ten minutes later Harper was back at the desk, the subpoenas outbound to the carriers with preservation letters attached. He leaned back, rolled his neck until it popped. A breath left him he didn't realize he'd been holding. Exhaustion hit like a truck. They'd been up all night with Silas, and he still hadn't slept.

Maguire slid into the chair across from him and set a fresh cup down. "You look like an affidavit grew legs and ate your soul."

"Judge should be able to read it without a headlamp," Harper said, checking his email.

A reply from Summers landed: Nice freezer detail. A reply from Fulton followed half a minute later: "Approved as drafted. Add plain-view clause for cash/ledgers." He added the line, re-sent, and watched the little paper airplane vanish.

"Okay," Harper said, mind already sorting the next stack. "Once the warrant is signed by the judge, we hit it. You run point on entry with Narcotics for the house."

Maguire sipped. "Got it. We'll knock-and-announce. Freezer first, phone under the tray. Bag it Faraday."

"And the nightstand drawers for passcode notes," Harper added. "Kitchen trash for wipes/packaging. Laundry for anything bleached. Then the bedroom closet: shoebox money, ledgers. Air returns, drop ceilings. We're not leaving without the burner and anything tying him to this."

"And the dinghy?" Maguire asked.

"Already sent a request to the CG station CO. They're gonna launch a boat, check the shoreline near Harbor Island where Silas said they left it. They'll expand the grid a mile past Alki. If Silas is telling the truth, the tender's either dumped or sitting in somebody's backyard with a spray-paint job."

Maguire nodded, then pointed to Harper's screen. "What's the tower dump window?"

"1800 to 2400 on the ninth." Harper's tone turned clinical. "If Kincaid, Hugo, or Cindy were smart, they kept their primaries dark. But they still needed to coordinate. If any of those burners overlapped towers near Shilshole or the dump zone, the carriers will cough it up. Then we subpoena the store for CCTV where the cards were bought."

Maguire cracked a thin smile. "And then we bring the prophet a little revelation."

Harper looked at Maguire, but found himself too exhausted to even smile at the quip. Thankfully, his phone buzzed. It was the judge: Warrant signed and attached. He printed two copies, slid one to Maguire, and stood. "Time to gear up."

Maguire pushed up, the old bones of the building creaking with him. "Ten says the phone isn't where he said it is."

"Deal." Harper grabbed his go-bag: Faraday sleeve, write-blocker, DSLR, evidence tape, and extra gloves. "If it is, we get the data. If it isn't, we get to bury him with the lie."

They moved for the door. Harper paused long enough to fire one more email: emergency preservation on Silas' Google and

Apple IDs—if they existed—and a quick note to Evidence to reserve a bench for immediate device triage.

As they stepped into the hallway, Maguire angled a look at him. "Finish line's in sight."

Harper nodded. "Let's roll."

•••••

They were stacked outside the small yellow house on SW Dawson Street by eleven a.m. Maguire and Harper moved up the cracked sidewalk, the porch sagging under their weight. The red-brown front door was shut tight, curtains drawn. Two narcotics detectives covered them from behind, pistols out.

Harper pressed an ear to the door. Silence. He gave it three heavy knocks.

"Police! Open up!"

Nothing.

Harper slid Silas' key into the lock, the bolt snapping back with a tired click. Maguire called out, "Police! Search warrant!" as the door swung open. Still no answer. The two narcotics detectives went in first, clearing fast. Seconds later, they returned.

"All clear," the first one said. Dirkson, Harper thought his name was.

"Thanks, Durkan," Maguire said.

Close enough, Harper thought.

Gloves on, Harper and Maguire stepped inside. The air was stale, tinged with old smoke and fried food. Harper went straight for the freezer. He yanked the tray up, and there it was. A gray burner phone, exactly where Silas had promised.

"Ha," Maguire said. "Guess I owe you ten bucks."

Harper slipped the phone into an evidence bag, and then into the Faraday bag. "Smartphone. That's a win. Messages, GPS, maybe even photos."

They split the house. The living room was barren except for a sagging couch and TV that hadn't been dusted in weeks. In the garage they found stacks of cleaning supplies—bleach, wipes, and scrub brushes—organized like someone had bought them in bulk for more than just spring cleaning.

But it was the bedroom that the real paydirt hit. The other detective, Murray, called them in. A duffel bag was half-tucked under the bed, unzipped enough to show fat rubber-banded stacks of cash and small baggies of fentanyl pills. Next to it sat a ledger book, with handwritten columns of dates and amounts.

Maguire flipped a few pages. "Looks like our boy was running weight."

Harper took the book, scanning the notes. Some entries were initials, others cryptic symbols. But one name showed up clear, over and over again. *TWF.*

"The Way Forward," Harper said aloud.

Maguire peered over his shoulder. "The pipeline. Drug money in, 'donations' out."

Tucked in the back of the ledger was a folded letterhead sheet with The Way Forward Foundation's logo. It was a receipt, phony and polished, documenting a "charitable donation" of $25,000. Underneath, in Silas' handwriting, was a note: *Picked up by AK.*

Maguire let out a low whistle. "And there's the tie to Kincaid. Washing drug money through the offering plate."

Harper snapped photos with his phone before bagging the evidence. "Phone, cash, dope, ledgers, and a receipt. Fulton's gonna love this. Now we just need the phone to back it all."

Before Maguire could answer, Harper's voice buzzed in his pocket. He pulled it out and answered.

"Harper."

" Agent Harper, this is OS3 Harrang, Sector Seattle watchstander," a male voice came through, calm but clipped. "We think we may have found your dinghy."

Harper's pulse jumped. "Yeah? Where?" He could feel the excitement that only came when a case was coming together.

"Pier near Alki Beach. Crew on scene found a burnt skiff tied off under the pilings. Still floating. I'll text you the coordinates. Can I use this number?"

"Go ahead," Harper said. "Appreciate it."

The line clicked off. A second later, his phone buzzed with a GPS pin.

"Bingo," Harper said, showing Maguire. "You good to wrap here?"

"Yeah, I'll finish bagging and log it in," Maguire replied.

"Perfect. I'll check the dinghy, then drop the phone with the techies after."

Harper slipped out the front door and into his sedan, pulling out from behind a line of unmarked units. Fifteen minutes later he was walking along the rocks near Alki Pier, the tang of salt air sharp in his nose. Out on the water, a Coast Guard small boat idled just offshore, the silver hull gleaming in the sunlight while the orange bow bobbed in the chop.

Next to it, half-hidden in shadow under the pier, a dinghy floated. Blackened from bow to stern, but still afloat, its tether rope looped tight around a barnacled piling. Even from shore, Harper could see the scorch marks across the fiberglass, the melted rubber curled like skin.

Fuck. Hope there's still some evidence left.

The small boat edged closer, the coxswain raising a hand. "Agent Harper? Head up top and climb down. We'll get you aboard."

Minutes later, Harper dropped the last two feet into the boat and felt it rock under his shoes. The coxswain motored them alongside the dinghy. Up close, the stench hit him. Burnt fuel. Charred fiberglass. Saltwater rot.

On the starboard flank, ghost letters clung stubbornly to the hull: *The Halc—*. The rest had been scorched to ash.

They had tried to torch the evidence. Harper exhaled once, cold and steady. He noted the GPS position, snapped photos from every angle, and dialed up Seattle PD.

"This is Special Agent Harper, CGIS. I need a forensic team dispatched to Alki Pier. Possible evidence vessel tied off under the dock. Burned, but still afloat."

CHAPTER
THIRTY-SIX

The forensics van arrived just after two, its tired crunching over the gravel near the Alki pier. Harper stood at the edge of the seawall, arms folded, watching the CSU team gear up. Gloves snapped, kits were opened, and the smell of the Sound— brine and diesel—mingled with the faint chemical tang drifting from the charred dinghy still tied off below.

Two techs climbed down with ropes and harnesses, balancing against the slick timbers until they reached the tender. One crouched low, flashlight beam sliding over the blackened interior.

"Definitely an accelerant," she called up. "But not straight gas. I'm smelling bleach, too."

The second tech swapped at the scorched bench seat, shaking his head. "Classic clean burn. They torched it and then tried to wipe what was left. Anyone riding in here? Doubt we'll pull a clean print."

Harper leaned over the rail, notebook in hand. "But you can confirm bleach?"

"Yeah," the first tech said, bagging a sample of damp residue scraped from the hull. "Enough of it pooled along the seams that it's still binding with the char."

Harper jotted the note. Bleach meant intent. *Too bad their cover up won't hold.*

The lettering on the hull stared back at him, the partial name tying it back to *The Halcyon Way*. It was all the confirmation he needed. Vindication singing in his veins, he looked at the techs.

"Tag it, photograph it, and get it back to the lab. Chain of custody stays airtight. This one's going to court."

The lead tech nodded. "We'll handle it."

Harper stepped back, pulled off his gloves, and checked his watch. The dinghy would keep. What mattered now was the phone bagged from Silas' freezer, the one that might finally connect all the names, the calls, and the plot to kill the Rainiers.

He turned away from the pier, already dialing Easton as he headed towards his car.

•••••

Harper pulled into Pier 36 just after four, the sedan's engine ticking as it cooled in the September haze. The base was alive with the rhythm he knew well: Polar Icebreakers at the dock, small boats humming in from drills, Coasties in ODUs hauling gear across the asphalt. For a moment it was almost comforting. Predictable chaos against the storm of the case.

Inside the CGIS office, it was humming. Racks of computers lined the wall, their screens lit with code and mapping tools. Francis, the technician, looked even more caffeinated than before. He looked up as Harper came in, holding up the sealed evidence bag.

"This the freezer phone?" he asked.

"Yeah, straight from his place. We need a full dump. Texts. Calls. GPS. Deleted files. The works. Prioritize link analysis with the numbers from the subpoenas."

The tech slid the bag onto the desk like it was radioactive. "Got it. You'll get rolling updates. This one's gonna run hot."

"Good," Harper said, already turning for the door. "Ping me as soon as you have coordinates or calls tying to other lines."

"Will do, Agent Harper."

The hall felt quieter on the way out, his shoes echoing against the tile. He signed off the chain of custody log, tucked the copy into his notebook, and finally let his shoulders sag. For the first time in days, there was nothing else to do but wait.

By the time he made it home, the afternoon light had already gone soft. Alyssa's car was in the driveway, a chalk rainbow scrawled across the walkway. Adelyn's handiwork. He let himself in quietly, the smell of grilled cheese and crayons hanging in the air.

Addie's shoes were by the door. Alyssa's laughter drifted faintly from the living room. He walked in, Adelyn running to his arms. "Daddy!" she said. "We're watching Baby Monster!" He set her down on the couch. He gave Alyssa a hug and kiss.

"I'm just here to crash for a bit," he said.

"Go. We're ordering McDonald's tonight. I'll order an extra burger and fries for you. It'll be in the fridge when you wake."

Harper slipped upstairs, loosed the Glock from his holster, and set it carefully in the safe in the nightstand. He stripped off his shirt and collapsed onto the bed. He barely kicked off his shoes. His eyes were closed before his head hit the pillow, the day's weight giving way to the dark pull of sleep.

•••••

Then.

Fourteen-year-old Jake crouched in the driveway with grease up to his elbows, holding a wrench that felt three sizes too big for his hand. The old Nissan sat jacked on blocks, its hood yawning open. Raymond lay on his back beneath it, worn boots sticking out.

"Alright, Jake," his father's voice came, steady and patient. "Tighten that bolt by the manifold."

Jake leaned over, twisting the wrench until it resisted, then stopped. He pulled back. "It's snug."

Raymond rolled out from under the truck, his face streaked with sweat and engine grime. He looked at the bolt, then at Jake. "Snug isn't tight. Do it again."

Jake signed and reached for the wrench. "It's good enough—"

"Good enough," Raymond cut him off, his tone sharp but not unkind, "is how things come loose at sixty miles an hour. And when bolts come loose, people get hurt. You don't half-do a job just because you're tired. You finish it right." He let the words settle before adding, quieter: "Integrity isn't what you do when it's easy. It's what you do when no one is watching you. When it costs you. Right now, the cost is a little more time, a little more effort. But the cost of cutting corners?" He shook his head. "That's always higher."

Jake gritted his teeth, put his weight into the wrench, and felt the bolt turn another quarter.

Raymond gave a single nod. "Now it's right."

Finish it right.

Always.

•••••

Now.

The buzz of his phone pulled Harper out of sleep like a hook to the chest. He blinked blearily at the screen before swiping.

"Yeah?" His voice was still rough, thick with sleep.

"Sorry to wake you, Agent Harper." Francis's voice came steady but quick, a hint of youthful excitement under the professionalism. "We've cracked the phone. Call logs, GPS, everything's ready.

Harper sat upright, the cold jolt of adrenaline forcing the fog from his head. "I'll be right there."

The screen lit with the time as he set the phone down. 8:00 p.m. He'd managed barely three hours. It would have to be enough.

He kissed Alyssa goodbye, murmuring a promise to be careful, and slipped out the door. The evening traffic had thinned, and he made it back to base in record time.

Francis was waiting in the hall with a thumb drive pinched between his fingers like a prize. "Since it's a burner, not much activity. But what's there is gold."

Harper thanked Francis and took the drive. He headed straight for his desk and slid it into the port. The screen blinked awake, filling with data.

The first files he loaded were the call logs. Harper leaned forward, scrolling line by line. Numbers. Timestamps. Exactly as Silas had described.

One set linked to Kincaid's burner. Another to Hugo's. Another to Cindy's.

The four of them, circling each other in bursts of activity. Multiple calls on September 9. One at 2:47 p.m. Another just before 3:30. And again at 3:40.

Harper's pulse ticked faster. He opened the AIS data on his laptop, dragging the timelines side by side.

The Rainiers' yacht departing Shilshole. A flurry of calls, then silence.

His stomach sank.

He opened the GPS file. The coordinates painted the picture with cruel clarity. The burner left Shilshole at the same time as *The Halcyon Way*. Its track bled north into the Sound, stopping at the exact grid where the yacht stopped. In the same area Silas said the anchor was dropped.

The cursor blinked on the screen, hovering over the coordinates where Daniel and Malia had disappeared beneath the water.

Harper exhaled slowly, forcing his hand to steady as he clicked onward. The track resumed. South again, into Elliott Bay, where the Yacht was set adrift. Then west to Harbor Island with the Dinghy. Finally, the line crawled to rest at the address on Dawson Street. Silas' house.

The whole story, plotted in cold numbers and timestamps. Exactly as Silas had said.

Harper sat back in the chair, the glow of the monitors washing his face pale. The evidence was almost ironclad now.

Murder, mapped by satellites.

His inbox chimed. Subpoena returns.

Harper opened the first file. It contained carrier logs, cell-site IDs, sector azimuths, and timestamps stacked in tight columns. Not GPS-precise, but close enough to sketch the night in radio waves.

He split the screen again, AIS on the left, phone record spreadsheets on the right.

Kincaid's handset: hits a sector covering Shilshole at 15:31, then sectors marching north along the Sound. Broad wedges that lined up with the burner's exact trail. At 18:04 the phone falls quiet, then reappears on a sector facing Elliott Bay. Later, a tower near Capitol Hill. Home.

Cindy's phone: same pattern, offset by minutes. Shilshole marina. Mid-Sound. Elliott Bay. Then a sector that served her block. Home.

Silas' cell: sectors matching the GPS already pulled off the physical phone, settling near Dawson around 22:00. Home.

Harper moved to the last file.

Hugo.

The sectors start at Shilshole. Sweep north with the rest. Reappear over Elliott Bay. But then west. Not toward Queen Anne or Ballard. A string of hits hand over to towers that blanket Alki. 22:47, 23:06, 23:28, each ping locked to sectors that face the waterfront. The final entry time-stamped 00:12 on September 10. After that, nothing. The phone was powered down or the battery yanked.

Harper zoomed in on the sector map overlay, tracing the fan of coverage that opened toward the pier. The same pier where the tender had been found burned and tied off.

"Got you, fucker," he said under his breath.

He tagged the files, dropped key screenshots into a quick summary: burner GPS track; Kincaid/Cindy parallel sectors; Silas home after Harbor Island; Hugo's westward drift to Alki and the midnight dark-out.

His cursor hovered over "Send." Then he attached the summary to a new email addressed to Maguire, Fulton, and Summers.

He hit send, grabbed his phone, and started dialing.

Maguire picked up on the fourth ring.

"Hey there, Coastie," Maguire said, his voice gruff with sleep.

"Sorry to wake you, Tate. I got the phone data back. GPS corroborates Silas' statement."

"Hell yeah, brother. You get the carrier info on the burner phones yet?" Maguire asked.

"Sure did. Tower pings place the phones in the same movement patterns as Silas. They all go north through the Sound, stop at the dump location, then back down to Elliott Bay where the Yacht was set adrift. Then they go to Harbor Island where they all get off and head home. Except for Hugo."

"Oh?"

"Yeah. Hugo's phone goes west toward Alki beach, overlapping with where we found the burnt tender."

"Boom."

"Yeah. One more thing to make this airtight though. The carriers sent over the IMEI data, and location where the phones were bought. Looks like a Target store off Barton St," Harper said. "And their cameras are usually gold."

"I happen to know their loss prevention guy. I'll call him and meet you there. Good work, Jake."

The Target off SW Barton Street was small. Harper pulled into a parking stall next to Maguire's sedan. Maguire was on the phone. After a moment, he put the phone down and stepped out of the car.

"The loss prevention guy, Brad Tidwell, is on his way. We used to work together a lot when I worked commercial crimes," Maguire explained. "He owes me a favor or two."

About ten minutes later, a blue Subaru pulled into the stall on the other side of Maguire's car. A male in his forties stepped out, balding and wearing glasses. He was dressed in jeans and a t-shirt.

"Brad, good to see you!" Maguire said, shaking hands with the man.

"You too, buddy. How's Thomas?" Tidwell asked.

"He's good. We're real good. Looking forward to our vacation next month."

"Oh yeah? Where you headed?"

"Maui. We haven't been in a while. We're ready to unplug a bit," Maguire answered.

"Especially with your job, Tate. How is homicide?"

"Well, that's actually why we're here. We're working a homicide case. The suspects used burners bought from here. We'd like to see who actually picked them up."

"No problem. And this is?" Tidwell looked over at Harper, extending his hand.

"Jake Harper. CGIS," Harper said, returning the handshake.

Pleasantries out of the way, Tidwell had them follow them into the store to an office behind customer service. The small office had a computer on a table and two chairs. Tidwell and Maguire sat. Harper chose to stand.

"Now, what was the date and time of purchase?" Tidwell asked.

"September 8. I have the IMEIs if that'll help," Harper replied.

"Oh, that'll help. I can search by those."

Harper gave them to him. Within just a few moments, Tidwell had the transaction pulled up.

"Looks like they paid cash at 12:07 p.m. One second while I pull up the actual footage of the purchase…"

Tidwell clicked the mouse, and the screen switched from the receipt to a crystal-clear image of a man at the checkout counter, sliding four phones across the scanner before peeling bills from a wad of cash. The man turned toward the exit, walking past another camera.

The frame froze just as the man looked up at the lens. An electric thrill went up Harper's spine as he stared at the still image, recognition igniting his fury.

"Here we go," Tidwell said. "Does this guy ring a bell?"

The man was lanky, ropey muscle coiled under pale skin. Tattoos inked both arms. A short, military-style crew cut. A patchy mustache that couldn't hide the smirk.

Oliver Hugo.

Harper's pulse quickened, the air in the tiny office thick. He looked at Maguire. Maguire met his eyes and gave a single nod.

"It's airtight now," Harper said, his voice flat but certain.

CHAPTER
THIRTY-SEVEN

September 17. Ten a.m.

Harper and Maguire stepped out of the Grand Jury courtroom, the heavy oak doors swinging shut behind them. Both men carried the same taut energy, the kind that came when days worth of hard work finally began to lock into place. They had laid it all out for the jurors: the AIS tracks from *The Halcyon Way,* the phone data pulled from Silas' burner, the carrier dumps that lined up with every movement. They had painted the connections between Oliver Hugo and Asher Kincaid, The Way Forward Foundation, and the cult orbiting Kincaid's pulpit. Cindy Glorevich's role tied the circle shut.

Now Silas would testify under the plea agreement, laying out the same details he'd given them in the box. And with his cooperation, they would have everything. They would have *indictment.*

While Maguire was testifying, Harper had been working. He drafted two more warrants to ride alongside the arrests: one for Cindy's house, one for Kincaid's office at the church. By the time they reconvened in the hallway, the judge had already signed them. All that remained was the grand jury's word.

A little after 11:30, Silas shuffled out, head down, shackles clinking against the tile. Deputies led him away without ceremony.

Fulton emerged seconds later, a thin smile breaking his courtroom poker face.

"We got the True Bill," Fulton said. "Aggravated Murder on all three. I'll have the signed arrest warrants in the system in 30 minutes."

Harper held up his laptop. "And I've got paper for Cindy's place and Kincaid's office. We're greenlit."

Maguire leaned against the wall, his grin hard and humorless. "Then let's go collect the prophet's flock."

•••••

They pulled up a few houses down from Cindy Glorevich's sagging craftsman, government sedans and SUVs nosed into a tight row along the curb, followed by marked Seattle Police cruisers. Harper climbed out, scanning the block. Curtains twitched across the street, neighbors already clocking the caravan.

Another car pulled up fast. Special Agent Kiera Lawson stepped out, her braid tight, jacket zipped. Harper met her halfway.

"Appreciate the assist, Kiera," he said.

She gave a curt nod. "You covered me last time. My turn."

Harper turned back to the house, voice pitched low to the assembled team. "Quick and quiet. I don't want her calling Kincaid. We get her out, we clear the house, then we move."

They moved in, boots and shoes thudding softly on the porch steps. Harper rapped hard, three sharp knocks that echoed through the wood. Silence. He tilted his head. Movement inside. Feet shuffling on carpet. Harper's impatience grew. He followed with five rapid knocks.

A muffled voice snapped back, irritated. "Alright, alright, I'm comin', don't get your panties in a—"

The door cracked open. Cindy Glorevich froze when she saw Harper. Her eyes widened, and she tried to slam it shut. Harper's hand shot up, palm flat against the door, forcing it open. He pushed his way in and grabbed her arm at the wrist.

"Ms. Glorevich, step outside."

"Uh, I don't—" She backpedaled.

"Now." Harper yanked her wrist, pulling her onto the porch. He flicked his chin to Maguire. "Go."

Maguire, Lawson and the others streamed inside, clearing rooms.

Cindy thrashed against Harper's grip. "What the fuck do you think you're doing—"

Harper spun her, cuffs snapping around her wrists. His voice stayed calm, clipped. "Cindy Glorevich, you're under arrest for the aggravated murder of Daniel and Malia Rainier. You have the right to remain silent..."

She cursed through the Miranda warning, but he finished without pause. "Do you understand your rights as I have read them to you?"

"Fuck you," she said, spittle hitting Harper in the face. "Lawyer."

"Noted." He marched her over to a waiting patrol vehicle, guiding her head down as he sat her inside. The door slammed shut with a heavy thunk.

When he turned back, Maguire was already on the porch. "House is clear. Mom must've taken the kids out."

"Good," Harper said. He adjusted his gloves, eyes hard. "We've got a Shepherd to grab."

Inside, the air smelled faintly of cigarette smoke and cheap candles. The front room was cluttered but not dirty. Kids' toys were stacked against the wall, a laundry basked half-full near the couch. Normal life.

"Bedroom first," Maguire said. Lawson peeled off down the hall while two detectives swept the kitchen.

Harper started with the living room desk shoved under the window. The top drawer stuck halfway, but he forced it open. Inside: envelopes banded together with rubber bands, most bearing Kincaid's church letterhead. Harper pulled one free and skimmed.

Dearest Sister Cindy,

Your faith and sacrifice are seen. Remember the prophet is worthy of double honor. Your obedience proves your devotion, and your reward will not be withheld.

Harper exhaled sharply, bagged the letter, and kept going.

In the bedroom, Lawson's voice called out. "Got something!"

Harper joined her. She stood by the nightstand, holding up a prepaid phone still in its packaging. A second, battered burner lay on the nightstand itself, plugged into a cheap charger. Its call log would be gold.

Maguire whistled low as he pulled open the closet. Stacks of shoeboxes lined the floor. He slid one out, popped the lid, and revealed bundles of cash wrapped in church offering envelopes. Another box held ledgers, handwritten notes of payments, initials and dates.

"Here's your link," Maguire said. "Church cash, straight into her closet."

Harper photographed everything before bagging it. "Phone, cash, ledgers, correspondence. Fulton's going to salivate."

One of the detectives stepped into the doorway holding up a small stack of printouts. "Found these in the kitchen drawer. Looks like email exchanges, her and Kincaid. He's calling her his 'faithful steward.' Tells her to notarize, to trust him, that she and *their* kids are protected."

Harper took them, scanning the words. Cindy's handwriting scrawled across the margins. *Yes, Father. I will obey.*

He closed the folder slowly. "She was never going to flip. She's devoted. A true believer."

Maguire zipped one of the evidence bags shut with a sharp pull. "We can nail him with his own words."

Lawson stepped out of the hall with another bag in hand. "Her laptop. Still warm. Let's get it to tech."

Harper gave a grim nod, scanning the small, cluttered room one last time. Every corner whispered of ordinary life—children's drawings taped to the fridge, cereal boxes lined up on the counter—but layered under the rot of Kincaid's control.

"Alright," he said. "We've got what we need. Let's move. The Prophet's next."

"Let's rip the collar off this motherfucker," Maguire agreed.

They walked off the porch, fury evident in their strides.

As Harper slid back into the driver's seat, the hollow feeling hit him like a stone in the gut. Two down. Two to go. Hugo was still in the wind. And Kincaid—the Shepherd—was next.

Cindy's defiance gnawed at him, louder now in the silence of the car. It wasn't just denial. It was faith. Twisted. Blind. Merciless. The same faith Silas had described when he told them how she struck Malia, hard, in her pregnant belly. How she helped

Hugo bind them back to back. How she laughed as the anchor clattered overboard and the Rainiers prayed through their sobs, dragged into the black water with no mercy, no future.

All of it, for the ego of one man.

Asher Kincaid.

Harper's hands tightened around the wheel, leather creaking under his grip. His jaw set, teeth grinding. He jammed the key into the ignition and twisted hard, the engine roaring to life.

It was time.

Justice would wait no longer.

CHAPTER
THIRTY-EIGHT

September 17. Evening.

The plan was set. Harper had half-expected Kincaid to cancel the evening service after Silas and Cindy went down. But either he hadn't heard, or worse, he didn't care. That arrogance was part of what made him dangerous.

From his spot in the lot across the street, Harper watched headlights sweep in. At 5:54 p.m., a black BMW turned smoothly into the *Living Water Church* parking lot. Asher Kincaid stepped out, Bible in hand, tailored jacket sharp against the evening sun. He carried himself like nothing in the world could touch him, striding up the steps with the casual confidence of a man walking into his kingdom.

Harper keyed the radio. "Target arrived."

"Copy. Rollin in two," came Maguire's reply.

One by one, the cavalry appeared. Unmarked sedans sliding into position, SUVs heavy with detectives, and marked patrol cars drifted into place along the curb in front of the church doors. Their lights stayed dark, but the air was charged, a storm about to break.

Harper's hand found the challenge coin in his pocket, the cool metal steadying him.

Right is right. No matter the cost.

The words were more than Foster's creed. They'd become Harper's scripture. In a world where pulpits had lied and leaders had failed, he needed something that didn't. This coin, this promise—it was the faith he could still believe in, forged in sacrifice, carried into every fight.

He slid out of the car, grabbed his vest from the backseat and threw it on, **CGIS** stamped across front and back. The nylon settled on his shoulders, a reminder of the justice he was now about to seek. He joined the cluster of detectives and patrol officers forming up at the curb, where Maguire was already talking them through.

"Alright, this is an evening service," Maguire said, his voice steady, but carrying the gravity of a warning. "Plenty of folks inside are just normal churchgoers: families, seniors, and kids. But don't let that lull you. Our subject runs a cult, and some of those people will likely be in there too. They'll protect him if he calls for it. Don't underestimate that."

Maguire nodded toward Harper, who stepped forward and held up a photo.

"Watch your backs. These people are devoted and fanatical. The men have let their wives sleep with him. The women are having his children. Some have even helped him cover up, and commit, at least two murders, including a pregnant woman. And this man—" he tapped the photo of Oliver Hugo, tattoos showing in the mug shot, " —is one of his enforcers. If he's in there, assume he's armed, assume he's violent, and act accordingly. We all go home tonight."

The line of investigators and uniformed officers studied the image, sober nods passing down the row.

"Alright," Maguire said, putting his folder away. "On me."

He and Harper pushed through the glass entry doors, the rest of the team fanning out behind them. The foyer smelled faintly of coffee and air freshener, shelves lined with glossy brochures and stacks of tracts boasting about "family ministries" and "life groups." The coffee bar looked more like a hip cafe than a church, complete with stools, chalkboard menus, and aprons hanging neatly on hooks.

Two men in polo shirts stood by the double doors labeled **Sanctuary.** One of them started forward, his voice wavering. "Uh, hi, officers–uh, can we—"

Harper brushed past without slowing, pushing the door open.

He and Maguire stepped into the sanctuary. The hum of voices, the rustle of Bibles, and the murmur of whispered prayers filled the air. Rows of padded chairs stretched to the stage, where Asher Kincaid stood under bright lights, mid-sermon. His voice carried smooth and commanding, every syllable dipped in charm.

Harper's eyes swept the crowd, scanning for Hugo, scanning for eyes too sharp, faces too still. Nothing yet. But at the podium, Kincaid looked up, and smiled.

As Harper stepped forward, he thought he saw a falter in Kincaid's smile.

Kincaid's voice rolled across the sanctuary, smooth as honey. He held a Bible in one hand, but his gaze stayed fixed on the crowd.

"Hebrews thirteen, verse seventeen. 'Obey your leaders and submit to them, for they keep watch over your souls as those who must give an account.'"

He let the words settle, then smiled. "That means obedience isn't just about rules, brothers and sisters. It's about trust. About faith. God places shepherds over the flock, men called to lead and to guard. And when the sheep obey, blessing flows. Safety flows."

A murmur of *amens* rippled through the rows. Harper began walking up the middle row between the pews. Congregation members began looking away from Kincaid and toward Harper as he walked down the center, and whispered questions could be heard over the preaching.

"Now, obedience costs something. It's not always easy. It might mean surrendering your pride. It might mean sacrificing what you thought was yours. But God says that obedience is the proof of faith. That your submission isn't weakness, it's worship."

He leaned forward on the pulpit, his smile sharpening just slightly. "So I ask you tonight—are you willing to obey the shepherd God has sent you? Are you willing to trust, even when it costs you?"

Harper was halfway down the aisle now, Maguire and the other agents fanning out behind him. The congregation shifted, whispering, sensing something was happening but not yet sure what.

Kincaid spread his arms wide, voice swelling. "Now, as I said earlier, obedience is the proof of faith. As your shepherd, I now call upon you—"

Up in the corner, Special Agent Lawson was already moving. She slid past the ushers and stepped into the sound booth, flashing her badge at the startled engineer.

"Cut his mic. Now."

The engineer froze, eyes darting between her and Kincaid's looming figure at the pulpit. Lawson leaned closer, voice like steel. "You heard me. Kill it."

His Adam's apple bobbed. Then his hand shot to the mixer, yanking the fader down.

Kincaid's booming voice vanished mid-sentence, the sudden silence falling heavy as stone. The sanctuary rustled with unease, leaving only the shuffling feet and hushed gasps of the congregation. A baby cried, and whispers rose like smoke.

Harper reached the pulpit steps, eyes locked on the man who'd styled himself untouchable.

Kincaid's face flushed crimson, veins rising at his temples. He bellowed without the mic, his voice raw and cracking. "I call upon you to aid your Shepherd in his time of need! Your prophet calls you! Stand with me! Obey the prophet! Defend me from the wolves!" He spread his arms wide, as if expecting the congregation to surge forward.

Several men from the night house gathering shoved to their feet, shouting in angry protest. Uniformed officers stepped forward immediately, hands on holsters, voices barking commands. The men froze, mid-step, fury in their faces, but none dared move closer.

Harper mounted the steps in three long strides before they could. He grabbed Kincaid by the wrist, spun him, and slammed him chest-first across the lectern so hard the wooden frame rattled. The microphone wobbled and clattered to the floor with a hollow bang that echoed like a gavel strike.

"Asher Kincaid," Harper said, his voice cutting across the sanctuary, "you are under arrest for the aggravated murders of Daniel and Malia Rainier. For conspiracy. For robbery. For murder at sea under the laws of the United States."

Gasps rippled through the room as Harper snapped the first cuff.

Kincaid roared, his voice shredding to a ragged shriek as he tried to pull away from the cuffs. "Lies! All lies! You dare touch the

Lord's anointed? You think your law means anything to me? I am the shepherd! I AM THE—"

Harper clamped a hand on the back of his neck and forced his face down onto the wood, silencing him mid-scream. The lectern rattled under the weight, the sound sharp and final.

"Enough," Harper said sharply. His tone carried farther than Kincaid's broken cries.

The men in the congregation froze. Their prophet's voice—once booming, untouchable—was gone. All that remained was his muffled struggle and the click of steel locking tight around his wrists.

Harper hauled him upright, his suit twisted, sweat darkening the fabric under his arms. His eyes darted wildly across the sanctuary, searching for loyalty, for obedience. None came.

"Walk," Harper ordered.

Maguire took hold of Kincaid's other arm. Together, they dragged him down the aisle. He tried one last time, voice cracking. "Don't let them take me! Without me you are nothing! I am your shepherd!"

A thud was heard as a Bible fell to the floor. But no one rose. No one answered his call.

For the first time, Asher Kincaid walked in silence.

They walked him out under the eyes of his congregation, Harper reading him his rights. Outside, patrol cars lit the church in red and blue, the storm finally breaking.

The rest of the team fanned out to execute the search warrant. In Kincaid's office they found what they'd expected, and more. Ledgers stuffed with coded entries. A box of burner phones, still in shrink wrap. Bank statements that bled into The Way Forward Foundation's accounts. Enough paper to bury him, and enough digital evidence to choke a jury with his guilt.

When Harper came back to the patrol car where Kincaid was seated in the back, he opened the door and crouched to eye level. "We found your ledgers. Your phones. Your receipts. The Foundation's nothing but a washing machine for dirty cash, and we've got the proof."

Kincaid's jaw worked, but he stayed silent.

Harper's voice dropped lower. "We have Cindy. And Silas. Where's Hugo?"

For the first time that night, Kincaid hesitated. The mask faltered, just a crack. Then he leaned back, lips curling in something that wasn't quite a smile. Harper felt his blood run cold.

"Call my lawyer," he said.

Harper stood, steel in his chest. Hugo was still out there.

The hunt wasn't over yet.

CHAPTER
THIRTY-NINE

September 21. Evening.

For days, the city couldn't stop talking about it. The arrests of Asher Kincaid, Ezra Silas, and Cindy Glorevich had led every news broadcast, every headline. The prophet in cuffs. The devoted mother turned murderer. The violent ex-con flipped into a state's witness.

Behind the scenes, Harper, Maguire, and the rest of the task force kept working. The burner phone recovered from Cindy's house had been cracked open, its GPS logs and call history stitching her role into the fabric of the case exactly as Silas had described.

The ledgers and phones seized from Kincaid's office were worse. An avalanche of proof. Page after page of coded entries, contact lists, and shell transfers tied him to the Foundation's laundering. It wasn't just spiritual rot, it was financial rot too, baked deep into every transaction.

But the most damning piece hadn't come from the Foundation. It had come from Kincaid's own front porch. While he'd been careful enough not to keep his burner from the night of the murders, he hadn't remembered to disable the doorbell camera at his residence. A search warrant to the service provider had delivered the footage straight to their inbox.

J.K. WOLFE

The clip was clear: Kincaid arriving home at the precise time the cell tower pings placed him there. In his hand, a phone he tried to hide from view. Then, with a quick motion, pulling the battery out before stepping inside. Proof not just of his movements, but of his intent to cover his tracks.

Hugo was still in the wind. The U.S. Marshals Fugitive Task Force had picked up the hunt, chasing leads in Seattle and Idaho. Harper knew it was only a matter of time before they caught him, but the thought gnawed at him all the same. One man still unaccounted for. One piece of the horror still walking free.

That night, Harper sat at the dinner table with Alyssa and Adelyn, a pizza box between them. Addie jabbered happily between mouthfuls of mac and cheese, telling stories in her tiny voice. Harper found himself laughing more than he expected. He'd slept most of the day after the church arrest, but for three nights in a row he'd been home for dinner, and he'd tucked Addie into bed each night. Normalcy, however fragile, had returned.

Afterward, he pushed Addie on the backyard swing until her laughter carried into the night. They played tag, Harper letting her win every time. Later, bath and bedtime.

"Goodnight, Daddy," she said sleepily as he pulled the door closed. "I love you. I'm glad you're home."

His chest tightened. "Me too, Addie-bear. I love you."

He turned toward the bedroom, where Alyssa was folding clothes into boxes. He joined her, packing a stack of sweaters.

"I'm glad you're home too," she said, glancing at him. "But I'm really looking forward to going back to our real house. I do not want to give birth here."

Harper chuckled. "Yeah. I'm glad the case is finally closing out."

"You have much left to do?" she asked.

"Not really. Just a few reports tomorrow. Easton says he can end the orders as early as Friday. I already reserved the U-Haul for Saturday."

Alyssa's smile broke wide. "That's amazing. Addie keeps saying she wants to go back to her 'real house.'"

"It'll be good for her," Harper said. "For all of us. And I appreciate you both doing this with me."

"Of course, love. We're a team."

Harper leaned in and kissed her. "Sure are. But I couldn't do this without you."

"Damn straight," she teased with a wink. "You'd be lost without me."

Just then, the power winked out. The house went black. Harper glanced through the window and saw the neighbor's porch light was still on.

The hair on the back of his neck stood on end. Adrenaline rushed cold through his spine as he remembered Kincaid's words at the house meeting.

Wouldn't it be a shame if temptation—or tragedy—visited your house before the harvest came due?

He sprinted to the closet safe, punched in the code, and yanked out two pistols.

"Jake, what's—" Alyssa started.

"Go to Addie's room," he whispered, thrusting a compact Glock into her hands. "Call 911 and let them know we have an intruder. If anyone but me comes in, shoot until they stop moving. Go!"

Fear shone in her eyes, but her grip was steady.

Harper pulled out his 1911. He slid a spare mag into his pocket, cracked the bedroom door, and scanned the hall. Empty. Pointing the pistol down the hall with one hand, he motioned Alyssa across. She darted into Adelyn's room and closed the door behind her.

A floorboard creaked from the kitchen. He could see the sliding glass door was open, the curtain flowing in the evening breeze. Harper moved down the hallway, barefoot, pistol raised. As he edged toward the living room corner—

WHACK.

Pain exploded through his hand as a club smashed the gun from his grip. It skittered across the hardwood into the shadows of the living room.

No hesitation. Harper lunged, wrapping the attacker at the waist. They both slammed to the ground, Harper on his back. The man straddled him, raining fists down. Harper covered, blocking with forearms, then bucked hard, throwing his hips and heaving the man forward.

The stranger braced the fall with his arms, landing with both hands on the ground. Harper snatched one, yanking it inward, rolled his hips, and twisted—flipped them both over.

Now on top, Harper drove his elbow down. **CRACK.** The man's nose broke under the blow. Blood sprayed. The man tried to buck Harper off, but Harper continued elbow strikes to the man's face and hands as he tried to block Harper's blows.

The attacker roared, hammer-fisting Harper's ribs. White-hot pain shot through his side. Another hook clipped his jaw and the world sparked white. Harper toppled sideways, rolling away just as the man scrambled up.

The man tore his mask off.

Oliver Hugo.

346

Hate filled the man's eyes as he spat blood on the floor and squared his stance.

"You don't have to do this," Harper rasped.

"Fuck you, cop. I'm going to enjoy killing you, and then your family." Before Harper could react, Hugo charged.

They collided, crashing through the wooden coffee table. Splinters flew. Both swung wildly—elbows, fists, forearms—some blocked, others cracking flesh and bone.

Hugo twisted behind Harper, an arm snapping around his throat. The choke crushed tight, cutting air. Stars bloomed in Harper's vision. He clawed at the arm, buying no space. Desperation flooded his veins, knowing that if he failed, his family would die.

Harper drove an elbow backward into Hugo's ribs. Once. Twice. Three times.

"Ugh!" Hugo grunted, grip loosening just enough.

Harper wrenched down on the forearm, pivoted his hips, and slipped free, rolling toward the darkened living room, his breath rushing back in ragged gasps. As he rolled, he felt a hard object under his thigh.

The 1911.

He scooped it up with his left hand and scrambled to his knees. Four feet away, Hugo staggered upright, clutching his side.

Harper raised the pistol.

POP-POP-POP-POP-POP.

Muzzle flashes lit the room like lightning. Hugo stumbled but kept coming, coughing blood.

POP-POP-POP-POP.

The slide locked back. Empty. Hugo dropped to his knees, then collapsed face-first onto the floorboards.

Harper reloaded on instinct, eyes locked on the body. No movement. He edged forward, pistol aimed at Hugo's head as he walked over, putting his fingers to Hugo's neck and checked for a pulse. Nothing.

Breath burning in his chest and throat, he cleared the kitchen, then the open back door. Empty. Quiet.

Harper turned and took one last look at Hugo's body. He had killed the man— in self-defense—but had killed him nonetheless. A burden he would carry for the rest of his life.

But it's over. He let out a sigh, then started walking down the hall. His face throbbed and he could taste blood in his mouth.

"Lyss, it's me," he called softly as he approached Adelyn's door. "It's me. You're safe."

The door cracked open. Alyssa clutched Addie, both of them sobbing. He tucked the pistol into the back of his waistband and pulled his daughter against his chest.

"Shh, shh, it's okay, baby girl," he said, stroking her hair. He pulled Alyssa to his side with his other arm, letting her bury her tears in his shoulder.

Keeping Adelyn's face buried in his chest, he covered her eyes as he guided them past Hugo's body and out to the front lawn.

Sirens wailed closer. Harper held them both, heart hammering, while red and blue lights grew on the horizon.

CHAPTER
FORTY

After medics checked him over, Harper gave a quick statement to CGIS and Seattle PD. The rental house was taped off, a joint crime scene that would take hours to process. SSA Easton, already on scene along with Special Agent Lawson and Detective Maguire, insisted Harper go to the hospital for a full workup. Alyssa and Adelyn refused to be separated from him, so they rode with him in the ambulance.

Later, in a quiet exam room, Harper sat on the bed with Adelyn curled against him. She traced a small hand along the bruises on his cheek.

"Daddy, are you hurt?" Adelyn whispered.

"No, baby, I'm okay," Harper said softly, covering her hand with his own.

"And is mommy okay?"

Alyssa was in another room, being checked for pregnancy complications after the stress of the break-in.

"Yes, mommy's okay, too. They're just making sure she and baby brother are healthy."

"Baby brother!" Adelyn giggled, then dozed off on his chest, her breath light and even.

A woman in a white coat entered quietly. Her name badge read *Erin Brockman, M.D.*

"Well, Mr. Harper, you're lucky. No broken bones. Some significant bruising to your face and neck, but no internal injuries. You'll be sore, but you'll be fine."

"Thanks, Doc. Think my family and I can get out of here soon?"

"The nurse will bring discharge papers. Your wife's still being monitored, but so far things look good." She smiled, handed him a lollipop for Addie, then slipped out.

The door opened again. Harper's shoulders eased at the sight of the tall man in the doorway.

"Hey there, Coastie," Maguire said, voice pitched low, half-grin in place. "You gave us a hell of a scare."

"Yeah," Harper said, shaking his head. "That was...something else."

Maguire stepped inside and shut the door gently. They both kept their voices down.

"Doc clear you?"

"Yeah. Just bruises."

"And Alyssa?"

"They're checking her. She started cramping when we got here."

Maguire exhaled. "Stress'll do that. Especially with some crazy asshole coming after you in your own house."

Harper looked down. Addie was still asleep, face tucked against his chest. He smoothed her hair, then glanced back at Maguire.

"Besides physically, you doing alright Jake?"

"I will be. But..." He took a breath, then slowly let it out. "I'm angry. Angry he came to my home. Angry he forced me into that fight. Forced me to kill him. Angry my family had to see the aftermath, that they had to hide, terrified. That our safe place—our sanctuary—got torn apart. We'll be carrying that for a long time."

Maguire didn't interrupt, just let him say it.

"And I'm angry at Kincaid," Harper went on, pulse pounding at his temples. "That his poison spread this far. That people like Daniel, Malia, their baby...they're dead because of him and his need to be worshipped. Hugo's dead. And my family was almost added to the list."

For a moment the room was still, just the hum of hospital machinery.

Maguire finally spoke. "I hear you. But Jake, you did your job. More than your job. You got Kincaid. The Rainiers are going to get justice because you didn't stop. And none of them—Kincaid, Hugo, Cindy—will hurt another soul again."

Harper nodded slowly, the weight still there, but steadied. "Thanks, Tate."

"You got it, puddle pirate." Maguire's grin returned, small but real. He held up a paper bag. "By the way, I brought you a change of clothes. Figured you wouldn't want to put the bloodstained ones back on."

The nurse came in with discharge papers, and Harper scrawled his name on the clipboard, careful not to jostle Adelyn asleep against his shoulder. He eased her onto the bed and changed into the clean jeans and shirt Maguire had brought. As he tugged the shirt over his head, another nurse hurried in, eyes wide.

"Mr. Harper? You need to get over to the birth center. Now."

Harper froze. "What?"

"Your wife's gone into labor," the nurse said gently but firmly. "Her blood pressure spiked, and we can't stabilize it. You're having this baby tonight."

For a split second, Harper just stared, blood turning to ice in his veins. Then his eyes snapped to Maguire.

"I'll take Addie," Maguire said immediately. "Go."

Harper pressed a quick kiss into his daughter's hair before lifting her, still sleeping, into Maguire's arms. "Thank you," he whispered.

"Go," Maguire repeated. "We've got you covered."

Harper jogged down the hall, following the nurse through double doors into the bright, sterile bustle of the maternity ward. He tried not to panic as the smell of antiseptic hit him, sharp and clean. A nurse handed him a sterile gown and booties. He pulled them on over his clothes, his hands trembling despite himself.

Another nurse appeared in the doorway. "Mr. Harper," he said. "Your wife is prepped. Because of the stress, her labor progressed fast, and with her blood pressure, we're going to perform a cesarean. She's stable, and so is the baby, but we need to do this right away. Follow me."

Pushing aside his own anxiety, Harper pushed through the swinging doors into the operating room. Alyssa lay on the table, pale under the lights, eyes wide with fear.

He rushed to her side and took her hand. "It's okay, love. I'm right here."

Her fingers squeezed his. "Where's Addie?"

"With Tate," Harper assured her. "She's asleep. Safe."

Alyssa exhaled, tension loosening from her face. She looked at him, tears brimming. "You ready for round two of parenthood?"

Harper bent close, smoothing a strand of hair from her forehead. "There's no one else I'd rather do it with." He kissed her

352

gently, smoothed her hair, then stayed by her side as the procedure began.

Twenty minutes later, the doctor lifted a squalling baby boy into the air. The sound of his cry cut through the sterile room like sunlight. Harper's throat tightened as the tiny body was placed in his arms.

"Congratulations," the doctor said.

Harper carried the boy to Alyssa, laying him gently against her chest. Tears streamed down her cheeks as she touched their son for the first time. Harper leaned over them both, his forehead resting against hers.

Later, in the dim light of the recovery room, Alyssa finally slept, exhaustion softening her face. Harper sat in a rocking chair in the corner, his newborn son bundled in his arms. The baby's breaths came steady, warm against his chest.

Harper rocked slowly, his ribs aching, his face bruised, but his heart impossibly full. For the first time in weeks, the case, the darkness, the weight of everything else, all of it fell silent.

He looked down at his son's tiny face and felt the echo of Malia Rainier's sobs, Daniel's steady voice in the dark, the two of them bound together at the bow, clinging to faith and each other. Their child would never take a breath, never see the light of day. But his had.

The thought carved deep into Harper, a reminder of why he fought, why he endured. Justice wasn't abstract. It was this. Protecting the future, the laughter, the small beating hearts who deserved to live.

He bent and pressed a kiss to his son's forehead, whispering so softly only the newborn could hear. "You're why I'll never stop."

As he shifted, his free hand brushed against his pocket. The familiar shape of the challenge coin pressed into his palm. The one Foster had given him. One side etched with St. Jude, the other with the scales of justice, and those words that had carried him through every dark night: *Right is right, no matter the cost.* He turned the coin over once in his hand, then slipped it back into his pocket, letting the weight of it anchor him while he held his son close.

The door eased open then, light spilling across the floor. Maguire stepped in, Adelyn perched on his hip, her eyes wide and curious. He smiled faintly at the sight.

"So," Maguire said quietly, "what do we call this little guy?"

Alyssa stirred awake just as Addie wriggled down and ran to the bed. Harper handed the baby boy to Alyssa, then scooped up Adelyn. He bent and gingerly set her on the edge of the bed so she could touch the baby.

"Addie, meet your baby brother," Harper said, looking at Alyssa.

Alyssa smiled, finishing the sentence. "Addie, meet Elliott."

Adelyn broke into a wide grin and kissed the baby on his forehead. "I love him so much already!" she cried.

"But let Justice roll on like a river, righteousness like a never-failing stream." -
Amos 5:24

EPILOGUE

The service was held on a gray morning, the kind the Sound seemed to breathe out of itself. The chapel was filled with uniforms, a sea of Coast Guard blue blended with family and friends. Harper had shaved and put on his service dress blues. The Investigator rating symbol on his left shoulder felt apropos, the scales of justice under the Coast Guard eagle. Three red chevrons below the scales marked his rank as first class.

The Coast Guard honor detail stood rigid at the front, their faces carved from stone, dress blues immaculate.

When the chaplain spoke Malia's name, her mother's sobs carried through the pews. Harper's chest tightened. He had seen grief before, raw and unfiltered, but today was different. This was a family mourning not just a daughter, but a grandchild they would never meet.

As the congregation sang the final hymn, Harper stayed silent, listening. The words rose up from broken voices and hung in the rafters like smoke. He didn't know what he believed about heaven anymore, or justice beyond this life. But he knew the weight of the badge in his pocket, the promise etched into Foster's coin, and the words his father had given him all those years ago. Justice wasn't just a job. It was promise.

When the service ended, Harper followed the slow line of mourners out into the gray light. He pulled his coat tighter, breathed deep, and carried the memory with him. Another vow carved deeper than words.

At the cemetery, the honor detail moved with mechanical precision. Three rifle volleys cracked across the gray sky, each report echoing off the Sound. The sharp tang of gunpowder hung in the damp air, brass casings tumbling into the grass. Then came the long, solitary note of taps, carried on the wind, bending around the mourners and breaking over them like a wave.

The caskets were empty. Everyone there knew it, and somehow that made the grief sharper. Symbols in place of bodies. Daniel and Malia's coffins stood beside an impossibly smaller one, white and almost delicate, a placeholder for the life Malia had carried but never brought into the world. No one wanted to look at it, yet no one could look away. Harper's throat tightened at the sight. The smallest casket he'd ever seen, and yet the heaviest.

The chaplain's voice wavered as he spoke of sacrifice and the sea, of anchors that hold even when storms rage. The honor guard folded the flag from Daniel's casket with slow precision, the kind of ritual Harper had witnessed too many times. When it was presented to Malia's parents, her father cradled it like an infant. Harper's vision blurred, his hand came up to his eyes, and came back down damp with tears.

He had worn the uniform before, but never before had it felt so heavy.

Harper's gaze drifted past the rows of mourners, out toward the water. The Sound stretched gray and endless, its surface hiding what lay beneath. Somewhere out there, the sea held Daniel and Malia. The thought hollowed him out and steadied him in the same breath. The case was closed, but the promise remained.

•••••

Several months passed since the close of the Shepherd's Wake case, as the media had branded it. Harper's temporary Coast Guard duty had ended, and he and his family returned to their home in Stonehaven. Because he'd served on active duty for more than 180 days, he was granted ninety days' leave before reporting back to

Stonehaven PD. He added six weeks of paternity leave on top of that, time he was determined to spend anchoring himself with his family.

Life settled into a new rhythm. Nights were shorter and mornings earlier, but the house carried a new warmth. Between late-night feedings, Harper learned the weight of his son in his arms, the way Elliott's tiny hand curled instinctively around his finger. Adelyn was adjusting too, trading her role as an only child for the proud title of Big Sister. Alyssa laughed more easily now, though the shadows of what they had endured still lingered at the edges.

On the night before his return to the department, Harper stood alone on the porch, the horizon painted in fading gold. In his palm lay Foster's coin, warm from his touch. He turned it over and over, tracing the words etched into the metal. He heard his father's voice as if it had never left him.

Integrity's not about how you feel. It's about what you do when it costs you.

The cost was still there. The case no longer haunted his sleep with the sound of Malia's drowned sobs, but the weight of her family's loss pressed on him still. It was always that way for cops, he knew, when cases cut too close to the heart.

Justice for the Rainiers had come, but it had taken something from his own family in return. Hugo's break-in had stripped the peace from their Seattle rental; they had never set foot in it together again. Maguire had helped him box up the house, and back in Stonehaven Harper installed cameras, alarms, locks—every safeguard he could muster—to make sure Alyssa and the kids felt safe again.

Later that night, lying beside Alyssa, Harper wrapped his arm around her and felt the rhythm of her breathing steady against him. And for the first time in months, he let himself drift into a peaceful sleep without the weight of vigilance pressing down.

But the peace would not last.

The phone buzzed on the nightstand. Once. Twice. Three times. Then it silenced. Harper stirred, pried open his eyes, and glanced at the clock. 3:30 a.m.

The phone buzzed again. He slipped out of bed, careful not to wake Alyssa, and answered in a hushed voice.

"Harper."

"Hey Jake. Sorry to wake you," came the voice of his old friend, Detective Sergeant Carrie Hurst. "But we need you here. We've got bodies."

Bodies. Plural. The word hung in the silence between them, heavier than sleep.

"Alright," Harper said. "Where do you need me?"

"Major crimes is converging on the scene," Hurst replied. "Jake, this one is bad. And I mean real bad. I need you to take lead."

He stood in the darkened living room, hand tightening around the phone, eyes drifting toward Alyssa, and then towards the hall where the children slept in their bedrooms. The stream of justice never stopped flowing. It pulled him forward now, cold and relentless.

"I'm en route," he said evenly.

He slid the phone back into his pocket and looked out the darkened window. Somewhere in the night, the city was already stirring with the weight of what waited for him. Something cold, sharp. A shadow taking shape.

And it was coming for him.

The end.

Book One of the Detective Harper series:

Shadows of the Badge

Introducing Detective Jake Harper

When power shields the guilty, justice has only one weapon left: the truth.

Detective Jake Harper thought he left the past behind. After false accusations nearly ended his career, he rebuilt his life in the quiet city of Stonehaven. But when a tech mogul is found murdered, Harper uncovers a trail of corruption that leads straight back to the department that betrayed him.

The deeper he digs, the darker the truth becomes, finding evidence of a trafficking ring, political cover-ups, and a conspiracy involving powerful men who still view him as a threat. Now, with enemies circling and old wounds reopened, Harper must decide how far he is willing to go for justice and what it will cost him.

Shadows of the Badge is a gripping crime thriller about loyalty, redemption, and the high price of doing what's right.

Out now!

www.jkwolfebooks.com

COMING SOON

Hostile Intent

A Detective Harper Novel

When a midnight fire tears through a rural wedding venue, Detective Jake Harper is drawn into a case that twists love, loyalty, and vengeance into something far darker.

As old wounds resurface, he'll learn that some truths are buried for a reason—and some killers never stay hidden.

The next gripping chapter in the Detective Harper series.

Coming 2026 from J.K. Wolfe

www.jkwolfebooks.com

To read more about Detective Harper's friend from the Coast Guard, Logan Cross...

Dive into *The Dark Waters Trilogy* by D.M. Webber:

For Boatswain's Mate First Class Logan Cross, a transfer from the Coast Guard's elite Maritime Security Response Team to a quiet Massachusetts small boat station should have been a chance at a normal life—a quiet billet, a chance to build a family with his wife, Melanie.

When a known trafficker is found murdered outside Gloucester, Cross suspects it's no coincidence. *Cold Front* follows him into a rising conspiracy as the body count grows and orders from his command fail to add up. When he and Melanie learn they're expecting their first child, the stakes climb higher. With violent threats looming, Cross must channel his past to stop the danger before it consumes everything he holds dear.

In *Storm Warning*, a conspirator silenced in prison should have meant the end. Instead, Blackwake regroups—deadlier than ever. Violence erupts, targeting his team, his station, and his pregnant wife. Pulled between protecting home and answering duty, Cross is forced back toward his most violent instincts. How far will he go to safeguard those he loves—and the service he swore to uphold?

Nor'easter's Wake brings the chilling conclusion. Two conspirators are gone, but a third remains—more manipulative, more calculating, a threat unlike any Cross has faced. When Blackwake turns the Coast Guard's own resources against him, the storm intensifies. As maritime industry deaths mount and danger closes in on his family,

Cross must uncover the final act of a ruthless syndicate that will stop at nothing. To end it, he must decide whether destroying the enemy means becoming the monster he's fighting.

The fight chose Cross. But some storms are too powerful for even the strongest of men. When this storm makes landfall, destruction will follow in its wake.

The Dark Waters Trilogy

• Cold Front

• Storm Warning

• Nor'easter's Wake

Part of the Storm Front Literary Universe

DMWebberbooks.com

The Storm Front Literary Universe, in chronological order:

Cold Front – D.M. Webber

Storm Warning – D.M. Webber

Shadows of the Badge – J.K. Wolfe

Nor'easter's Wake – D.M. Webber

Shepherd's Wake – J.K. Wolfe

Hostile Intent – J.K. Wolfe

ABOUT THE AUTHOR

J.K. Wolfe is a veteran police officer with years of experience in criminal investigations. He is also a U.S. Coast Guard veteran, bringing a disciplined, mission-focused perspective to both his service and his writing. His crime thrillers draw from real-world investigations, written to reflect the weight, cost, and purpose of police work. Through his stories, Wolfe explores the bonds of family, the struggle of faith, and the integrity it takes to do what's right. Because justice is not just a job. It is a calling.

JKWolfeBooks.com